Copyright © 2014 by Megan J. Parker & Nathan Squiers
Edited by Nathan Squiers for Tiger Dynasty Publishing
Cover art by ShinyShadows (DeviantArt)
FRONT Formatting Art by Samantha Jenkins
Design by Eden Crane Designs
ISBN-13: 978-1-940634-22-7

This is a work of fiction. Names, characters places, and incidents either are the product of the author's imagination or are used fictitiously. Any resemblance to actual persons living or dead, events, or locales is entirely coincidental.

If you purchased this book without a cover you should be aware that this book is stolen property. It was reported as "unsold and destroyed" to the publisher and neither the author nor the publisher has received any payment for this "stripped book."

All rights reserved. No part of this book may be reproduced or transmitted in any form or by any means, electronic or mechanical, including photocopying, recording, or by any information storage and retrieval system, without the written permission of the Publisher, except where permitted by law.

DEDICATION

"To all the lovers and fighters out there; here's to always having what it takes to face down your demons"

ACKNOWLEDGEMENTS

We'd like to send out our thanks to YOU! All our readers who have been following both of us through all of our works! This series wouldn't be here without your love and support. We are so excited to share this final piece in the Scarlet Night series. We'd also like to thank our local friends & family who back us up and support our work & cheer us on.

Anyway, thank YOU for all the support we have received and we hope that Serena and Zane's final book in this series.

(Don't worry; Serena and Zane are FAR from gone!)

"It was not well to drive
men into final corners;
at those moments they could
all develop teeth and claws."
              -Stephen Crane (1871-1900)

"From there we came outside
and saw the stars"
-Dante Alighieri (1265-1321)

Prologue

HE COULDN'T RECALL BEING BORN. Couldn't recall much of anything anymore. Still, he doubted it hurt as bad as this...

Unable to move or see—unable to even *function* beyond the simple sense that he *was*, in some way or another, *existing* once again—he simply floated in the void of his own growing self-awareness and let the jagged, ugly deposits of whatever reality existed beyond his blindness grow more and more obvious:

Voices. One was unmistakable; a voice that, for some time, he'd grown to know as a part of himself...

The vampire called Zane.

Though he couldn't be certain if he even *had* lips anymore, he was certain the name would have brought a sneer to them.

The other voice, though…

The unmistakable pitch and sensuality of a woman though tarnished with an undeserving pride and intellect.

Ah yes… he mused to himself, *The blue-haired whore!*

The name escaped him, though the face shimmered just beyond the veil of his memory. One of Zane's comrades; one of the psychic types, if he wasn't mistaken. She was close to Zane, he remembered, though he'd never bedded her. No, she was more of a sister to him…

One of the reasons he'd always wanted to personally break her; to take her in the worst ways possible and leave Zane to soak up the guilt of the aftermath…

But, with Zane's voice ringing *outside* of his head, it was clear that his *unique* relationship with the vampire playboy had been terminated…

Though, if he could figure out a way to *operate* whatever vessel he'd been placed within, perhaps the circumstances could be turned in his favor.

"You *know* she's going to taunt me about being right when she wakes up, right?" the blue-haired whore said.

"Can't really blame her," Zane's voice was solid and confident; *happy!* A deep rage boiled deep at that realization as he listened on: "She was right about *everything!*"

"Can you do me a favor and *not* feed her that gloating right for at least a day?"

"Only if you do me a favor."

A groan from the whore, "What?"

"I am *dying* to get a Slushie and a cheap, nasty gas

station hot dog in my belly, and I'm sure Serena would love to have a Snickers and one of those magazines she's always reading." The echo of freedom in Zane's voice was only fueling the rage, then, "Do you think you could drive me to the city and front me the cash to grab the goods?"

"Why can't you drive and buy your own garbage?"

"Because then it wouldn't be a favor."

A chuckle? He was actually *laughing*?

This wouldn't do!

"I guess that makes sense... sort of. Alright, fine."

A pregnant pause offered the hope of miscarried happiness.

"Why are we keeping that *thing* in here?" Zane asked, the familiar jagged edge of fear clinging to his voice.

Another pause.

"Because that's a corpse..." the inflection at the end was more taunting than fearful, "And we're in the medical center. Would you rather we kept it in the cafeteria?"

A corpse? Is that what he'd been dumped into? Unacceptable!

"I guess I just don't like the idea that it could suddenly wake up."

Yes! *There* it was!

The fear!

The concern!

After all that had happened, he *still* had Zane by the manhood...

And it was the right time to twist and pull!

"Doubt it. It's not that it's not going to wake up *eventually*, but *that's* been out without *any* sign of life—no pulse, no brain activity, and barely any measureable auric activity—for *days*, where Serena's breathing and dreaming no differently than if she was just napping. Between the two of them, I'm willing to bet that Serena's going to be the first to open her eyes."

Not if I have anything to say about it, bitch!

His sense of smell resurrected then, offering two *very* pleasant-and-familiar scents:

Zane's fear; his succulent, delicious terror!

And, painfully near to him, Serena. *His* Serena!

His buttercup baby!

Yes, Zaney-boy! Do run along with the whore! Immerse yourself in your delusions and leave me to my devices. Nothing will be alright; not while I remain!

Zane's anxious sigh sang such glorious potential, and the motivation to drag himself from this mock-death grew so powerful he was certain he'd awaken in his new body cackling.

Finally, Zane sealed his fate:

"You promise?"

*I swear it, Zaney-boy! I fucking **swear** it!*

It had taken a bit longer for Zane and his blue-haired colleague—who was finally identified as Zoey through the rest of their incessant banter—to finally leave the room; to finally leave him alone to his devices. The time, however, didn't feel quite as wasted in hindsight, as it was a period that allowed for even more senses and awareness to return to the seemingly dead creature laid out not far from them.

Once they were gone, though…

About fucking time! he growled, though entirely internally, his new body still not able to respond to his commands. Despite this, he was otherwise fully aware. His internal senses told him that he was on his back, that whatever he was lying upon was cold...

And then there were the senses he *hadn't* expected.

The skin of whatever he was in was somehow able to *feel* the presence of light and heat; somehow able to tell him the presence of ultraviolet and neon waves without being able to actually *see* them!

Simply fascinating! he mused to himself as he tested this alien ability. Underground; every nerve of his being screamed that he was underground. Part of him was pleased with this—feeling a sense of security and secrecy in it—but yet another part was furious with the total lack of meat...

Save for morsel that he'd been able to smell since almost the very start!

Then there was *his* part. The part of his mind that was neither hardwired to this new body nor sympathetic to its comforts and preferences. The part that he'd carried with him from the start, long before he was in this body or planted inside Zane as the creature known as *Maledictus* or even when he'd been occupying the makeshift reliquary he'd buried his essence into. The only part of himself that he had left.

That part didn't care about his new shell's comfort or contentment, and he certainly wasn't going to offer up the morsel to its simple appetites.

Not when his own appetites—appetites that burned just below his new body's rumbling stomach—were so much more demanding; so much more *satisfying*.

No, he chortled to himself as he willed his mind to hurry the process of claiming the body's motor functions, *I have MUCH more delicious plans for that one! But if you behave,* he internally addressed his new body, *then I'll feed you the cartoon-headed cunt with Zaney-boy's still-beating heart plopped on top like a plump cherry.*

The body lurched.

A labored, hissing growl oozed through a parched throat.

His legs tensed and kicked as his arms flexed and flopped with the sudden waves of backed-up neurological commands.

Something at the base of his spine twitched and rolled.

A serpentine tongue lashed out, tasting the air and filling his mind with even more details about his surroundings—none of them pleasant. As he'd heard the blue-haired one say, they *were* in a medical center, and the air—the very air—was *teeming* with the rancid artificialness of it all; sanitizers and cleaners and cold, bloodless metal upon even more cold, bloodless metal. His mind thrashed and hissed at the total lack of death and rot and agony…

But, despite this, his dry, chapped lips peeled into a grin as the thought screeched in his head.

"Oh, I think I'll like you very much," he offered to his new body; relishing in its need—its sheer *demand*— for the forced procreation and agonizing extinction of *everything* around him.

Those fools had actually planted *him* inside a creature that outright *thrived* on rape and murder!

Perfect! Then let's begin!

Finally cooperating, his eyes opened and he was met with the harsh and unnatural glow of synthetic lighting that his skin had already warned him about. Curiosity grew as he shimmied to the edge of metal slab he'd been lying upon, and he dragged his hands into his view, marveling at the scaly, clawed digits that occupied his sight.

Reptilian? he marveled, running one elongated finger across the back of his opposite hand and smirking at the cold, bumpy texture of his new flesh. "How fucking delightful!" he chortled and stood, glancing down at the stilt-like pair of clawed, brownish-green legs that now supported him, "In their haste to be rid of me, they put me in a blood-thirsty, cold-hearted *weapon?*"

Spotting a mirror above a sink set into a nearby wall, he allowed himself a long moment to take in his new face. While there were some notably simian qualities about the head and jaw—looking more like the brutish sculpt of one of the human's slightly more primitive, tree-dwelling ancestors—there was definitely an unmistakable, lizard-like aesthetic. A pair of stretched pupils nestled amidst a pair of hazy, piss-yellow bogs that surrounded each of them, that should have belonged in the skull of a giant snake narrowed at their own reflection as he leaned in to inspect his visage. Two teardrop nostrils flared then, and his mouth—seeing that what he'd previously passed off as chapped was, in fact, a total lack of actual lips and just an angry gash cutting through the scaly surface—parted enough to let a long, forked tongue jut forward and vibrate angrily against the glass in an attempt to sample the air around their doppelganger. He smirked at the simplicity of the response, and the gesture reminded him of an alligator exposing its assets. The brownish-green hue appeared to be a constant throughout, save for the paler area of his chest and abdomen and…

He snarled.

"My dick!" his hands flew to the body's scaly-yet-flat crotch and began frantically searching for something—*anything*—resembling a pair of genitals. "Where the *fuck* is my…"

Then… there!

A… pocket?

He sneered as a portion of his pelvis dipped into itself, offering an opening for his fingertips to slip inside.

"Did those fuckers seriously stick *me* in the body of a *fema—*"

His enraged monologue was cut short as a clawed fingertip grazed the topside of his new penis and a hungry hiss leapt out of instinct from his throat.

"Well then… *that* might take some getting used to," he laughed to himself.

Still, it would be all the more worth it to see Serena finally succumb to him when he was holding such an *unconventional* member over her.

He erupted into laughter. As his body convulsed and pitched in its own excitement, he felt the twitching at his lower-back again and caught sight of a long, wicked tail in his peripheral vision, and another round of laughter issued. The sound of the cold, hissing echoes rattled about the room and reverberated in his skull, pushing his cackles that much farther.

And then she awoke…

It started as a murmur—the innocent, garbled whimper of a mind roused from slumber too early for its liking—and quickly turned to something more befitting of its owner:

"Either the laughter ends or I rip your junk out through your ass—" Serena's threat cut short as she whipped her blonde head around to face the source of the laughter and her purple eyes widened at the sight. "What the fuck…?"

"A pity," he offered, turning away from the mirror to face her, "I've always found your threats to be something of an art form, Serena. Not unlike a fine painting, or a well-structured poetic stanza…"—he smirked again, and Serena's response told him that she was, while perhaps not impressed, at least stricken by the sight—"… or a well-orchestrated slaughter." He chuckled, stepping towards her and letting the perched talons of his feet clack down as he did, "People like you and I, we *savor* the art of malice, do we not? We…" he shivered with growing anticipation, "We live for it; we fucking *feed* from it! When you're making your opponents cower under your hollow, air-headed words and when I'm plunging dagger and dick alike into whatever quivering sow I've claimed as mine… *that's* when we're in our elements! Ain't that right, princess?"—another step—"Well? Ain't'cha gonna talk? Don't you have something to say to me, bitch?"

She slowly dragged herself away from him, pushing her body across the plush, soft bed they'd given her to stand. "*Mal… Maledictus?*"

He hissed. "You know, you sound like a real cunt when you say it *that* way; like a real *ungrateful* cunt!"

Serena's face shifted at that and the sneer he'd come to recognize so well found its place. "Ungrateful, huh? And why should I be grateful to *you*, you walking ghetto handbag?"

He leapt then, slamming down atop the metal table that had been his new body's resting slab moments earlier, and leaned towards the arrogant blonde vampire like a gargoyle; his claws skewering through the stainless steel and causing his prey to flinch at the series of shrill, metallic screams.

"A handbag, am I? A bold statement coming from you, since we *both* know I could punch through your lady-parts and drag you inside-out if I suddenly decided to accessorize!" He raised his hand and mimed locking his mouth before continuing, "I'd watch my fucking words if I were you, my brazenly arrogant pet; I'm not above beating a dog, and you're just the *worst* kind of bitch!"

Though Serena's face showed little give, he could see her mind working towards being more selective with her phrasing. "Okay then," she took a step away from him, "so what *exactly* do you think I should be grateful for?"

"For *saving* you and you're entire fleet of dickless fuck-wads! For helping you defeat that congealed jizz-stain you called a brother! But, more than *any* of that other shit, for *not* burying myself into every single nook and cranny your pink ass has to offer, *girl!*" he hissed as he let the weight of his upper body fall then, letting his long, reptilian spine distend momentarily as he caught himself on his hands and scuttled across the floor, allowing his legs and, finally, his tail to follow as if on their own accord.

The cold, soulless sound of his body scuttling across the linoleum floor made Serena shiver, and his tongue darted out then, tasting the fear and uncertainty that she'd just saturated the air with.

Despite all the evidence to the contrary, Serena hid her fear. "You didn't do a goddam thing, *Maledictus*! Zane could've just as easily—"

"ZANE?" he roared and lurched forward, suddenly standing upright again as he cleared the distance between them in a flash and pinned her to the wall. "That... that *boy* is a pussy! A spineless, pity-wielding sack of shit hiding behind *my* power in the hopes that nobody will call him on being nothing more than a child with a pair of balls that *miraculously* sprouted a few big-boy curlies! Make no mistake, you stupid cow, *I* am all that was ever right about that loser!"

Serena's lower jaw set as her fists clenched at her sides. "Before you try talking shit about my man, I suggest you take a look down and ask yourself if you have any right talking about the state of *anybody's* balls!" She laughed, "Do you even *have* a—"

"OH IT'S THERE, WHORE!" He bellowed and slammed his fist into the wall before reaching behind her and grabbing her by the hair, "BELIEVE ME, YOU'LL BE ACQUAINTED WITH IT SOON ENOUGH!"

Before Serena could react, he turned, letting his tail whip around behind him and sending several trays and a table around him toppling to the floor before allowing it to crash against the wall. Crying out at the sudden yank at her scalp Serena struggled, shrieking as the tuft of hair in his grip was ripped from her head. Free from the hold, she leapt past him, trying to get across the room towards the door. An enraged hiss grew as he tossed the matted blonde mess to the floor and lunged after her, making several desperate grabs at her before finally getting a grip on the back of her neck.

The frantic vampire howled and thrashed in his grip, and he began to feel the tugs of her aura against his scales—the desperate attacks tearing bits and pieces of his new body from his frame and raining the bloodied chunks to the floor—and he grinned through the discomfort at her efforts.

"A fighter to the end, eh Buttercup Baby?"

Before she could consider a snide remark, he slammed her head forward into the doorframe, chuckling as both her body and the invisible attacks from her aura went still.

She was finally his!

Releasing the grip on her neck, he let the

unconscious body of Serena Vailean start to slip to the floor before reclaiming his hold on her hair, this time making sure to keep his grip at the base of her scalp, and began to drag her into her new life with him, starting to hum as he did:

"*Go-ing to the chap-pel and we're… go-o-onna get ma-a-a-arried! Yes, I'm… go-ing to the chap-pel and we're… go-o-onna get ma-a-a-arried!*"

Chapter One
Nightmares & Chaos

THREE DAYS.

Three god forsaken days.

Three days' worth of tension weighed down Zane Murdoch's shoulders as he paced back and forth in the community room of the Clan of Vail. Zoey, Isaac and Raith, all sitting on a nearby couch, watched their friend-and-clanmate stalk across the same path over and over; watching with a still and quiet awe as he continued to pace like a caged animal that could, at any moment, rip free of its confinements.

And, in this comparison, they weren't inaccurate; Zane had long since been recognized as the vampire clan's hot-head, though the *true* threat behind his temper had been removed from his body three days earlier.

Three god damned days earlier…

A cage of time since his lover, Serena Vailean—the new leader of their clan—had been kidnapped by the very being that he'd been so eager to be rid of. And each day that passed was another cake of rust on the animal's bars; another burning need to break through and cause some damage until, somehow, it brought her back.

"Three fucking days," he growled to himself. "*Three* days and *zero* sign of Serena *or* Maledictus!"

Maledictus…

He shivered at the mention of his name; the gut-wrenching title given to his waking nightmare of the past twelve years; a waking nightmare that they'd put into its own body and turned into a *walking* nightmare.

A walking, dirty-talking, murderous, rape-happy nightmare that had been holding *his* lover and their clan's leader who-knew-where for…

Zane sighed and finally stopped pacing.

Running his hands through his disheveled hair, he turned his attention to the others in an attempt to find some sort of salvation.

"She must be out there, Zoey! How fucking far could that monster have gotten?" he snarled.

"Zane… you need to calm down! This is no way to fix the problem!" Zoey turned her bright blue eyes to him.

"She's right, mate," Raith, his best friend, agreed.

Zane groaned and looked down, feeling the rage pass and a new wave of depression and guilt slam into him.

"I can't lose her, Zoe…" he whispered, letting the sudden current of relaxing energies to flow through him, knowing they were coming from his auric friend.

"I know," Zoey offered, the pain of Serena's disappearance burning in her own eyes. "But we can't allow ourselves to lose hope, Zane. If there's a chance for her, it starts with us staying positive that we *will* get her back."

"You haven't slept at all. Why don't you go get some rest, mate?" Raith stood up and offered a reassuring hand on his shoulder, "We'll continue to search while you do. Zoe's right, have hope, and have some faith in us."

Zane only gave a weak nod—the force of his exhaustion coming down on him; no doubt another mind-trick from Zoey, but one that he didn't mind succumbing to—before turning down the hall and heading for his room.

Pushing the door shut behind him, he eyed his bed like a long-lost friend before letting himself fall onto the unmade mess, not even bothering to undress or turn off the lights before letting sleep drag him out of his three-day burden.

"*Serena?*" *Zane called out, stepping through a canopy of clouds and seeing his lover chained to a stone wall.*

Serena's face contorted in pain as her lips opened and called to him, but no sound came out. The need to protect her grew and he started towards her to help.

With every step he took, she grew two paces further.

Desperate, he ran faster, watching in horror as she continued to grow more and more distant.

A cycle of trying to close the gap between them only to have her grow that much farther away continued until darkness began to shroud her, threatening to take her from his sight. Zane looked around, trying to see through the darkness to find her.

He needed to save her.

Then—suddenly—there was sound!

Laughter.

Serena's laughter...

"You'll never get to me, Zane. You are too weak on your own," Serena's voice mocked him.

The darkness ebbed and Zane was confronted with Serena lying back with a large shadow above her. Zane felt a tremor snake down his back as he watched a set of large fangs grow from the shadow as a pair of piercing red eyes took shape within the darkness. Serena's condescending gaze held his for a moment longer and she smirked, running her hand over the shadowy figure.

Maledictus!

"You'll never make it, Zane... you aren't strong without him!" Serena laughed, running her hands across his shoulders.

"Ha! YOU are NOTHING without me, bitch-boy!" Maledictus cackled, "Without me saving your ass at every fucking turn, you won't even be able to survive!"

The words sunk into Zane's chest and he froze, helpless to say anything or do anything. The darkness swam across him as he watched Serena succumb—and outright ENJOY—Maledictus' embrace. Her mocking laughter growing into an all-consuming roar that taunted him as her cries of ecstasy pierced through the veil and he fell to his knees in loss.

"Serena... no!"

Serena opened her eyes to the sound of rattling chains and glared over at the metal pipe that she was bound to. The pipe that Maledictus had dug free from an otherwise off-white padded wall that made up one of six equally padded and equally off-white surfaces—walls, ceiling, *and* floor—in a room that, though she'd only been in there for three days, already felt like a jail cell to her. Though, all things considered, this wasn't too far from the reality. While the length of the chain allowed for *some* moving room, she already knew full-well that it wasn't long enough for her to even reach the other side of the already laughably small space. Were it not for the growing rage and panic, she might've admitted that Maledictus' decision to hold her hostage in an insane asylum was *almost* clever.

It certainly seemed like an appropriate place for him to hunker down.

As she collected her bearings from yet another unpleasant set of dreams rousing her from yet another uncomfortable round of sleep, she tried to stand and and whimpered at the struggle to perform even the simplest of tasks.

Her refusal to eat was beginning to take its toll on her.

She glared at the pile of dead vermin—rats and mice mostly, but Maledictus *had* made a big deal about tossing a still-twitching squirrel into the room the previous night—that littered the floor around her; all of them lying just out of her reach. This, however, had been her doing; an effort to keep herself from potentially succumbing to the hunger and accepting her kidnapper's "offerings."

She'd sooner die than give him that satisfaction.

As she leaned her head weakly against the metal pipe, she looked up towards the padded, off-white door as its hinges groaned loudly.

Then, standing there like a nightmare, was Maledictus.

Serena sneered at the changes that had already begun to show in the ykali body he'd stuffed into; an already hideous creature that was being made even more revolting by the repugnant being occupying its form. Long, bony barbs had begun protruding out of his shoulders, and his limbs had begun to warp with the recent growth, causing an uneven and hobbled effect whenever he walked or gestured. She looked up to meet his shifty reptilian gaze and fought the urge to instantly look away, refusing to let him see what sort of power he already had over her. The ykali's face had already taken a turn away from the lizard-like and a long drive down the road of the demonic; his brow and temples already darkening, and a long, too-wide of a grin lined the lower half of his face.

Serena fought the urge to look at his clawed ykali hands as he held out a few more dying vermin, dropping them within the range of her shackles before beginning to rub his hands together like a fly perched atop a dog turd.

She bit her lip, feeling the growing hunger emerge even as she fought desperately to control it. She just had to hold onto hope that Zane and the others would find her soon.

In a desperate act of self-control and forethought, she began throwing the offerings out of her reach before burying herself back in the corner.

"Still not eating, I see," Maledictus leered. "That's quite foolish."

She narrowed her eyes as he kicked one of the vermin in front of her with a gangly lizard leg and sneered at the still-twitching creatures. Looking to her as a challenge, she once again swatted the offering away. "I'd rather starve than take charity from *you*," she spat. "*Especially* when that charity is every bit the vermin you are! So unless your prepared to open a vein—or all of them—I suggest you stop trying!"

Maledictus frowned at that, "It's been three days now. That's three days that *nobody* has found you." He crouched down in front of her, hooking one of his ykali talons behind one of the dying rats and inching it closer to her, "You'd imagine that your friends would be clever enough to track you down in that time, yes? That, if they *truly* cared, they would've stormed this place and left not a single bit of me left for what I did. But they haven't—they haven't even come *close*—and still you deny me. *Me!* Me who has offered you shelter," he inched the rat closer to her, "Me who has offered you nourishment. When will you open those pretty little purple eyes and see that *I* am the only future you have left?"

Serena narrowed her eyes at that and hauled back, collecting a wad of phlegm from her sinuses and hawking one of the best loogies of her life in his face. Maledictus roared and pulled back before backhanding her and sending her careening across the room, the heavy links of chain rattling as her body sailed and finally slammed into the wall behind her.

"You have always been one to take the hard way with everything, eh buttercup baby? Well that's just fine with me," Maledictus sneered as he itched at a slight protrusion on his chest and a fresh, bony barb exposed itself beneath a chunk of dead, scaly skin that fell onto the ground beside the rejected offerings. "Believe it or not, I actually prefer it."

Chapter Two
Past to Present

Zoey turned to the others after a moment of long silence. She sighed, leaning into Isaac as Raith and Nikki watched the hallway for a moment.

"He's asleep," Zoey whispered. "I can't believe this; we finally had something *right* going on. Zane finally was free of this beast, after all the years."

"Seeing things from, well, behind his eyes was hard enough… but now that Maledictus has his own form," Raith shook his head. "I can't even imagine what he's going through."

"Before Serena… I don't think Zane would've been able to handle it honestly. After Serena came in, Zane changed for the better. I know you were watching, Raith, so I'm sure you can attest for that."

"Not only Zane though," Nikki smiled, "I may have only met Serena earlier this year, but watching her handle her power-hungry, Council-seated asshole brother, Keith, an—"

"Why would they even give him a seat? He was so young," Isaac interrupted.

"Well, at least we don't have to worry about Keith anymore, seeing as he's in an auric induced coma."

"Anyway, seeing her interject *him* and that Kristine broad's new clan, Sere—"

Isaac scoffed, "what is it with you fang-heads attracting power-hungry psychopaths? This is why us therions—"

Nikki slammed her fists on the table, "if you interrupt me one more time, dog-breath…"

Isaac looked down and paused on the discussion and sighed, feeling Zoey's hand on his shoulder.

Nikki sighed, "Either way, Serena has grown just as much as Zane from these past occurrences."

"Well, Kristine had ties to Serena's dead lover, Devon," Zoey sighed. "Serena's ex-fiancé was killed the night he was to propose to her *by* Kristine. His aura had tied to Serena's before Zane's anger and partially Maledictus' power destroyed him for good. That auric still had a thing for Devon and then, from there, you could see the vendetta grow. She allowed that revenge to grow, to the point where she used innocent people, people like Axle and his friends, the orphanage, and others to gain power."

"You're telling me that that auric *mimicked* an entire clan for the sake of getting Council backing just to get back at Serena for an ex-lover? That seems strange,"

Nikki shook her head, turning to Raith who had been fortunate, if they could use that word, to have taken Axle's body as his own.

"Do you think there could be a greater power here somewhere?" Zoey tilted her head, looking over at Nikki.

Something did feel strange about this. Zoey paused, knowing she felt this way with Keith, Serena's brother, and how he had so easily taken ahold of The Council.

"We don't have time to worry about the past, Zane can't handle another loss... *especially* from Maledictus' hands," Raith scowled.

"What do you mean by that?" Zoey asked.

"Zane was previously engaged to a sangsuiga vampire named Celine. She was with Zane when we started to work together," Raith sighed. "She didn't agree with Zane working with me and in my opinion, she was a heinous bitch. But Zane loved her..."

"What happened to her?" Zoey bit her lip, afraid to know the truth.

"After our curse, Zane went back to the house. He lost control and when he came to, he was surrounded in blood. *Celine's* blood," Raith shook his head. "It broke him..."

"How exactly was this curse created? I know that Zane and you were hoping to obtain something at Nikki's clan, but the details weren't exactly something Zane was ready to get into."

"I had asked Zane and Raith to take something—a relic—from my village," Nikki chewed her lip. "It had begun to taint my tribe; burden them with an unstoppable rage. They stopped acting themselves and had begun to worship it. Prior to this, my people never worshiped objects; it was considered a sin of sorts. I had hoped that Raith and Zane could steal it and get it far enough away from my tribe to clear their minds. But instead... well, you know."

"Before that curse, Zane was a different person entirely," Raith sighed. "He was carefree and upbeat about everything. Not a god damn thing could've ruined his optimism on anything. He was my best mate and even now, I promise to stick by his side."

Nikki smiled, running her hand up and down Raith's back, noticing the tension growing in her lover. Zoey turned to Isaac, who had been noticeably quiet and smiled, resting her hand on his leg and he turned his green gaze to hers. Without Isaac, Zoey couldn't imagine going through all this. With him by her side, she knew they would be able to work through it.

Somehow they'd find a way.

"This obviously has everything to do with that receptacle that we pulled out of Zane. What the hell is that thing anyway?" Zoey asked.

Chapter Three
Valuables

~DECEMBER 28TH, 893AD~
~ARMENIAN OUTSKIRTS; JUST OUTSIDE OF DVIN~
~PALACE OF MELEILZSI SHAYKH NAQSHBAND~
~SHORTLY AFTER SUNDOWN~

THE GREAT HALL TREMBLED ONCE MORE as Meleilzsi Shaykh Naqshband's bellows for his chalice became more enraged. Slave and concubine alike flinched at their master's roars, and the very walls of his palace—walls that were rumored to contain the thousands-upon-thousands of bodies that had fallen in the efforts to erect them—shook; seemingly humming with a fury that matched Meleilzsi Shaykh Naqshband's own.

Those who knew of his power and the magic he wielded *also* knew better than to question this, just as much as they knew that the phenomena was not an unrelated or random one. There was no question in the minds that Meleilzsi Shaykh Naqshband had allowed to still *have* thought that there were, in fact, corpses within the walls...

But they were far, *far* from restful.

While many believed great Meleilzsi Shaykh Naqshband to be a Mage—after all, the rumors of his magic *were* the stuff of legends, and it was no secret from any, both within his palace *and* without, that he had an affinity to working with the dead—it was clear that his workings were something *far* more sinister and, moreover, reserved for his gain alone.

That the walls now rumbled with the fury of the palace master's demands was proof that the flames of his magic were growing, and it would not be long before all within the palace walls would burn if those demands were not soon met.

It was the victorious shouts of Arezoo, Meleilzsi Shaykh Naqshband's most coveted of concubines, that finally stilled the rising storm. The soft-yet-steady patter of the young girl's nimble feet echoed through the still-bloodstained halls, and any set of eyes that were privy to the sight of her swiftness shimmered with a bastard hybrid of awe and terror. And while, on any other day, this *might* have been in response to her alien beauty, their gazes cared little for her appearance at that moment. Undeniably, with her almond-toned flesh that offered the same smooth flawlessness as the porcelain treasures of the far-East and a mane of hair so golden it put the treasures of sultans to shame, she was a sight to behold; a goddess, some would say. However, on that night, all beauty and splendor for not, it was the threat that Arezoo's swiftness with the palace-master's chalice, his most beloved of relics, that forced the air within their chests to still.

If she were but to stumble or waver...

Should just one drop of the chalice's contents breach the rim...

Meleilzsi Shaykh Naqshband would surely let none of them live.

None, of course, but Arezoo.

No, she and she *alone* held privileges that her master offered to none other. Few knew of just *where* Meleilzsi Shaykh Naqshband had found his most coveted of concubines—what grand reaches of the world their master had dredged this strange creature from—and even fewer knew *why* she, over so many other young, nubile girls that just as eagerly lived to serve his every lustful whim, should be *his* favorite. And while the mysteries of Arezoo's birthplace *or* the name she'd carried before Meleilzsi Shaykh Naqshband had stripped her of all identity but the title of *his* cherished one were a mystery that none would dare press to be solved, it was certain that, at that moment, she held all of their lives in her hands...

And she was *laughing*!

Violent, enraged thoughts teemed in the minds of all witnessing the spectacle, but none dared make a move upon her. While the chalice and its contents were most certainly a prevalent demand at that moment, Arezoo took precedent in Meleilzsi Shaykh Naqshband's eyes before all else. Any harm that could possibly befall her would be returned a hundred-thousand times over on the heads of not just her attackers, but all within the palace *and* the lands beyond.

There was no question that, were Arezoo to meet an end, all of Egypt would see a wrath from Meleilzsi Shaykh Naqshband that would put the plagues of the Testament to shame.

Meleilzsi Shaykh Naqshband would leave no survivors, and, in creating so much death, his powers would be enough to vanquish any of the gods: old *and* new.

And so, while the arrogant creature might have been audacious enough to laugh with the fate of so many at stake, neither slave nor fellow concubine made a move or protest to correct her.

They already knew there was no getting through to Arezoo.

Meleilzsi Shaykh Naqshband was halfway into another tremendous bellow in the old language—still refusing to let the dialect of the Tajiks sully his home—when his eyes fell upon the glorious sight of Arezoo's ample bosom rolling about her chest as she sprinted down the hall towards his chamber, his chalice held proudly over her head as she exclaimed again and again that she came to her master with *both* of his treasures.

The broad, arrogant grin that birthed across their master's face then brought a sigh of relief that traveled throughout the entire palace; the angry hum within the walls fading into a nothingness that held promise that the new day's sun *would* be a spectacle for all eyes to see.

Arezoo's laughter doubled in triumph as she neared the doors, and she paused but only a moment to admire the massive, gaping hole that occupied the wall; letting what it symbolized send a tremor of excitement up her back before finally crossing the threshold.

Once she was through, the chamber doors slammed shut behind Arezoo, and Meleilzsi Shaykh Naqshband shifted himself within his seat to prepare for his consort. Seeing this, Arezoo smirked and leapt—still gripping his teeming chalice—into his lap. The scarlet contents sloshed and rolled, and Arezoo offered nothing more than a giggle as a portion of her master's drink slipped over the rim and splashed across her breasts.

Were any of the other servants to bear witness to this, they'd surely have dropped dead.

A deep, low growl emanated from deep within Meleilzsi Shaykh Naqshband's body—his intense gaze honing on the spilled liquid as his lip curled; on the opposite side of the palace, one of the walls quaked with activity from within—and the master's body began to shake.

Arezoo smirked and cocked her head as her deep, intense purple gaze—one of the unique traits that had brought her master's attention to her all those years ago—shimmered; a sound not unlike the cooing of a dove issuing from her partially opened mouth.

Swelling her chest and letting the liquid adorning it trail further down her cleavage, she silently willed her master to act.

Meleilzsi Shaykh Naqshband's hands found either side of Arezoo's hips and yanked her forward with enough force to make her yelp. His parched mouth found purchase, and he quickly began to lap at the myriad of scarlet trails that had begun to descend towards her abdomen, starting from their freshest point and working back to their source before starting again on another.

And Arezoo bathed in the attention; relished in the power that the two of them recognized as hers.

Though their union was, in the eyes of all others in the palace, nothing more than that of Meleilzsi Shaykh Naqshband's typical activity with any of his concubines—albeit his undeniable favorite—there was an intense passion shared between the two behind closed doors and safe from prying eyes.

Meleilzsi Shaykh Naqshband was a man of great power and strength—at least, he *had* been a man before his mortal body had perished so many years ago—and, with all of his power, there was little that he couldn't obtain. He'd lavished the halls of his palace with all shapes and shades of feminine flesh, sending his most prestigious of buyers far and wide to procure the best specimens from all around the globe. Each and every one of his concubines was well-versed, well-trained, and well-rewarded; never a fear of want or of worry creasing their perfect brows…

So long as they obeyed.

But it was in their relentless obedience that Meleilzsi Shaykh Naqshband was cursed with boredom.

Arezoo was not only content in her lifestyle, but outright *flourished* within it; her body knowing the carnal demands of *both* sexes long before her chest bore fruit or her loins were graced by the hair of adulthood. All manners of pleasure and the demands she was expected to fulfill had been introduced to her long ago, and it was through not only her acceptance of these pleasures but also her *manipulation* of them that she discovered just how lucrative they could be.

With but a warm, wet orifice and a few simple noises, she could claim anything she'd ever wanted.

Especially power!

And, in the chamber of Meleilzsi Shaykh Naqshband, she had not only power, but security, as well.

~*Present day*~

Flashes of his old life, visions of power or of faces that seemed so dreamlike now, were coming to him more often. He still couldn't remember his name, only the title he'd been "reborn" inside Zane with:
Maledictus.
"Cursed one."
He laughed at that as he gazed into the barely reflective surface of the aged mirror; if it could be called such a thing. The building he'd taken—a crumbling, graffiti-covered mess that was absolutely *teeming* with the twisted, angry energies of misery and pain; a long-since abandoned mental asylum—was a prime location for him for any number of reasons, not the least of which being its ambiguity and a means to keep his soon-to-be bride locked-up and...
"LET ME OUT OF HERE, MOTHERFUCKER!"
The neighboring room went into delicious chaos as Serena began throwing one of her increasingly predictable fits; the barrier spell he'd put up, however, was just as predictable and contained the outburst. She was no-doubt using her aura to create the racket—there wasn't enough length on the enchanted chain he'd tethered her with to build up that much momentum with her body—and *that* meant that the counter-spell would be activating right about...

"AAAAAHHHHHHHHHHH!"
Silence.
He chuckled and shook his head. "You're not exactly the learning type, are you?" he mumbled to himself, not expecting an answer from Serena.

Just like every other time she'd tried using her aura within the enchanted space, the counter-spell he'd put up as a precaution against the powerful-and-brash she-vamp reacted when her auric activity reached a potentially dangerous level. When the auric levels reached a critical point, the spell was awakened from its dormant state and shifted the charge in the ions within the room, delivering a crippling shock that, each and every time, knocked the sparky blonde unconscious.

Sparky.

He chuckled to himself and returned to the mirror; his irritation at the warped and rusty metal sheet that offered little-to-no reflection rising once again.

"Fucking pussies!" he griped, finding enough of his reflection to resume the process of picking the looser scales from his face. "If the batshit crazy bastards you bolted down in this shit-shack were demented enough to take their lives with *glass* mirrors then you should've just *let* them!" He growled as he once again lost his reflection in the tarnished surface and drove a fist into it, sneering at the sight of the twisted sheet of metal he was rewarded with.

Nowhere *near* as satisfying as broken glass.

"Fucking pussies!" he muttered again.

Abandoning the hope of using sight to aid him in his cosmetic efforts, he began to simply rake his talons across his face. As more and more scales popped free—some needing more passes with the clawed hands than others—the small, stained sink became increasingly filled with the product of his efforts. The greenish-brown flakes looked like a pile of festering toenails, and the fresh layer of blood-covered bits reinforced the illusion of some sort of torture scene.

But he—he sighed in resignation at his stubbornness and finally just accepted the title he'd been wearing for so long: *Maledictus*—had never felt better.

At least he didn't *remember* feeling better.

Though there was something—some ghost of a memory haunting the back of his mind—that made him certain that Serena, that spunky, resilient, and delightfully defiant purple-eyed blonde, would somehow make things even better.

Finally, Maledictus' claws had "shaved" the last of the scales from his face—and more than a fair share of his flesh, as well—and he went to work with the incessant itches that crowned the top of his head. As he began to work the area of his forehead, he discovered three hardened spots that had risen slightly under the skin of his brow, and he went to work picking around the myriad of tears he'd earned in his previous task. A memory that he'd vicariously acquired through Zane—a moment from his *human* childhood—picked up on his subconscious, and the chiding words of young-Zane's mother echoed on his lips.

"*Don't pick at it. It'll never heal.*"

Maledictus cackled.

Healing?

Healing?

There was no growth in *healing* from something; there was no strength to be found in letting something knit and rest. To grow a muscle, it had to first be worked and torn; tortured to a point of realizing that it must either perish or push to thrive.

Push to rise above all else.

Continuing to pick and tear away at the flaps of skin on his head, Maledictus finally was rewarded. Tossing a chunk of bloodied meat into the sink, he yanked the warped hunk of mirror-metal from the wall and worked to angle it so that he could look upon…

A *horn?*

He beamed at this.

For the past few days he'd been pushing his new body to shift; the lizard-like exterior, though entertaining at times, simply not offering him the personal aesthetic he demanded. Granted, it was a definite improvement on the weak and simple humanoid form he'd been locked within, but when he'd been condemned to occupy Zane's body there had at least been the *transformation*; the process by which he could twist and break past the simple pink flesh and become something more powerful and fear-inducing.

After taking the abandoned mental asylum and locking away his future wife, he'd taken a tour of the establishment. While relishing in the lingering traces of suffering that had caked themselves into every nook and cranny the building had to offer, he saw any number of messages—desperate and futile calls to sympathetic passersby—that had been left by the patients. Messages that were carved into the walls with crude tools or— judging from the bits of yellowed fingernails littered about the site or embedded within the surfaces themselves—with the scribers' bare hands; messages written in blood, feces, and, less frequent, pen or marker.

HELP ME! I AM IN HELL!
BEELZEBUB MADE ME DO IT
I AM HIS VESSEL. LORD SATAN RIDES WITHIN.

THE DEMONS DEMAND MORE CORNBREAD!
ABASHED THE DEVIL STOOD...

Everywhere that he'd looked, there had been references to whatever name the mad men and women had attributed to evil. This devil—whether it was referenced by some religious title or, his personal favorite, simply referred to as "he"; as though the walking embodiment of evil could be *anything* but a woman—seemed to be an ongoing theme for all that pain and suffering; the very pain and suffering that had led him there in the first place.

So, naturally, he decided that this devil, no matter what others thought it to be, would be the role he'd assume now that he was free to walk the streets within his own body.

Horns?

Talons and a tail?

Viciously inhuman?

None of these descriptors were outside his reach. True, a great deal of the references demanded a *red* devil, and his brownish-green scales were certainly far from that, but, seeing the sinewy and bloody mess he'd made of his face in excavating the first horn he'd birthed from his forehead—feeling at least five more beneath the surface of the skin around his head—he was certain that, with time, even his hue would follow.

After all, he'd gotten this far on willpower alone.

With nothing more than his *hope*, he'd willed his body to begin changing into his vision of the humans' "devil."

A pained tickle in his mouth made him flinch, interrupting his glee as he poked at the still-small hunk of curved yellow bone that protruded from just above his left eye. Reaching into the back of his mouth, he

SCARLET DUSK

poked about. A screaming pain as the flesh-and-blood coated claw met one of the teeth along the top row of his jaw gave away the culprit, and, getting a firm grip on the offending tooth, he yanked it free of his face. A brief moment was spared as he admired the jagged, reptilian thing, contemplating what his body would birth in its place, before tossing it into the fetid pile of waste within the sink.

"Look at you, you magnificent motherfucker!" he swooned over his partial reflection. "There's no way that stupid bitch will be able to resist you much longer."

At that moment, as Maledictus playfully batted his freshly-grown and still crusty eyelids at himself, his left eye—which *had* been growing increasingly pale and been itching with an ongoing set of twitches—ruptured in its socket and began to leak out into the sink.

He couldn't help but laugh at his own body's timing.

"No-fucking-sir!" he whistled, "No chance of resisting *this*!"

Chapter Four
Forget Me Not

THE SAME BAR.

Zane shouldn't have been as surprised as he was when he found himself walking into the same bar he had before he met Serena. The same bar that always seemed to be the place he showed up when he was troubled. Stepping forward, he made his way down to the bar and placed a seat right in front of the SAME German bartender who looked at him with both an annoyed and frightened gaze.

"Same as usual, Fuhrer!"

"Haven't seen you here in a while," the bartender sneered, "but I guess nothing truly does change."

"You have no fucking idea," Zane snarled, reaching forward and grabbed the bartender's collar, pulling him closer. "Now, I'm not here for chat, or trouble, but if you don't just make with the drink and keep your Nazi mouth shut—I am not against making some."

"R-right," the bartender quickly pulled back as Zane let him go and he watched as he scurried off to make his drink.

Sighing, Zane allowed himself to calm down again as he pulled out the small bottle that was nearly empty. He sneered, remembering how much he relied on the mythos drug before and shook up the bottle as he waited for his drink. The bartender quickly handed him a bottle and made his way to the other side of the bar.

Good. Zane thought as he pressed the smaller mythos potion to the bottle and began to pour it down. He sighed, pressing the bottle to his lips and allowed himself a good swig as the effects of the potion began to set. He grinned, allowing the haziness to envelop him as the numbing started.

Serena…

He glowered, realizing his fists were clenched and he quickly placed the bottle down as to not start a scene, any more than he already had. He found himself smirking as he thought of what she'd say about his present state. She'd most likely go on about how he was being a little bitch-boy and he had to grow a pair.

Grinning at the sudden fond memory of his snarky lover, he allowed that moment to sit in him as he chugged another sip of the potion beer.

He narrowed his eyes, catching something, *someone,* familiar out of the corner of his eye. He turned and the warmth he had previously been feeling grew cold. Walking towards him was a piece of his past thought destroyed and as she made her way closer, he felt his nerves begin to grow and the haziness dissipated.

"C-Celine..." he whispered, "w-was it you? I thought I saw you...just the other day when I was with...was i-it you?"

"It was me..." Celine chewed her lip for a moment, "I couldn't tell if it was you or not but when I saw you walk into this bar, I had to follow."

"H-how? You're, I mean, you *were*..." he shook his head, "I thought you were dead," Zane stammered, stunned at the sudden events as he stared at his fiancé.

He shook his head again; *ex*-fiancé.

"I... I'd been following you for a bit," she shrugged nervously. "What with all the rumors of the Maledictus curse and your finally getting rid him, I... I had to know the truth, to see it for myself," she whispered as she took a seat next to him and he could still hear a faint trace of her Scottish accent.

He frowned at her closeness but chose not to say anything as he gazed forward at nothing.

"I guess I should start the beginning," she coughed at his silence. "When Maledictus had... well, when he'd showed himself, he *had* targeted me. Luckily, I was able to get away... barely. Afterward, I was taken in by some nearby friends of my family."

"They told me not go after you again; that the curse you had would kill me and I chose to wait. I hoped that you'd be able to find a cure, and I had to wait in hopes that you'd find a way."

"And that's why you are here *now?*" Zane tilted his head, feeling unnerved by her story. He frowned at his own doubt, realizing he had no reason to judge her.

Anyone would've done the same if they had watched someone close to them transform into a raging beast.

Except Serena.

"I've missed you, Zane... *all* this time," Celine pressed her hand to his arm. "I was hoping to... well, I was hoping to spend some time with you."

"I-I don't know, Celine," Zane forced himself not to frown, "A lot has changed since..."

"*Please*, Zane... I have nowhere to go right now," she whimpered, squeezing his arm, "The only other place I had to stay..." she shook her head, "The plans fell through, and now I don't have anywhere to stay."

Zane sighed, turning to her for a moment and felt a pang of guilt for the past. He had an obligation after everything that he had put her through in the past to at least offer her somewhere to stay. "I...I can offer you a place to stay, but that's all," he sighed and looked away, suddenly realizing how much time he was wasting *not* looking for Serena. "That's all I can ever offer you."

"That's more than enough for now, Zane!" Celine smiled and hugged him, "Thank you again!"

"Yea, sure. No problem," he quickly pulled away and finished his beer before he turned towards the door. His doubt grew, and he began to wonder if it *was* a good idea to be offering *anything* to *anybody* at that time, let alone a place to stay to a past lover he'd presumed dead for so many years. Once again, he found himself wishing that Serena were there to help guide him. But it was too late to retract the offer now; not comfortably, at least. "Let's go," he called out as he made his way for the exit, "I've got things to do."

Zoey smiled lovingly at Isaac, her therion lover, as she wrapped her arms around his neck. It had been so long since she'd been able to have a private moment with him and she needed the intimacy he was offering.

"Are you alright, love?" Isaac smirked down at her.

"I just want this moment," Zoey smiled.

"Oh?" he smirked, tilting her head upward, "well, let's not keep the lady waiting any longer."

Zoey moaned as Isaac's lips crashed down on hers and she shivered at the pleasure that came with her lover's kiss. She gasped as he squeezed her breast and he took the moment to slide his tongue in her mouth, running it against hers. Deciding that it was her time to take control, Zoey allowed her aura to rip their clothes off as Isaac pressed her back against their bed.

"Mmm... have I mentioned how much I *love* having an auric vampire for a lover? It makes undressing so much easier, and so much more fun," Isaac smirked, running his finger across her bare chest as he teasingly ran it around her nipple.

She gasped, arching up, begging him to touch her, begging for the teasing to stop. She needed him inside her. It had been so chaotic for *too* long and Zoey cherished these moments with her lover. She watched as he leaned his head down, flicking his tongue across one of her nipples as his finger found her other. The shock of electricity running down her spine caused her to arch further up and she found herself pressing against his hardened member.

"Looks like someone's ready to go," she purred, running her hand up and down his length, watching in pleasure as her lover rocked forward against her fist.

Isaac clenched his eyes shut in pure bliss as she continued to jerk his shaft and finally, he was able to find the willpower to remove his lover's grip.

"Careful, love..." he smirked, "I don't want to be finished *too* quickly."

She smirked playfully and spread her legs, allowing her sex to be in full view for Isaac and she watched as his eyes widened at the sight before he smirked and moved his hands down her torso, moving towards her glistening folds.

"I-Isaac! Hurry touch me!" Zoey cried out, no longer able to hold in her arousal.

Isaac smirked, quickly remedying his lover's thirst as he began to slide his fingers inside her. She cried out as he readied her for his shaft and before long, she was climaxing on his hand. Breathing hard, Zoey looked up at Isaac as he positioned himself over her and leaned down, kissing her hard as he allowed himself to finally thrust inside his lover.

"Oh! That's it!" Zoey shivered, wrapping her legs tightly around his waist as he quickly picked up the pace.

Isaac had finally gotten over his fears of hurting Zoey with his size and had *finally* realized that Zoey liked it rough. She smiled up at him, letting him know there was nothing to worry about, dousing any fear her lover may have had. Leaning up, she pressed her lips to his in a passionate kiss as he continued to dive inside his lover's folds.

Shivering in ecstasy, Zoey could feel Isaac's body tense as he reached the edge and she cried out, falling with him as they both reached their climaxes together. She wrapped her arms around his neck tightly and kissed him hard as they slowly came back from their bliss.

Isaac fell to Zoey's side, not bothering to pull out of her as she snuggled against his chest. He smiled, looking down at her bright blue hair and ran his fingers through it as she rested her face over his heart.

"Mine," she murmured into his chest.

"Always," he agreed.

"What's on your mind?" she turned her bright blue gaze to his and he smiled, her gaze perfectly matched the color of her hair.

"Your blue-ness," he grinned.

She chuckled and teasingly slapped his arm, "no, really, what is on your mind?"

"How can you expect me to even be able to speak, let alone *think* after that?" Isaac arched his eyebrow down at her, "what's on *your* mind?"

"Honestly? I'm hoping we find Serena soon…" Zoey bit her lip, thinking about her missing best friend.

Not long after she'd first met Serena, the two of them had bonded; forming a nearly sibling relationship. This bond, though having nothing to do with their shared auric abilities, was tight enough to give them insight to one another's wellbeing, and she knew then that her friend needed her just as much as she needed Serena.

"I know. I'm worried about Zane too in that regard, I mean, I don't know much about him," Isaac sighed. "But, I'm worried about how he's taking this whole kidnapping thing."

Zoey nodded slowly, "I know he can seem scary at times, especially in the past considering what his anger brought out," she paused for a moment. "But, Zane is like a brother to me and despite all the appearances he puts up, he is truly a passionate and loyal comrade. He is loyal to the Vailean clan."

"I see..." Isaac frowned, "But what do you think he's feeling about losing the curse?"

"I'm a bit worried about that honestly," she sighed, "I mean, on the one hand I do sense a great deal of relief, but on the other..." she shook her head. "I sense a growing concern for how he's feeling about not being able to handle these new threats. That he isn't strong enough *without* Maledictus serving as some sort of ace in the hole."

Isaac narrowed his eyes at that and looked over, "You mean he feels inadequate without Maledictus?"

"Though it *was* an awful curse, Maledictus' strength and power were, in many ways, a safety net for Zane. Now that that strength and power are gone, he's afraid—though I know he'll never admit it—that he might not be able to handle things on his own. I mean, I..." Zoey paused, looking away. "We need to go," she sighed, using her aura to retrieve a fresh set of clothes for the two of them from the drawers.

As they rushed out the door and down the hall, the two spotted Zane walking into the community room along with a redheaded woman; a sang.

"Zane? Who's this?" Zoey asked, nodding a quick greeting to the newcomer standing beside him.

The woman's aura, originally filled with an awed intrigue, shifted to nervous as Zoey and Isaac both approached them, and she moved closer to Zane. Narrowing her eyes at this, Zoey watched the woman, unsettled by something about the way she moved, before returning her focus to Zane.

Zane bit his lip, his aura shifting with unnerved movements as the newcomer came in close to him. "This is Celine," he finally confessed, "my... well, we *were* engaged a long time ago. She heard that the

Maledictus curse had been lifted and came to town to see if it was true."

"Engaged? You mean the fiancé that Maledi—" Zoey's eyes widened as she looked back to the woman, "So she isn't dead." Zoey forced a smile, hoping to not come off as rude during such an uncomfortable reunion. "Well, it's a pleasure to meet you, Celine. I'm glad to hear that you're alive and well," Zoey started to offer her hand for a more formal greeting, but decided against it when she noticed the nervousness growing in her aura. Though curious about this, she decided not to pry out of respect for Zane.

"Yea, I guess she got away from Maledictus before… well, before he could do what he's known for," Zane nodded, and Zoey could see he was forcing the words and gestures just so he could be rid of the need to do so. "Anyway, she doesn't have anywhere to stay, so I figured I'd offer her a room here until she gets back on her feet."

"That was nice of you," Zoey nodded before clearing her throat. "So, any progress on Serena's whereabouts?"

Zane shook his head, "No. I got a little sidetracked while I was out and…" He glowered, "I *will* find her, though. I *need* to. She's in danger out there with *him*, Zoe, you know that."

"I know," she nodded, setting a hand on his shoulder—sensing a swell in the newcomer's aura as she did—and offered him a reassuring smile. "We have to have hope and just stay focused. In the meantime we just have to keep a level head on our shoulders and not get distracted."

"I would never let anything distract me from this," Zane looked into Zoey's eyes and she smiled, seeing that Zane wasn't in any way deterred from his goals due to the Celine situation. "Nothing will stop me from finding her."

"Good! I'll continue keeping an eye on all the city's public camera networks and the police broadcasts to try and find any clues," Zoey smiled.

"Sounds like a plan. I'm going to go back out there while there's still some time until sunup," Zane's voice had shifted back to his serious, *not* forced tone. "Have someone show Celine to her room and call me if you find anythi—"

"I'll go with you," Celine suddenly offered, closing the distance between them yet again. Biting her lip, her aura shifting with embarrassment as she realized how her suddenness had come off, she cleared her throat, "P-please, Zane. I… I want to help you. If this girl—"

"Serena!" Zane narrowed his eyes at her.

"R-right. Serena. If this Serena means so much to you, then I want to help you find her." Celine blushed and let her gaze shift between Zane and Zoey. "It's… it's the least I can do…"

Zane sighed and shook his head, his aura shifting as he abandoned any cruel-worded rejections he'd wanted to respond with. "Do what you want. Just don't get in the way. Zoey," he turned back towards his friend, "if anything—and I do mean *anything*—turns up on any of the frequencies, don't hesitate to call me."

"Will do," Zoey went to turn towards the clan's resource room, spotting Isaac a few paces back. As she walked by, he followed and fell into a pace beside her as she made her way to the surveillance room.

"You were awful quiet back there," she nudged him, smirking. "You shy?"

"I don't like strange vampires," he confessed.

"Yea, and she was plenty strange, wasn't she?" Zoey chuckled, shaking her head. While this Celine seemed to be more of a nuisance than a danger, she knew that she'd have to keep an extra eye on her.

Something in her gut told her that something wasn't right with her sudden appearance.

"You alright?" Isaac asked, tilting his head.

"Yea, I'm fine. I was just thinking about what else I could do to search for Serena. I feel like I'm not doing enough." Zoey bit her lip and shook her head before realizing that Isaac was beginning to look nervous. "It's alright, baby, I'm just in business-mode, you know? I'm going to be pretty wrapped up on the computers—boring stuff—if you want to wait for me in our room you can." She smiled and nudged him, "Without me to complain about the weak plot lines, you could watch your cartoons in peace."

"No, I'd rather stay with you," Isaac nodded, taking her hand in his. "While all that technological stuff still bugs me, I don't want to leave you alone. And if I can help find Serena, I'd rather do that than watch cartoons," he nudged her back, "besides, I *like* it when you point out stuff like that, it reminds me how smart you are."

Zoey blushed at that, "Like you need a reminder."

Chapter Five
(un) Dead Heart

~893AD~
~ARMENIAN OUTSKIRTS; JUST OUTSIDE OF DVIN~
~PALACE OF MELEILZSI SHAYKH NAQSHBAND~

MELEILZSI SHAYKH NAQSHBAND AND AREZOO, unlikely and unconventional as their union might have been, had something special between them; something genuine.
   Something that compelled Meleilzsi Shaykh Naqshband to do the unthinkable...
   In his mortal life, the powerful master had sired no

children—produced no heirs to his conquests—out of spite and greed. To him, allowing a rightful successor to his glory was an acknowledgement that his goals for immortality might fail, and he felt that any such sign of doubt was, even if only to himself, a weakness that could fester and spread like an infection. So when the night finally came that he'd sent all of his servants away and barricaded himself deep into the cold, dry depths of his ceremony hall, there wasn't a doubt in his mind that he'd emerge three days later an immortal.

There were the tales of the life-feeders that scoured the lands at night. Few, if any, had not sat—wide-eyed and awed—and listened to the stories of the legends. And while many put little faith in the tales—tales of beings that wore the shape of men and dragged the young and elderly from their beds to consume their blood and rip the very souls from their hearts, and still others of men who abandoned their human skins to take to the nights as great beasts that consumed all they came across—there was rarely any who took the chance at such encounters. The magi were, for the most part, entrusted with keeping such evil from entering the great cities, and though Meleilzsi Shaykh Naqshband had no interest in repelling such creatures—not while they held so many delectable secrets—it was not his interest to come to them as anything less than their equal.

Meleilzsi Shaykh Naqshband was far too proud to claim his legacy from any hand that was not his own.

And so it was that, when he'd grown satisfied with his research and his spells, it was with his own hand that he tore out his heart and allowed his mortal body to fall within the geometric grid he'd drawn for *exactly* that purpose and die there in the cold, dry depths of his ceremony hall.

All his work.
All his hopes.
All his power.
All invested with such faith and determination that he'd entrusted everything he was—everything he'd achieved and everything he'd become—to the unquestioned hope that, as he spent his last moments, clutching his own heart within his trembling grasp, he was creating a new beginning rather than simply engineering an end. Forcing the gurgled chants to breach his quivering lips, Meleilzsi Shaykh Naqshband set his heart within a small hammock fashioned of virgin hair that hung just over what was to be his mortal body's final resting place.

The fading sight of his heart offering one final, futile pump of spurting life within the dark, woven strands had been a vision of hope.

Hope...

Unquestioning, unwavering, and undeniable.

Meleilzsi Shaykh Naqshband *had* woken up, though a full day ahead of schedule, and as he found his first breath and, with it, his first pained-yet-victorious shrieks within the empty confines of his ceremony hall, he knew that his hope had held merit. It was with this pride and profound new power coursing through his body that he'd stood and torn his mortal heart from its resting place and took his first bite.

He'd been feeding on death ever since.

Those creatures—those *monsters*—that Meleilzsi Shaykh Naqshband had once seen as something to be envied had become nothing more than animals to him. Everything that *was* ate something; the lions had their zebras, the peasants had their livestock...

But all of them—each and every thing that ate of

anything else—perished.

Meleilzsi Shaykh Naqshband, however, had become a Liche; a being empowered *by* death!

And if anything was more certain than life, it was death!

Immortality *was* his, and he owed all of it to his hope.

A hope that had returned to him when he'd found Arezoo…

A hope that he would not be burdened to traverse the path of an unending life alone.

A hope that, though he had sacrificed any possibility of ever producing a new life—life being the one thing he could not create—he might find a companion in death.

And so it was that Arezoo, nothing more than a concubine in the eyes of all others within the palace walls, became not only his lover…

But his apprentice.

Holding once more to his hope, Meleilzsi Shaykh Naqshband taught Arezoo the ways of death—the energy and possibilities that could be drawn from life's greatest of mysteries—and shaped her mind and body for the day that she, too, would descend into the cold, dry depths of his ceremony hall and, like him, watch her mortal heart's last beat and be reborn an immortal.

Despite all of his aspirations and romances, however, did not deter Meleilzsi Shaykh Naqshband from finding the time—he *was*, after all, an immortal with all the time in the world—to take pleasure in the powers he had earned. Nor was the great Liche master without his fair share of rivals.

Shortly after his rebirth, he'd discovered that the legends and stories were not only all true, but grossly dulled and lacking in the glory they were deserved. Though they *were*, as the legends described, seemingly human in appearance, the vision his new powers offered him made spotting them within the crowds during his outings as simple as plucking the overripe dates from a proffered bowl. Challenging them, however, proved to be something of a challenge, as, though they were every bit as vicious and powerful as the legends credited them, they were infinitely more cunning. Whether they avoided Meleilzsi Shaykh Naqshband advances out of fear or urge to maintain their secrecy, none seemed willing to face him as anything more than just another predator amidst a sea of prey; an alligator among wildcats…

Again and again he struggled to challenge one of the immortal creatures whose legends had motivated his unholy metamorphosis, but none were willing to offer him such satisfaction…

Until night that the eight-fingered creature declaring itself a son of Sekhmet arrived at the palace gates…

~*Present day*~

"Still no sign of them. *Nothing!*" Maledictus leered at Serena, "And you know why? Because your lover-boy is *nothing* without me! I was *everything* that made him who he was!"

"That's a bold line coming from the *freak* with a lizard-dick!" Serena scoffed.

It was the sort of snarky response he'd come to expect from her, but, rather than letting it boil his blood and motivate some violent response—something she seemed to outright revel in despite the obvious torture—

he let it slide. There was no point in letting her think that she could keep manipulating him, and he could already see that, despite all her forced boldness, hunger and weakness were beginning to take their toll on her. Her outbursts were less frequent, her fits were less violent and rarely grew strong enough to even awaken the dormant counter-spell, and, more and more, she was flinching at every move he made. She was scared, and, through that fear, he knew he would break her sooner or later.

He squatted down to her level and offered a wide grin, smirking as she recoiled from the sight.

It *was* true that, in the ongoing process of his metamorphosis, he *had* become something of a visually acquired taste. The majority of his body's lizard teeth had fallen out—though a few of the more stubborn stragglers remained—and allowed the far-more enticing, needle-like replacements to come in. The bulk of his facial wounds had healed into a network of angry scars that bisected his shifting skin-tone, which had begun to take on the color of burnt flesh. He'd finally succeeded in digging out all seven of his horns, which had grown quickly since and now adorned his skull like an organic crown that stretched nearly half-a-foot above the top of his head, which had recently begun sprouting clumps of platinum-silver hair. His new, bright blue, catlike left eye, contrasted sharply with paling snakelike right, and he was certain that he'd be shedding it soon enough. In one of his prior visits to Serena, he'd remarked that, like Zane, he now sported a pair of mismatched eyes and asked if she felt any more attracted to him for this reason.

Somehow, despite having not eaten in some time, her body had found something to vomit.

The rest of his body was, for the most part, still covered in scales, though portions of his upper torso and shoulders—which had begun to sprout a series of bone-spike protrusions like those that adorned his head—had been stripped in moments of boredom. Though he'd done little to transform his reptilian lower-body—outright adoring his new tail far too much to even consider parting or modifying it—he'd begun training himself to walk more upright than his body seemed initially willing. Because of the bulky mass of his tail and the otherwise weak upper-half, he felt naturally inclined to lean forward to accommodate; several times coming to walk on all fours without willing himself to do so, though the reaction he'd earned from Serena on these occasions *had* been worth it. Despite this, the arched figure—far too reminiscent to the lumbering form of a tyrannosaurus rex or other such relevantly extinct creature—was a major deterrent in his goals of reshaping himself into something far more regal. As an unexpected result of his posture regiment, his chest and shoulders had begun to broaden and his previously smooth, pale abdomen had taken on a more dense and rigid form. While it had not been his intention, the overall effect was not only the desired upright posture he'd strived to achieve, but *also* a far more muscled and intimidating appearance.

The entire package proving to be, though an emotional deterrent to his advances, an effective way at drawing out the fear and uncertainty in his future wife.

So while his appearances weren't what he wanted them to be just yet, he was perfectly content with the fear they elicited. If nothing else, it was helping him to break Serena's spirit; bringing her to lose hope in Zane and the others; the only thing that was keeping her resilient to his goals.

He needed to strip her of that hope…

And perhaps something else.

"You seem quite fixated on the subject of my dick, my dear, hollow-headed harlot," he chided, wetting his newly-grown lips with his forked tongue. "Is that all it takes then? A deep dicking; a sordid affair; a promiscuously casual romp in your loin-garden? Are you really such a simple trollop? Can you really be *that* much of a stupid slut-cunt? Is that why you're so insistent that he's something special? Because of that first night you met *us*—make no mistake, my air-headed princess, I *was* there—and you *fucked* us? Is that all the persuasion your feeble fucking mind needs to create the illusion of this thing you call love?" he chuckled and shook his head, "You stupid cow! Did it even occur to you—do you even remember—that it wasn't *either* of us *controlling* his body when you were riding him? Your loser ex—that brain-fucked *ghost* you clung so pathetically to!—was *controlling* his body the entire time! Zane"—he couldn't help but cackle then—"couldn't remember that night if I personally tore into his skull and *dug* for the memory! So is *that* the moment you feel you felt something between the two of you? 'Cause I got news for you, bitch: *I* remember that night all too well; I could send every sopping detail to Penthouse for their gaggle of retards to viciously jerk off to. Then you could feel some romantic sense of obligation to *everyone!*" He spotted tears welling in the she-vamp's eyes and, as she tried to turn her head away to hide her face, he caught her by the throat and forced her to look at him. "You *fucked* me on that night too, you cheap, loose-cunted sack of shit! So, if *sex* is the only thing that defines romance for you, then you'd better be ready to love me just as fucking much as that loser!"

Serena was shaking; her face a constricted mess of pent-up tears and pain that was growing beat-red around his clawed grip. Despite this—despite the growing agony that he could practically *see* welling within her—she resisted her own weaknesses and spit in his face. "You could arrange a fucking *gangbang* with the entire cast of 'Magic Mike,' and I'd *still* wait for him rather than settle with the likes of you!"

Weakening or not, a lesson had to be taught.

He couldn't bring himself to grin in the face of her defiance when her mucus was trickling down his cheek.

His fist landed with enough force to send her back, ricocheting off the padded walls of her cell and toppling back into him; the enchanted chains binding her jangling with the sudden movement.

Maledictus rose to his full height as his grip on her shoulders tightened and he growled in her face. "At some point I'm going to have to make a note of correcting the wretched habit of your flapping tongue!" He threw her back into the corner with a meek sense of pride as she cowered in his shadow, reaching to the crotch of his body to work his genitals free of the accursed "pocket" they were nestled in as he took a step towards her "And, at the rate you're going, that time will come sooner than you'd like!"

Serena struggled to muster her strength, sensing a fight coming up. "Take another step and I'll be flapping my foot up your scaly ass!"

Maledictus smirked at the threat. "Time to see if you can follow through with your chatter!"

He came down upon her, dropping the full force of his weight against her to overpower any efforts she might've been planning. Serena's left fist hooked around and slammed into his ribs—something snapping and shifting beneath his leathery hide—before she sacrificed her balled fists in an effort to push the impending force off of her. Muffled grunts and whimpers oozed into Maledictus' shoulder, which he propped against the thrashing blonde's throat to keep her pinned and still while he hooked one of his talons under one of the straps of her stained tank top. Serena growled against the restraint and lunged, trying to bite at the side of her attacker's face; her teeth snapping as her fangs left a pair of ruby trails across Maledictus' cheek. Hissing at her resistance, Maledictus cocked his head towards her and slammed several of the solid-bone horns along the side of his head into her face.

Serena's attack faltered and her eyes went cloudy as they rolled about in her skull.

"Good little sluts should learn to sit still!" Maledictus growled as he yanked his talon back, cutting the first strap—sagging half of her top over her chest—and reaching across to do the same with the second.

"Then maybe you should stop squirming, bitch!" Serena's words, though every bit as snarky as he'd come to expect, were muddy with her dizziness.

He raised his opposite hand and pinned her head against the wall, keeping her from biting him as he worked to rid her of her clothes. "Ever the defiant little shit, aren't you?"

She grumbled something.

Curiosity got the better of him and he paused to look up at her, sneering. "What was that, bitch?"

Serena's vampire speed caught him off guard then. He hadn't seen her right arm move at all, yet, in the blink of an eye, her hand was wrapped around the horn just behind his left ear.

"I said," her eyes came to settle as the defiance returned to her tone, "that your punk-ass hasn't even *seen* defiance yet!" She gave a sharp yank, an elongated cracking sounding both outside *and* inside Maledictus' head as the horn was snapped from his skull. "But I guess you don't hear so well without any ears, huh?" Serena mused, spinning the pointed hunk of bone in her palm and pulling it back, "Let's fix that, SHALL WE?"

Maledictus shrieked in agony as his horn was stabbed into the side of his head, raking against several of his new teeth as it breached the back of his jawline.

"Aw shit! Missed your brain," Serena offered him a fake pout as she worked to yank her makeshift weapon free. "Let's try that one more time!"

"LET'S NOT!"

Maledictus pulled the horn from his face and jumped back, kicking down on Serena again and again until the blind fury at her attack subsided to a slow boil. Serena cried, her body quaking under the assault as the burden of her wasted burst of energy—that momentary flood of adrenaline—began to wear off.

"Enough of this dumb brute business!" Maledictus growled, cupping his left hand over the gaping wound on the side of his head. Extending the fingers of his right hand, he willed his old magic to take hold of the she-vamp and, as he watched her body strain against the invisible force, slammed her against the wall; binding her body with the enchantment.

Serena struggled, and, as the realization that she was magically pinned settled in, she narrowed her eyes and opened her mouth.

"Uh uh! No more of your snark, missy!" Maledictus pinched his thumb and middle finger together and Serena's jaw snapped shut and locked. He smirked,

"Why in the fuck didn't I think of that before?"

Serena's muffled whimpers went from angered by her forced silence to panicked as Maledictus once again closed in on her. The need for brash, full-body attacks was past him—his magic hold on her offering him the ability to go about his task with more flamboyancy than ever before—and he felt himself fall into a swagger as he approached and worked one of his claws behind the remaining tank top strap.

"Do you ever just stop to appreciate the power of the naked body, buttercup-bitch?" he asked as he offered the strap a few teasing tugs, refraining from using enough force to sever it just yet. "You look at all the shit out there that people can appreciate the sight of—fucking art and nature and all that whimsical crap—and you realize that nothing else—fucking *nothing!*—has as much demand for repeat views as, say, a nice pair of tits." He sliced through the strap and Serena's top fell halfway down her breasts, teasing the moment; he smirked at this. "Or, even *moreso*"—he accentuated his rant by dragging the claw down her cleavage and over the top of the tortured garment, tearing the fabric in a few places but leaving it intact enough to not completely fall off of her body as he worked ever downward—"a waiting cunt."

Serena let out an enraged howl behind her locked lips, the impact coming off as a garbled growl with a few high-pitched moments where the air fueling the protest hiccupped in her no-doubt aching throat.

She *had* been screaming and crying an awful lot.

"See, a person can see a fine piece of art *once* and feel content with that; they could squat on their deathbed and say, 'At least I got to finger my asshole to the Mona Lisa that one time,' or *whatever* those dumb fucking meat-puppets think to themselves over such trivial nonsense. But you never—not even fucking *once*—will hear an old fart succumbing to that sweet, finalizing sleep utter the words, 'I've seen enough tits in my life' or 'What I wouldn't give to bury my face in one last—'" he sighed, realizing he was rambling. "Well, you get my point. Just look at you, for example: luscious golden hair," he pulled his claw away from her lower belly and ran it through the strands that fell across her left shoulder—her right shoulder noticeably bare from the asymmetry he'd caused when he'd yanked the tuft out during his escape—and ignoring the stifled shiver that worked beneath his magic hold on her. "Then there's these purple eyes of yours"—he teased the claw just in front of her terrified cornea—"and, of course, this body!" He finally ripped the tank top from her body, tossing it to the other corner of the room where she'd be unable to retrieve it, and freed her breasts from the confines of the black bra that waited beneath; opting to yank it off and letting the snapping material sting against his victim's flesh.

Then, just like that, there they were…

He scoffed and shook his head, "It's not like I haven't *seen* them before, either. I mean—fuck!—I was nestled in Zaney-boy's noggin since day *numero uno*; I have *literally* sat front-row-fucking-center for *every* lewd and depraved act. All the things you did to him—to *us*— and all the things you let him do to you; hell, *begged* him to do to you!" He smirked and leaned in, dragging his forked tongue across her right cheek; the open wound on the side of his face gliding across her jaw as he moved, "You know, most girls aren't so fond of the back-door action, and your enthusiasm was certainly not going unnoticed."

Another stifled howl.

Maledictus backhanded her, "Shut the fuck up, bitch! That was a compliment! *All* of this has been! You fucking think I'd go through all this trouble for just *any* piece of pussy? Huh?" He moved to hit her again and smirked when he saw her eyes twitch—the fear making itself known—and he chuckled, offering, instead of another strike, a few soft pats on her cheek. "There *is* something about you, Serena; something engaging; something compelling," he narrowed his eyes at her, taking in the vision of her naked, heaving breasts, "Something... familiar."

His hand dropped to his side as his gaze wavered at a distant sight.

Something...

Familiar?

Where had he seen her—

Another of Serena's muffled cries broke the swirling void of the ages in his mind, and, enraged by her interruption, he struck her again.

And again.

And again.

"WHO IN THE FUCKING HELL ARE..." he paused, looking at the quivering, bloodied girl before him and spit out the last of his lingering rage on her naked chest. "Lesson over, bitch! Now it's time for extra-credit!"

He moved his hands—still shaky from the strange, ghostly shadows of whatever memories were calling to him—to separate Serena from her jeans. Again and again he fumbled with the task, growing evermore enraged by his own weakened resolve at—

He paused.

Weakened resolve?

Then his magic would also be…

Serena's energy flared, and a wave of glowing purple strands—his body's interpretation of the aura he'd seen her use so many times before—began to break free of his weakened magic hold on her.

The hold on her mouth broke, and she took in a sharp inhale; the sight of her fully extended fangs offering a morbid mixture of arousal and concern in Maledictus.

"Shit…"

"'Shit' doesn't even begin to *cover* it, you rape-happy smegma-stain!" she roared and threw herself from the wall, tackling Maledictus. As the two of them fell to the floor, she worked the enchanted chains that bound her around his throat. "Fucking disgusting, power-hungry, twisted freak!" Punch after punch was driven into the side of his head; the enraged blonde she-vamp targeting the wound she'd inflicted on him; each impact sending wave-upon-wave of searing hot pain coursing through his pinned body.

Pinned…

All around him, the purple strands held him to the floor—making him think of glowing thread that had him stitched to the padded surface—and forced him to endure the pummeling.

Oh sweet irony…

She was *so* the girl for him!

The sheer perfection drew a series of cackles out of him as she continued her assault. Enraged by his reaction, she drove a knee into his groin; his laughter doubled. She drove her elbow in the broken rib she'd given him earlier; he howled in amusement.

It was all too perfect!

"Ruin everything"—Serena caught him across the

face with a left hook and then—"Think you're badass"—she jabbed her locked fingertips into his windpipe; stifling the laughter for a moment before it flared up again—"Think that lusting after death and destruction are power"—a wave of punches rained down on his chest; Serena's fists moving too fast to see—"Show you! Once and for all, I'll show you!" Eager to inflict pain on him, she moved to gouge his eyes…

And his right eye finally ruptured.

"About fucking time!" Maledictus cackled.

Serena shrieked in disgust, fury still causing her body to shake as she jumped back and began to shake the vile fluid from her left hand.

Free of the onslaught and Serena's auric hold on him, Maledictus swung his tail out—sweeping the retching blonde off her feet—and bee-lined to for the door.

"NO!" Serena spotted his efforts and threw her aura after him, slamming into his back and throwing him against the door.

His right arm, taking the force of the impact, popped free of his shoulder—the reinforced siding of the door warping and a portion of the padded wall tearing around the seam—and the limb dropped several inches before swinging lamely at his side like a dead hunk of meat.

Maledictus hissed in pain as he struggled with the jammed door. "Fucking bitch!"

Serena fought against the enchanted chains, trying to free herself. "Yea, you better run, you fucking coward! Next time you bring that shit in here you'd better bring a pair of balls with you!"

Finally getting the door open, Maledictus turned an infuriated eye on the she-vamp—unable to find any pleasure in her still-naked breasts and what they represented at that moment—and sneered. "Know this, rancid harlot: when I *do* take you, I'm going to make sure it hurts you!"

The door slammed behind him.

Serena stood, staring at the door for a long while. She wasn't certain if she was waiting for the monster to return or if she was in some temporary form of shock and unable to will her body to do anything more than stare.

The attack was still too fresh.

She couldn't bring herself to shrug it all off; couldn't stream any sequence of vulgarity to make what she'd just endured alright.

Maledictus was just as strong, just as stubborn, just as vulgar…

But she… she had limits; boundaries that even she would not allow herself to cross.

Like lying to herself.

It was one thing to deceive an enemy—or, hell, even a friend—if it meant she could work it to her advantage. Telling Zoey that she'd be more careful the next time she drove was just her way of ensuring that her friend would be willing to hand over the keys on their next adventure. And convincing a rape-happy lizard-monster carrying the single-most destructive and evil force she'd ever encountered that she could be every bit the bitch she'd worked so hard to convince the world she was *was* her way of trying to keep it afraid of her. But she couldn't, in all her acts of deceit, come to try to lie to herself; no matter how many promises of safe, slow car rides she'd offer to Zoey, she could never believe that she'd be so reckless as to actually *endanger* her best friend.

Nor could she bring herself to believe that she wasn't absolutely terrified.

Serena's body crumbled under her own weight then, fear and despair and exhaustion—her already starved system beginning to turn inward; punishing her for calling upon energy reserves that didn't exist to fight— and she shivered with the realization that she wouldn't be able to fight back if… she shook her head, once again unable to lie at herself—wouldn't be able to fight back *when* Maledictus came back to finish what he'd started.

She wasn't even strong enough to retrieve her shredded tank top with her aura…

Tears rolled down her cheeks as Serena began to sob, curling up on the floor and shivering against more than just the cold. "Zane… please, I need you… Where are you?"

Chapter Six
Lighting the Way

"WHERE'S ZANE?" NIKKI ASKED, STEPPING INTO THE community room. Looking around, she noticed that it was emptier than usual and bit her lip. After the kidnapping of the clan's still-young leader, half of the clan had vanished—seeing the disappearance as a chance to focus on their current missions without concern of *new* assignments or a curfew—while the other half had abandoned their previous missions and gone out on their own extended patrols for any clues to her whereabouts. This, it turned out, left the clan's headquarters uncomfortably empty. "Damn," Nikki shivered at the ghostly silence, *"that's* eerie."

"Tell me about it," Raith said, looking over at her. "Zane went out to meet with an informant that he thinks might be able to help. Why? What's up?"

Nikki frowned, "Did that Celine-chick go with him?"

Raith cocked a brow, "Yea. He didn't look too thrilled about it, but she was pretty adamant about going along. Why?"

Nikki rolled her eyes and took a seat beside him. "I don't know. I've just been worried about him. I mean, with his ex popping up like this—piled on top of the disappearance of Serena—it just seems rough, you know?" She sighed, shaking her head, "There's only so much someone can handle, *especially* a guy."

"You mean a guy like Zane?" Raith looked over at her.

"I know what I said," Nikki gave him a look.

"Alright, fair enough, but Zane *is* stronger now; *a lot* stronger." Raith smirked, "Since hooking up with Serena, he's has become a lot more focused and dedicated, and while the situation *is* creating a shit-ton of chaos, I'm confident that Zane can handle it now more than he would've been able to before."

"You have a lot of confidence in him," Nikki bit her lip, "and I do too, please don't think I don't…"

Raith leaned forward, "But…"

Nikki shrugged, "*But…* that Celine-girl seems to have her own plans, and I don't like the way she's always hovering around Zane. Plus, the way she looks at him… well, it just gives me the creeps!"

"Honestly," Raith smirked, sitting back again, "I don't like her either—never have—but if she thinks she can get to Zane just because Serena's gone, she's sorely mistaken and in for a *very* rude awakening. Zane's totally head-over-heels for Serena; hook, line, and sinker. Celine doesn't stand a chance this round."

Nikki chuckled, shaking her head. "You never got along with her, did you?"

"Of course not, she's a bitch! And, in my defense, I *tried* to get along with her for Zane's sake, but that girl had it in for me since day one! I thought she was just some clingy girlfriend who didn't like her man's friends, but she honestly treated me like…"

"Like a dog?" Nikki looked over.

"No," Raith shook his head, "*that* would've at least made sense. She treated me like some sort of nark; like every time I was around her she was on edge that I might attack her or turn Zane against her or something; she was always warning Zane about me—despite *never* having met me before, mind you—and…" He shook his head, "I don't know, she just always seemed like she was keeping something from him that I was somehow going to spill the beans about."

"Not that any of that made any difference to Zane, I see," Nikki smirked. "Friends to the end, huh?"

"Yeah, guess so," Raith smirked. "It's why we were such good mercs; we could accomplish anything when we set our minds to it. I guess that must have scared her or something; maybe she thought that we'd get overconfident and land ourselves in hot water." He scoffed at that, "I suppose that wouldn't be too far from the truth."

"You suppose?" Nikki shook her head, "Though maybe you two would've been fine as you were without me getting in the way and mucking it all up."

"Don't you dare blame yourself for what happened, Nikki!" Raith glared at her. "The curse was not *your* fault;

you were just trying to help your people. There was no way *anybody* could've known what was going to happen."

"But—"

"No 'but's!" Raith growled, "Zane and I both knew the risks going into your tribe and we were too confident in our approach. Our stupidity and that *damned* curse are what are to blame. Nothing—and no one—else!"

"I still don't feel that's the complete truth," Nikki looked down.

"Well it is," Raith assured her, "and even if it wasn't, it sure as hell wouldn't be your fault."

Nikki bit her lip, looking over at her lover. She knew that Raith didn't blame her for what had happened to them back then, but somewhere inside of her she couldn't help but think what would've happened if she hadn't sent Zane and Raith on that mission. She knew that it would've been a matter of time before *somebody* was burdened with breaking the ever-thinning final straw and being the one to bear the curse, and though she felt terrible thinking it, a part of her wished that somebody else—anybody else—had wound up being the one to carry the *Maledictus* curse.

Shaking her head of the bad thoughts, she turned back to her lover and moved to sit closer to him, resting her head on his shoulder. She had finally gotten used to his new body, what had once been the body of Axle Travers—a small-time therion rogue before Kristine had had her way with him. After she'd killed him so that she could put Zane's disembodied aura—an unexpected burden she'd acquired after attacking him and releasing Raith's consciousness into Zane's body—into the empty shell of Axle's body in the hopes of manipulating the "new" Axle. Her plan, however, had fizzled out, and Zane's personality returned, taking control and seeking out Serena, who'd been driving herself crazy—in much the same way Zane was driving himself searching for Serena now. When the craziness had finally settled, Zane's aura had been returned to his body and Raith, with the deceased Axle's body then without an aura, finally had a chance to be his own therion once again.

While having Raith back in a totally different body had taken some getting used to, the personality of the therion that she'd fallen in love with—and the perk that Axle was quite the looker, as well—had made the transition a relatively painless one.

Body-swapping, Nikki smirked to herself, *who knew?*

"What are you smirking about?" Raith lifted her chin to face him, his forest-green eyes lighting up with mischievous intent.

"Hmm... that depends; what are *you* smirking at?" she countered, leaning forward to brush her lips against his.

"Let me show you," he purred, lifting her body in his arms with ease.

"W-whoa!" she blushed, "You do that *way* too easily!"

"What do you mean? You barely weigh a thing," he smirked. "Maybe you should get fat or something."

"Thanks, I guess," she chuckled.

"Now, let's stop talking," Raith smirked, pulling her down and kissing her hard.

Nikki gasped as his tongue swept into her mouth and she returned the kiss with just as much fervor. Raith smirked, once again lifting her and hurrying through the hall and to their room.

With that, the two lost themselves in the other. Forgetting all their troubles for the time being.

Chapter Seven
After the Dragon

ZANE SAT AT THE BAR OF THE NIGHTCLUB, KEEPING an eye on the bar as Celine settled in close next to him. Feeling cramped and shifting away to give himself elbow room, Zane kept his gaze locked on the bar, only slightly aware of Celine's heavy sigh.

He was anxious.

Moreover, he was impatient.

After less than three minutes of inactivity—not even a damn drink order!—Zane growled and stood, pushing through the crowd and honing in on one of the club's staff.

SCARLET DUSK

"Is Ben ready yet?" he growled, "I don't have all fucking night."

The staff member, a scrawny sang—pure-born if his age was any real indicator—with a frosted set of bangs that hung over his left eye, leaving only one, panic-stricken blue orb visible, began to stammer and shake under Zane's gaze.

Zane didn't offer him any sympathy. "Why don't you get on that fancy walkie-talkie of yours and get my night moving before I move you through a fourth-floor window?"

Things got moving.

There was a buzz of static as an impatient message crackled over the distorted frequency, and the still-shivering staff member nodded to Zane, "R-right this way. Mister Ben is expecting you."

"*Mister* Ben?" Zane chuckled and rolled his eyes, "bet he *loves* that." He started forward a few steps before he sighed and turned to Celine, motioning for her to follow. "C'mon!"

Celine jumped from the barstool and stepped up a little *too* close to Zane as they were led to the backroom. He frowned at this, nervous that somebody that might know him might see and get the wrong idea; even more nervous that, if Serena ever caught news of it, he'd be in for a butt-kicking. He toggled with the idea of telling Celine to back off, but decided that teaching her boundary issues could wait for a less pressing moment. Letting out a content sigh, she leaned her body closer to his, and he rolled his eyes; realizing that she must have taken his silence as some sort of approval. Still opting for silence, he took a longer step forward and let his body dip slightly away from her, falling back into a pace behind the staff member with a renewed—and

71

refreshing—distance from Celine as they were led into a large, extravagant office.

"I see the bastard still has a taste for the finer things, eh?" Zane mused, letting himself fall into one of the cloud-like leather chairs and quickly letting his arms fall across *both* of the arm rests so as to not offer any unspoken invitations to Celine to sit on one of them, Zane let his eyes drift around the room.

The staff member, still shaking from Zane's earlier stare-down, asked if they'd be needing anything else.

Zane nodded, "Yea. I'd like you to tell *Mister* Ben to quit jerking off and roll his ass in here double-time." He narrowed his eyes at the wide-eyed young vampire, "And if you change so much as *one* word of that request, I'm going to cut your balls off and feed them to my associate here."

The staff member bolted from the room before he had a chance to see Celine flinch at the suggestion.

Zane chuckled, *Mister Ben...*

"Zane, you sonuvabitch!" Ben, the club's owner and one of Zane's more trusted informants, gave the tires of his wheelchair a sharp push and, free to raise his hands in resignation, let himself roll into the room, "Not even in my club more than *ten* fucking minutes before you're making my employees piss all over themselves. 'Least you haven't started in on my *female* staff members, though"—he let his eyes shift to Celine as he reclaimed control of the wheelchair and began maneuvering behind his desk—"it would appear you'd have no need to." Smirking and settling in behind the polished mahogany desk, "I'm sorry, I haven't had the honor; you are?"

"She is with me on business, Benny," Zane interjected before Celine could think to offer her name *or* her role in this visit, "*Clan* business! You play along—give me the information I want—and I might even leave her here for a few hours to let you two get acquainted while I follow through with my investigation."

Celine's eyes widened, "What? Zane, I—"

Zane gave her an icy glare, silencing whatever was about to come.

Ben took all of this in, an intrigued and entertained arch taking hold of his brow, and reached for a silver-plated letter opener on the corner of his desk before beginning to clean his already manicured nails with it. "Not that I'm not enjoying all of this, but you *have* come in at a rather busy hour, and I *am* a businessman who's presently losing money with every passing second. Would you mind terribly if I insisted that you cut to the chase, big-league chew?"

Zane straightened up and leaned forward, "One of our clan members was kidnapped." Though he wasn't aware of doing so, he realized that his left hand had worked its way into his coat pocket and he was beginning to rub his thumb across the banded length of blonde hair. Despite being aware of this nervous reflex, he didn't stop himself from indulging; finding the effects somewhat therapeutic to his growing tension. "The attacker's in a—" He shook his head, "The attacker's an ykali, so I imagine he'd be hard to miss."

Ben chortled at that, "An *ykali*? Yea, I'd imagine something like that *would* be hard to miss… if there'd been any around. Are you pulling my leg with this shit, Zane? You come into *my* club—*my* place of business!—and drag me away from my work so that you can tell me some fairytale sob story? Does this clan member even exist, or are you shitting me with *that* too?" He shifted the letter opener to scratch under his chin before pointing it towards Zane, "What's this really about? And why are you toting this ginger around? Word on the street is you're banging Vailean's kid; some blonde spark-plug if I heard correctly."

Zane growled and leapt from the chair, bringing both of his fists down on the center of the desk. The polished mahogany surface split, caving in under its own weight and sending all of its contents to the floor.

Ben watched the display with bored eyes, still fidgeting with the letter opener.

Zane, breathing heavily, glared at his informant. "This... *is*... serious—"

"Sorry to interrupt your bitch-fit, Zane, but would you mind retrieving the intercom for me?" he motioned to a small, silver box with a call button on the top. "While I'm positive that all *this*"—he waved a hand at the mess that was once his desk—"I'm afraid that my men *will* be responding to the racket in their own, bullet-fueled way if I don't call them off. So, if you'd like for us to continue..." he waved his hand towards the intercom.

Zane bared his fangs but knelt down and retrieved the device, slapping it into Ben's waiting hand before returning to his chair.

"Daniel? Yes, yes I'm fine. A good friend of mine decided to let a dumb animal out of its cage and it caused a bit of a commotion. I've got a handle of the situation, though. Tell Mira that I said you and the boys are entitled to free drinks for the evening, alright?" The intercom buzzed out as Ben lifted his thumb from the call button.

"Mira, huh?" Zane smirked. "She stuck with you all

this time? Hard to imagine anybody taking you in such large doses."

Ben smirked and nodded, "I know, right? Stroke of good luck in an otherwise unlucky world. But the girl gets me, and the good lord knows I love the hell outta her." He let out a deep sigh then, taking another absent glance at the remains of his desk and then at the intercom in his hand. Rolled his eyes, he tossed the silver box back into the heap of splintered wood and office supplies. "This has officially become the most expensive visit I've ever received from you, Zane, and I don't think I need to remind you that your visits are *never* cheap. Though I guess I should be thankful you didn't let that rage-beast in you free. *That* thing would've—" He looked up at Zane, narrowing his eyes, "Wait… you could never control that renegade monster." He straightened his shoulders and pressed his fingertips together one-by-one, "Can you actually *control* that thing now?"

Zane sighed and shook his head. "Alright, Ben, I suppose it's only fair that I tell you everything…"

Ben listened while Zane told him the story of Maledictus and Gregori and, finally, of Serena. As he let the words flow, Zane was startled by how easy the rest of them followed; surprised that, despite their relationship and mutually abrasive personalities, he somehow felt comfortable opening up and being himself with his informant.

Venting to Ben just felt right.

And, when it was all over, the arrogant informant offered an understanding nod.

"Guess I'm not the only asshole on the block who found himself an angel who gets him, huh?"

Zane smirked and shrugged, "That's one way to put it, I suppose."

"Bullshit! Chick puts up with you—*all* of you; even that… that fucking psycho-thing, Mega-dick-fist—"

"Maledictus," Zane corrected him.

Ben shrugged, "Whatever. *Him*. This point is you got something special—a real angel!—if this girl of yours put up with all *that* and hasn't run for the hills yet; though if she's *anything* like her mother she'd sooner just smear the streets with your insides and laugh at how it looked like a Jackson Pollock painting."

"You knew Serena's…" Zane shook his head, "Nevermind. Forgot who I was talking to for a moment; *Mister* Ben: holder of secrets and lord of the assholes."

Ben smirked at that, nodding. "Long as you know who you're answering to, asshole."

"Watch it!" Zane smirked, "Or I'll roll your ass into traffic."

Celine gasped at that, but both Zane and Ben burst into laughter.

"Oh, fuck, man! I *needed* that!" Ben lifted his glasses and wiped a laughter-born tear from his eye, "You know that most of these punks treat me like a damn cripple; fucking pussies think that just 'cause I'm *half* the vamp I once was that I'm not still *twice* the ass-kicker they'll ever be." He navigated his chair over to a nearby filing cabinet.

Zane snickered, "Just means you ain't gonna feel anything after somebody breaks their foot off in your ass."

Ben nodded, punching a code into one of the cabinet drawers and yanking it open after a low tone buzzed.

"Damn straight! And while they're wearing me like a shoe I'm going full Chuck Norris on their nutsack." He ran his fingers through the stacks of papers before drawing a file and flipping through it, nodding. "This might help with your kidnapped angel, bud." He used his left hand to spin the chair towards Zane and tossed the file onto his lap. "Few nights ago some therions came in; real nondescript crew, y'know, rocking the goth gear and whatnot, but nothing that screamed trouble. They were all pretty jittery—buying drinks like they'd just come out of the damn Sahara!—and telling Mira about how they'd been hearing all this crazy shit lately, right? So Mira, knowing to keep this kids talking—keep 'em *buying*— keeps asking all the right questions, and they start in with this crazy talk about—get this—*the devil*!" He shook his head, laughing. "Now those in their right minds like you and I *know* that if the *real* devil was coming to visit, he'd probably be setting a goat-foot somewhere a bit more exciting, right; somewhere that didn't already have Mondo-big-tits—"

"Maledictus," Zane corrected him again. "And you *do* know I'm an atheist, right?"

"Whatever," Ben pointed to the file, "So Mira's got these therions rambling—got 'em good and drunk—and the stories keep rolling: humans talking about ghosts and demons and whatnot strolling around here, even told a story of some horny punks looking to score some tail at the cemetery down on Railway Street even seeing a body come tearing up through the ground."

"What," Zane cocked an eyebrow, "like a zombie?"

"Who the fuck knows! It's probably bullshit, anyway," Ben pointed to the file again, "but after I did a little sleuthing I found that there *was* a body that had been dug up over there?"

Zane frowned, finally opening the file. "So—what?—on top of Maledictus being out-and-about in a new ykali body we've *also* got zombies roaming around?"

"Zombies? Maybe," Ben rolled forward and pulled one of the pages from the file and planted it on top of the others, pointing to the police file of the event; a grainy black-and-white picture showing the response team circled around a dug-up grave and, next to it, the corpse. "But if the dead *are* coming back, they don't seem to be getting too far. This particular corpse," he turned the page around to read from it, "one, 'Mister Stephen Dravus, was found five feet from his desecrated grave site.'" Ben shrugged, "Now *I'm* going to be the first to say this is just some random grave-robbing that's gotten mixed in with the chaos of everything else, but, since it was in there with all the shit those kids were rambling, I figured I'd include what I found in the file."

Zane flipped through the pages. On their own, the set of police records, newspaper articles, and hand-written accounts seemed like nothing more than a bunch of random happenings and claims.

Still, there was something to them…

Celine, who'd been peering over Zane's shoulder and had finally abandoned her chair to hang over the back of his, shook her head. "Why did you make this file if you don't believe any of the stories?"

Ben motioned to Zane, "Because this guy keeps coming back here to peek at my sweet ass, but after the foreplay he always demands information about anything-slash-everything that's happened around here. If I didn't keep shit like *that*"—he motioned to the file on Zane's lap—"then I'd have to put up with a lot more of *that*"—

he pointed back towards his destroyed desk.

"I see…" Celine paused. Then, "What do you think, Zane?"

"I think I can feel your breath on the back of my ear and I don't like it," Zane offered absently, still sorting through the papers. "And I think that—"

Zaney-boy.

Looking over his shoulder, Zane could only see Celine—still too damn close—and the rest of the empty room. But then…

He slapped the file shut and pushed it into Celine's hands. "Hold that. Keep it safe," he ordered, quickly raising to his feet and starting for the door.

Ben frowned, "Hey! What's up, man? Aren't you going to stay for a drink? On the house!"

Zane shook his head, "I can't; I mean, not now. Give me a rain check or something. There's…" He felt it again; a nauseating wave. It was something in the air, like a vibration or a scent; something that made his muscles ache and his head throb.

Something familiar.

"He's here!" Zane growled, starting for the door.

Just before jumping into overdrive, he heard Celine calling out to him.

Zane sprinted through the club in overdrive, plowing through the time-frozen dancers and partiers as he made his way through. Reaching the stairs, he started up them two at a time and shoved past another seemingly-frozen patron who'd just entered before he crashed through the still-slightly ajar door. There was no sound as the door ripped free from the hinges and catapulted into the street before getting snagged by physics and slowing to a stop in midair; Zane leaving the club further and further behind him as he sprinted after the familiar energy.

Though he wasn't an auric and had no way discerning one aura from another, he *knew* Maledictus, and he couldn't forget *that* feeling!

A feeling that was just as suddenly gone.

What the fuck... he stopped, letting his body fall out of overdrive.

Behind him, the patron he'd plowed past started cursing up a storm and the sound of the airborne door sounded against the opposite building as it shattered into splinters and bits of glass against the concrete siding.

"Where the hell did you go, you bastard?" Zane demanded to nobody in particular as he swung his head around, trying to pinpoint the source. "Come on! Don't do this to me; don't let the trail go cold. Don't force me to—" The energy spiked again—coming from behind him—and he turned in time to see a shadowy figure dart around the building and disappear down the next street at the end of the block.

"Got you!"

The patron he'd pushed, a still cursing sang, appeared in the street as he dropped out of overdrive—obviously eager to offer some payback to Zane for slamming him against the wall—and glared at him.

"You owe me an apology, asshole!" the pudgy, balding vampire demanded.

"Sure thing, pal," Zane offered, starting towards him solely to get to the end of the street and follow the figure, "I got a really heartfelt 'sorry' written down for ya. Buried it pretty deep in my ass, though; hope you don't mind fishing it out with your teeth!"

The vampire's eyes widened. "You arrogant little punk!" he growled, turning to a nearby motorcycle and quickly mounting it.

"Picked the *wrong* night to get stupid, dipshit," Zane rolled his eyes at the sound of the bike's engine as it roared to life and he continued his determined pace back towards the club—positive that the angry biker thought it was for *his* sake that he'd turned around—and clenched his fists. "Still… I like your bike."

The vampire bared his fangs as he revved the engine and peeled off towards Zane, who quickly scoped the area to make sure that there weren't any humans to see the supernatural showdown. As eager as he was to take down the hotheaded sang, he couldn't risk exposing human witnesses to something that would only bring him more problems. Satisfied that the street was vacant, he opted to be quick and, for once, lenient. Though brash displays were one of the major 'no-no's in The Council's eyes, being the foundation of more than half of the laws they'd put into effect, he didn't think a death penalty was appropriate in this instant. Then he spotted the bits of busted door—a product of his own inhuman brashness—and a bit of his self-righteous pride deflated.

Well, he thought to himself, *at least there* weren't *any witnesses.*

The roaring biker-vamp accelerated towards him, preparing to drive his motorcycle directly into Zane and *still* demanding an apology.

"I'm sorry for the bruises you're going to have by sun-up," Zane offered, stopping in the middle of the road and squaring his stance.

The heat of the tortured engine and the rubbery stink of overworked tires grew as the bike closed in on Zane, and, just before the front tire had a chance to clip his feet, he side-stepped to the right and reached across the width of the bike with his left hand, snagging the handle bar and squeezing the clutch. The motorcycle lurched, and the vampire, caught in a moment of panic, swerved away from Zane in an effort to reclaim control of the bike. Maintaining his grip, Zane kicked off the pavement and let the speed of the bike carry him—swinging his body in a wide arc and kicking the startled vampire off the roaring vehicle—before he fell into place on the seat.

As proud as he was of the maneuver—and the fact that the calculated effort hadn't, like many of his other calculations in the past, failed miserably—Zane invested little time as he threw his bodyweight into turning the motorcycle around; the tires squealing as the bike drifted a short distance further down the street before Zane got the rear end to straighten out. The motorcycle's engine roared as Zane tortured the throttle and started down the street after the shadowy figure.

"ZANE!"

Tracking Zane's movement hadn't been hard for Celine. After offering a quick thanks to the informant, she'd tucked the file under her arm and hurried out after Zane, finding a trail of dazed and confused club-goers who'd been thrown to the ground. The floor is a mess of broken glass and spilled drinks, and as the confusion in the club gave way to outrage the patrons began to turn on one another, eager to blame their neighbor for the chaos.

Celine cried out as she was forced to jump out of the way to allow a pair of sangs to come crashing out of overdrive; their fangs bared and their hands wrapped tightly around each other's throats.

Ben, wheeling out as fast as he could, cursed as he got a look at the mayhem. "Motherfuck—goddamit, Zane! Do you have any idea how much this is going to cos—*ENOUGH!*" The roar of Ben's voice sent a unified tremor through the entire club, Celine even feeling a wave of dread as the sound assaulted her ears. Ben, seeing Celine's surprise, smirked and nodded. "Half the vamp; twice the badass," he winked.

"I can see that," Celine nodded before using the calm to run after Zane, starting up the steps as Ben reclaimed his club behind her.

Reaching the exit—hadn't there been a door in front?—she heard the rumbling of an engine and looked down the street in time to see Zane kick a motorcyclist off his vehicle and start back towards her on it.

"Zane!" she called out to him.

He didn't stop.

He didn't slow down.

He didn't even warn her.

His vice-like grip snagged her as he passed, lifting her off the ground and planting her behind him on the motorcycle. Her breath caught for a moment—awestruck by the sudden rush of movement and Zane's ease at plucking her from the side of the road—and she reveled in the surreal moment of—

"—got it?" Zane called behind him.

She blinked. "Huh?"

"THE FILE!" he roared, though she could tell it had nothing to do with the loudness of the stolen motorcycle's engine. "DO YOU STILL HAVE IT?"

Celine blushed and nodded, pulling the bundle of papers from under her arm to show him.

Zane's face relaxed at the sight and nodded, turning back to face forward as he navigated the streets, weaving in and out of traffic.

"Why... u-uh, wh-why did you s-steal this motorcycle?" Celine asked, blushing as she realized that the machine's vibrations and her closeness to Zane were having some serious impacts on her anatomy.

"Because I needed it," Zane's voice was flat. "I'm hunting somebody."

Celine frowned, "Hu-hunting some—Why w-wouldn't y-you just chase them in over... ah! Er, overdrive?"

"Are you going to be alright back there?" Zane growled.

"Yea..." Celine blushed, realizing her increasing arousal wasn't going unnoticed.

Zane sighed, taking a sharp turn and forcing Celine to grip his sides to keep from falling over the side. "If who it is turns out to be who I *think* it is, then I can't risk burning up all my energy in overdrive."

"Who you think it is..." Celine's nerves seized and her arousal fizzled away into nothingness, "You don't mean *him*, do you? You don't mean M-Mal-Maledictus, do you? *Do* you? I-is *that* who you're after; is that who took Serena?"

"Yea, Celine, it is, and I'm not sure if what I'm sensing is him," Zane confessed, cutting across an intersection. "But it sure as hell *feels* like him."

Chapter Eight
Battle with the Dragon

MALEDICTUS WAS OUT THERE SOMEWHERE, AND, SOMEHOW, Zane was able to track him; to *feel* his presence and chase after it. Celine's head darted about, oscillating to-and-fro in response to anything that her growing paranoia screamed to her *might* be the creature she'd encountered so many years ago.

When Zane had brought back the curse from his mission with the taroe tribe...

She felt a whimper scuttle free from her throat and she forced away the memory of the looming creature that had *literally* burst from Zane's body. It hadn't taken much—a bit of confusion and a stubbed toe, if she remembered correctly—and he'd doubled over, crying and cackling all at once; the new tattoos that littered his body burning like hot coals. He was no more than a turned sang, she knew that better than anybody, and when his body began to shift and warp like a therion's she'd known that she didn't want to stick around. Unlike all the dumb bimbos in the horror movies, when her man started screaming in pain and monstrous extremities began sprouting across his glowing body, she did what a *sane* woman *should* do:

She ran.

Maledictus, as *its* name—or title or classification or *whatever*—turned out to be, hadn't been too thrilled to see its first victim making a run for it, and he'd ripped the house apart in trying to chase after her; the sound of his vulgar rampage beckoning their neighbor to come knocking…

While it was tragic to a degree, Celine had never been too close with the old man. So when he went and called attention to himself, drawing the homicidal creature's attention away from her long enough to jump out the bedroom window, she didn't bother to go back to help him.

An old man dies; a young vampire lives. Probably not the fairest trade in the world, but she'd already come to grips with the idea of living off the death of others.

It *was*, after all, what made them what they were.

She could only imagine in hindsight what it must have been like for Zane when he'd come to after all that. Dazed. Confused. Covered in blood. Alone. It made sense that he'd come to the conclusion that the monster he'd brought back inside of him had killed her, and, in many ways, it was better that he thought that.

The Maledictus-monster thrived on the fear it

crippled him with, so if it had gone through the arduous chore of tracking her down it would've had to sacrifice the ruse that it *had* killed her. Knowing that truth *might* have offered Zane some sort of hope then; a hope that he might overcome what had happened to him. Obviously this was not something Maledictus had been willing to risk, so it allowed Celine to live—a small sacrifice in its campaign of keeping Zane tortured by the belief that it—and, in essence, he—had killed her.

But now that Maledictus had his own body and Zane was aware that Celine's death had all been a lie, there was no safety net for her.

No safety net *but* Zane.

"Do you really think you can kill him?" she asked, giving Zane's shoulder a light squeeze.

"Thinking isn't really my thing, Celine," Zane answered, steering the motorcycle onto a new street. "I *know* that that twisted fucker has Serena, and I *know* I need to get rid of him." He glanced back, the determination and commitment burning in his mismatched gaze, "I *have* to kill him!" He turned back and started off towards a lumber yard in the distance, "Besides, we put him in an ykali body. Those things might be ugly bastards, but they're hardly a major threat when you—"

Zane's reassuring words were cut short as something—something that cut through the air and howled like a banshee—slammed into the front of the motorcycle. Both Zane and Celine cried out as they flipped over the handlebars and crashed down on the sawdust-covered ground; the upturned motorcycle slamming down on Zane's right arm. Celine whimpered against the ringing in her ears and the ache of her own impact, looking around for any sign of what had hit them. When she spotted nothing but the silhouettes of stacked logs and machinery looming like waiting monsters ahead of them, she began to crawl towards Zane, hoping to reestablish some of her shattered sense of security by being nearer to him.

A slow, wet, serpent-like chuckle begins to ooze from the darkness that the attack originated from; the sound slowly shifting to a sharp, hissing intake followed by a satisfied, growling sigh.

"That, my dear boy, looked rather unpleasant from my angle," a serpentine voice chirped from the darkness.

Footsteps…

Celine felt her breath seize in her lungs as her heart rate tripled.

The hollow *thud* of one step resounded, followed by three sharp *clicks*. The pattern continued—*thud, cli-cli-click; thud, cli-cli-click;* a soft, almost inaudible *swooshing* overlapping the sequence—as it drew nearer; the ghostly outline of their attacker taking shape as he stepped out of the shadows cast by the nearby machinery.

Celine's eyes grew wider with every step; her body quaking that much harder with every inch that was lost between them.

Another snake-like hiss oozed across their ears, rattling and squealing like a child's laughter as it grew in pitch. "Oh my! Zaney-boy, you brought an old friend!" The rattling hisses continued, "Well, well, aren't *you* a sight for sore eyes… well, *a* sore *eye.*"

Celine didn't understand what the still-shadowed figure meant, but she instinctively scuttled away—away from him *and* away from Zane—in the hopes of opening up enough distance to build up a sprint. She knew that, if he was too close, she'd never get that far.

"Y-you… you remember me?"

Another rattling hiss, "Still a dumb fuck, I see. Yes, of course I remember you, bitch," she heard a sharp inhale then, followed by a satisfied groan. "I never forget the stink of a cunt, and, trust me, the way you hightailed it the last time I saw you, that pink ass was all the view I was offered. Why don't you bend over for me and let me see how you've grown?" Maledictus stepped into the light then.

Celine whimpered and scuttled back further, "Oh god! Oh god no, please! Don't let it… don't let it… don't let it… Don't—"

"Shut up, Celine!" Zane growled, looking up at the creature, "That's the sort of reaction he *wants*!"

"Oh don't you just know me oh-so-fucking well, you infected chode-wart!" Maledictus glared down at him with the only eye in his head, the other ocular cavity occupied by a small, reddish orb that was barely big enough to keep the lid held open. His body—no longer simply that of an ykali's—looked like something out of an exorcist's nightmares; a massive, hulking frame adorned in bony spikes at every joint perched atop a pair of legs that would've been more appropriate on something long-since extinct. As he took another step, the three talons that capped each of his reptilian toes rose and fell—*cli-cli-click*—against the ground, kicking up more dust and woodchips as they did. Seeing the two of them taking in the sight, he beamed—his face warping into something horrific—and held out his long, clawed hands. "Like what I've done with it? Lizard is *so* last year!"

Zane grunted, clearly still hurt from the fall, "Where is she, you son of a bitch? Where the fuck is Serena?"

"Oh, her?" Maledictus shrugged, "She's resting; with all the pussy she's been throwing around lately I haven't had a chance to—"

"SHUT THE FUCK UP!" Zane roared, starting to drag himself *and* the motorcycle from the ground.

Maledictus pouted, "Aww, still suffering from some separation anxiety, I see?" He nodded, "Alright, I'll spare you the creamy details—and I *do* mean 'creamy'—and focus on catching up with my *favorite* fuck-stain." He absently scratched at his chest, letting a few loose scales rain down in the process, before gesturing to Zane, "How you been? I mean, *aside* from that fall..." his face shifted and he chattered his teeth as he cocked his head, "Please tell me that that *was* as painful as it looked," he let out an orgasmic hiss, "Give me the satisfaction of knowing that you're in *PAAAIIINNNNN!*"

Zane steadied himself on his feet and stood the motorcycle up beside him, gripping one of the handlebars to keep it upright. "Sure, dick-cheese. A real pain in the balls," he lunged forward then, dragging the motorcycle behind him. "But I've come to expect that from **YOU**!" he roared as he jumped into the air and used the momentum to swing the motorcycle—whipping about in his grip as though it were nothing more than a lawn chair—at Maledictus.

Maledictus finally looked *exactly* like what Zane would've imagined.

Before, when he was still nothing more than a curse that shifted Zane's body whenever he took control, his appearance was nothing more than a warped shadow of whatever it truly was. Since the creature had never attracted much attention or left many alive long enough to pose, he'd never gotten the chance to actually *see* what he looked like when the curse took hold.

And, for that, he couldn't be more thankful.

What stood before him now, however, was in every way a product of Maledictus' vanity; a Halloween costume built of the recycled ykali skin they'd given him. And while Zane was certain that whoever or whatever Maledictus had been prior to that moment, it wasn't nearly as horrible as what he was facing.

A massive, disgusting, horny creature…

Fitting.

It just made him want to kill the thing all the more, and the high-speed impact of over five-hundred pounds of American engineering straight to his skull seemed like a great way to get the job done.

Swinging the motorcycle for all he was worth, Zane aimed for the center of his bone-crowned head; spotting the gaping wound on the left side of his face.

Serena, he couldn't help but smile at the sight as he came down on the monster, *you magnificent psychopathic bitch. I love you!*

Glaring up at him, Maledictus whipped around; a long, thick tail covered in a row of razor-like bone spurs coming into view as it sliced through the body of the motorcycle. The rear half the vehicle—spitting various fluids from the severed engine and lines—careened off into the distance, shrieking with a metallic exclamation as it crashed into one of the fixtures in the distance.

Zane landed on his feet and glared at the remains of his makeshift weapon before casting it aside. "Like I said: 'a pain in my balls.'"

"You always were quite lippy about your genitals, boy!" Maledictus scoffed, "You seem quite attached to your balls, yes?"

"Not that you'd know anything about that now, lizard-dick!"

Maledictus hissed angrily, "Haven't heard Serena complain yet!"

Zane's blood went hot with rage. "FUCKING BASTARD!"

Eager to see his long-running nightmare finally dead, Zane jumped into overdrive and rocketed towards Maledictus. No matter what he'd done to his new body, the monster was still bound by the abilities of an ykali; he had their strength, their swiftness, and their agility, but there was no way that he could keep up or fight back against a sangsuiga at their speed—a speed that could only be seen and followed by *another* sangsuiga; a speed that rendered bullets in flight seemingly motionless in midair. There wasn't a chance Maledictus would survive—

Unless he was somehow able to *also* jump into overdrive…

Unless he was to match Zane's superhuman pace and begin leading him deeper into the lumber treatment yard…

Unless every expectation of his capabilities was suddenly proven wrong…

Exactly like he was doing now.

Oh, sweet, naïve, dumb-as-a-fucking brick Zaney-boy! Always acting on emotion and emotion alone! What a predictable dipshit you are! Maledictus' voice echoed within Zane's head as he chased after his target, proving that he *also* had retained at least some of his psychic abilities; and if he could move like a sang and manipulate minds like an auric he was even more dangerous than Zane could've imagined. *Didn't stop to think that me ROTTING in your guts for all those years might actually have offered me at least* some *benefits upon our parting, did you?*

Zane didn't respond. He couldn't. Only a perfect vampire—one like Serena with *both* sang and auric abilities—could send psychic messages while in overdrive. Sound didn't work at that speed, though this didn't stop Zane from roaring in a rage as he charged after Maledictus.

Zane rocketed up a steel staircase to an overpass that bridged between three towering wood chippers that formed a triangle grid around a massive pile of woodchips partially covered in a series of tarps. The glimmer of sleeping blades beneath him created a foreboding illusion of a hellish creature's hungry mouth waiting beneath the long, narrow bridge, and Zane quietly entertained the idea of hurling Maledictus over the railing and into the waiting—

Banking around a corner to intercept his target, he ran directly into Maledictus' waiting elbow.

Zane pitched back, clutching at his broken nose and stumbling out of overdrive as blood poured down his face; the throbbing burn in his face blinding him. Beyond the rolling, hot waves of red, he caught a blurred glimmer of movement a split second before one of Maledictus' giant fists plowed into his stomach with enough force to lift his feet off the steel platform. His breathing faltered through his broken nose. His eyes strained against the well of tears that had erupted in response to the assault on his sinuses. His guts folded and rippled within his stomach around the kinetic force still rolling through them. Sensing his body drifting in midair, he made a desperate grab for the railing before he was fed to the sleeping-yet-deadly teeth of the machines beneath them.

His grip faltered on the railing, dropping him another three feet until the fingers of his right hand found purchase on the platform.

Then one of Maledictus' talons pierced through the back of his palm and through the grating beneath his hand.

"Oh no, no, no, Zaney-boy! You ain't dying *that* easy!" Maledictus chided, reaching over the railing and dragging Zane up by his arm and planting him back on the platform. Zane teetered and strained to focus on Maledictus, succeeding in getting a clear view of the monster as both of his hands clapped around his head, boxing his ears and kicking up another round of ringing in his head. Staggering forward, Maledictus maintained his hold on Zane's head, dragging his face down as he drove his bony knee into his face—sending another wave of agony rolling through his already broken nose—before tossing him back onto the platform. "There's still so much I wanna show you, old friend; especially now that I've got a chance to show you first-hand what I've been making *you* do for *years!*" He laughed and started towards him, "Like what I'm going to do when I take that whiny cunt down there *and* our favorite blonde bitch all at once!"

Zane couldn't bring himself to rage at that point. He could barely see, his vampire senses were warped by the scent and taste of his own blood, and he felt as though the slightest movement on his part would force not only every meal he still had within him but *also* most of his organs out one of his ends…

If not both.

"You don't look too good there, little buddy," Maledictus squatted down in front of him, resting his forearms across his knees and letting his long tail snake between his feet and inch closer to Zane's face. "And I can't help but feel like this isn't at least *partially* your fault." He stood, "Now I can't give you *all* the credit—that wouldn't be fair to me, after all—but it was *you* that underestimated me; if you'd have stopped and considered all the sweet, tender fucking years we'd had together as 'roommates,' you *might* have anticipated what I'd be capable of on my own. After all, you can't just *hand* a lizard an evolutionary advantage like *me* and expect it to *remain* a simple lizard, can you?" He scoffed and shook his head as his tail began to gently brush Zane's cheek, "I'm just as fast as you now, and I can—as I'm sure you've seen—even manipulate and change my body"—he made a note of framing his face between a square of paired clawed thumbs and pointer fingers—"courtesy of that crotch-sniffing mongrel buddy of yours."

Zane groaned, fighting to get his bearings; to get back up; to fight. "So how do you explain the—"

"The mindreading?" Maledictus beamed, yanking his tail back and cutting the left side of Zane's cheek on one of his barbs in the process. "Oh come now, Zaney-boy, I should be allowed at least *a few* fucking secrets, shouldn't I? Like what I intend to do to you, for example. Sure, I've got all sorts of plans for that red-headed codpiece of yours down there, and all the squirming little dingleberries scurrying about the Vail Clan—oh, the things I'm gonna do to that blue-haired cunt; do you think the carpet matches the drapes with that one?—but you… oh *you*, Zaney-boy, are in for an outright amusement park of torture. And what makes my plans for you all the sweeter?" He leaned in, gripping either side of the railing in his hands and lowering his body—shoulders popping and unhinging as he brought his face so close to Zane's he was certain the monster would try to kiss him—so that he could whisper, "I can bring you back from the dead to do it all over again."

Zane's eyes widened.

Back from the dead?

He looked up at the monster's leering face, studying it for *any* sign of deceit. There was none.

The body at the cemetery… had that been—

Maledictus nodded in response to his thoughts, "It's taken a little practice, I'll admit. Whatever I *was* capable of has grown a tad rusty, but I assure you that I have the means to make the dead walk. And when I'm back to full strength, I wanna try a little trick." He stood, his shoulders once again popping and grinding as they returned to their sockets, and he made a note of shrugging to show that no damage had been done in the process. "See, I've been having this dream—least I *think* it's a dream; could be a memory, 'cept the fucking thing is just so goddam… well, you get the point—and, in this dream-memory-thing, I am causing all sorts of sweet fucking mayhem; like, fucking *world changing* mayhem. And I *like* it! And it won't be long 'til I'm strong enough to do it here," he smirked as his tail whipped excitedly back-and-forth, slamming against the railings with each pass. "I'm going to torture, rape, *and* murder *every-fucking-one* that has ever meant a damn thing to you, then I'm going to rip you apart piece-by-bitchy-bloody-piece and *then* I'm going to stitch you back together and bring you back. Again and again and a-fucking-gain, Zaney-boy! And I'm going to get stronger and stronger each time I do; your agonizing deaths and rebirths are going to charge whatever batteries I've got waiting inside me. *Then* I'm going to bring the entire world—vampire, mythos, human, ghost, angel, My Little fucking Ponies,

God... all of it!—to their fucking knees!"

Zane groaned and shook his head, scoffing after he'd spit a wad of blood over the edge of the platform, "Obviously putting you in a lizard body was a mistake; same old insanity, half the brain capacity, eh, Mega-dick-face?" He sneered up at the leering monster, hoping that stealing one of Ben's "accidental" interpretations of Maledictus' name might spark him to keep talking. Anything to give him just a little more time. "Hell, you were better off sharing a mind with me!"

"YOU'RE A FUCKING FOOL!" Maledictus hissed and lurched forward before catching himself in mid-lunge. Zane smirked at that. He really *didn't* want to spoil his plans by just killing him then and there. His enraged hiss drew on a moment longer as his talons clacked incessantly on the platform, "I'd have been better equipped sharing the body with a fucking earthworm!"

Zane grinned, fighting through the pain to look entertained by his opponent's rage. Just like Serena had taught him. "Kinda says something about the dumb fuck you've gone and evolved yourself into, huh?" He made a note of mockingly framing Maledictus between a square of paired thumbs and pointer fingers, "My speed, Raith's transformation, the auric abilities from the land of eerie-mysticism-and-bullshit... and a crippling retardation courtesy of peanut-brain filled to the bursting point with raw, ludicrous insanity and the lingering rage that you *still* can't find your dick in that hand-bag you call a body!"

Maledictus' body shook with rage as he backhanded Zane, sending him skidding across the platform. "THE TWO OF YOU FESTERING FUCKWADS HAD BETTER LEARN TO SHUT-THE-FUCK-UP ABOUT MY DI—"

Zane, though hurting, laughed at that, "The two of

us, huh?" He finally mustered the strength to drag himself to his feet—clinging to the railings as he forced his legs to accept the burden of his weight—and narrowed his gaze at Maledictus, "You deceitful cocksucker; all that talk of being with her—all your cocky, arrogant swagger—and you can't even *scare* her into fucking you, can you?" He cackled, nearly toppling over under the force of his own laughter. "You... you *pathetic* little iguana! You're nothing but a—"

He didn't see Maledictus coming, but he felt the aftermath as the two of them careened over the railing and slammed into one of the stairwells before chaotically rolling down the narrow, steel column.

Zane groaned, looking up at the furious face of Maledictus when they'd finally come to a stop, "Oh my... did I find a tender spot, princess?" He nodded towards the wound on Maledictus' face, "Are you still fuming that my girlfriend got to penetrate you but not the other way around?"

"Maybe I'll kill you now, after all," Maledictus growled, "So that I can carry on your torture *without* being forced to listen to your relentless fucking banter!"

Head still swimming, Zane's eyes swam in an effort to focus on his attacker once again. In the daze and confusion, he caught sight of something that brought a smile to his face, and he felt a flower of confidence bloom in the back of his mind.

"That sure does sound swell, asshole—it really does—but, before you go through with all that, y'know, killing and bringing ponies to their knees and whatnot, you might wanna work an extra step into your plan."

Maledictus sneered and started towards him, clenching his fists. "Not that I particularly care what a dumb shit like you thinks, but *what*—pray tell—are you babbling about?"

Zane was already laughing at what he knew was coming.

"You might want to watch your back."

Raith had never met Zane's informant, Ben, nor was he particularly trusting of the call that the club-owner had made to the clan. Though he'd been curious how somebody would have access to their private line, the message took precedent over any other questions he might have had.

Tracking the signal on Zane's phone, Raith had been able to follow his friend, who Ben had expressed a concern for after leaving his club in shambles to pursue a suspect. Raith knew that Zane was a heavy-handed warrior, but it wasn't his style to terrorize huge groups if he could avoid it. Not that Zane was particularly kindhearted when it came to strangers, but, for him, taking the time and energy to break a few strangers' faces was time and energy that could be better applied to breaking their target's face. The only exception Raith, or any of the others who were privy to the call, could make was Maledictus.

To get to him, Zane would've bulldozed the entire city and never once batted an eyelash at the bloody mess he was leaving.

So if this Ben's club was recovering from Zane rocketing out of the scene like a bat out of hell, it was a safe bet that the target he was pursuing was one that Raith was every bit as interested in seeing brought down.

And, as luck would have it, his deductive reasoning

wasn't wrong.

Unfortunately, Zane had obviously bitten off more than he could chew in trying to take on Maledictus in his new body on his own.

Raith was already in his therion form and putting more and more distance from the Dodge Viper he'd used to get to the lumber yard. Ahead of him, near a trio of wood chipping towers, he saw Zane—looking like he'd just called the late Joseph Stryker's mother a "whore"—cowering in the shadow of…

Well, somebody's been doing some reconstruction!

"—want to watch your back," Zane, despite his appearance, was laughing at Maledictus.

Whatever he'd just said sparked some suspicion and Maledictus, and the towering, tail-wielding, horned creature started to turn to face what was coming.

Raith, however, was faster.

Raith, moreover, was eager.

Zane had only made half of the turn to face the incoming threat before the incoming threat came down on him. It was no longer incoming, it was no longer waiting—no longer stalking or planning or sneaking—and, as the whirlwind of Raith—a flurry of teeth and claws slicing air and flesh alike to a chorus of ravenous snarls and grunts—collided with the monster Maledictus had become, the threat became relevant.

Raith's powerful therion hands pinned Maledictus' arms to the ground and he began snapping his jaws at his face. Before his teeth could sink into the monster's sneering face, though, Maledictus' tail wormed over his shoulder and twisted around his throat, holding him back.

"My my, aren't you a big doggy," Maledictus growled. As they continued their struggle, the monster's only eye glistened and widened. "Wait! Are you…?" he cackled and kicked Raith off of him, shooting to his feet, "Yes! That *is* you! You're the dog that *lived* inside Zaneyboy with me for all those years! I see Zane was polite enough to put you in a fellow fleabag's corpse. Isn't that precious!" He frowned as he took in the sight of the now-heaving, snarling creature before him, "Too bad, though. I liked you better then; not nearly so fucking panty and growly." He shifted his one-eyed gaze to Zane, smirking, "I'm afraid your doggy went rabid, boy; we had to put 'im down!"

Zane's body shook with rage, the act causing his tortured muscles to ache. He wanted to get up; wanted to help his friend and finally take down the monster that had plagued them for so long; wanted to, but he was too damn weakened from his injuries.

Looks like somebody could use a pick-me-up, Zoey's psychic voice echoed in Zane's mind, and a small flask dropped between his knees. *Drink up, Prince Valiant, we need you at your best.*

"Z-Zo—"

Nuh uh! Hiding myself from tall, dark, and truly heinous is tough enough with his new auric awareness without you advertising that Raith didn't come alone. Now drink!

Zane looked down at the flask, shuddering at the idea of what he *knew* was inside it, but scooped it up and began twisting the cap. Ahead of him, Raith had dropped to all fours and had begun a slow, calculated process of circling Maledictus; arching around him and forcing him to turn his back to Zane to keep him in his field of vision.

Smart, Raith, Zane smirked, opening the flask. Even with the blood caked in his broken nose, the smell of Zoey's enchanted synth-blood made him recoil. The stuff was potent, the contents within the flask alone having the raw, revitalizing impact of a full grown human's blood supply, but with the added medicinal and rejuvenating effects that only magic could supply. Though Zoey was a powerful fighter, Gregori's initial interest in her when she'd been brought into the Vailean Clan was her research in blood. Coupled with her science and the magical abilities of somebody known only as "The Gamer," who seemed to exist only as an online entity consisting of chemical formulas sent via email and way too many World of Warcraft screen-caps, they'd co-created the vile-yet-miraculous elixir.

Zane sighed, asking himself if being broken and bloody was *really* so bad.

ZANE MURDOCH!

Zane flinched and nodded, setting the flask down long enough to reset his nose—groaning in agony as he did—before retrieving and gulping down the disgusting substance.

He lurched. His body tried to reject the liquid from its taste alone…

Until his vampire anatomy sensed what it offered.

Then…

Clarity!

Strength!

Vitality!

Zane inhaled sharply, his vision and senses coming in so clear he could count the mosquitoes in the air and *feel* the trace amounts of blood inside each and every one of them. Sounds came in sharper and clearer, the nerves of his skin went electric with the heat waves surrounding him—each cell of his body telling his vampire mind which directions led to a warm body teeming with blood—and, with his strength returning to him, the urge to destroy Maledictus followed.

He has a broken rib, Zoey offered. *Second from the top on his left.*

Zane smirked, thinking Serena's name, knowing that Zoey would be able to "hear" it.

Of course. Zoey answered what they both knew, *She's been making his life a living hell, but she won't be able to hold out much longer.*

Zane frowned at that, mentally bringing up the possibility of Zoey getting Serena's location from Maledictus' mind.

You think I wouldn't have tried that already? Zoey's voice, even without the benefit of actual sound, made Zane flinch. *Pain receptors work differently than memories. Wherever he's holding Serena, he's taken the steps to not be read by anybody!*

Zane sighed, *So much for being a dumb shit...*

"Well look who's up and walking," Maledictus taunted Zane, "I was wondering when your bitch-ass would—How the hell...?"

Zane smirked as the realization that he was no longer crippled by his injuries dawned upon Maledictus, and the monster turned quickly to look back at Raith, hoping that the therion might have some clues as to how such a thing was possible.

Instead, he got a clawed hand ripped across his chest and a giant, wolf-like leg driven into his gut.

As Maledictus was thrown from his feet and launched towards Zane, the revitalized vampire vaulted into the air. Using the airborne monster' shoulders as a makeshift springboard, Zane flipped over him; drawing his legs in as he cleared the hurdle's frame and delivered a powerful kick into Maledictus' blood-gushing chest—centering the attack just below his heart; taking a morbid satisfaction in feeling the already broken rib shifting under his feet.

The added force of the kick sent Maledictus—shrieking in agony—soaring ever upward before he slammed into the siding of one of the massive wood chippers, catching his midsection on the railing as he fell back onto the stairwell beside it.

Zoey shimmered into view then as whatever auric shield she'd been hidden under was lifted and she focused on the platform.

Almost instantly the metal began to squeal.

As the fixture groaned and rumbled, more and more of the supporting beams—spitting nuts and bolts under the auric strain of Zoey's efforts—buckled and pitched. Finally, succumbing to the compromised support system, the stairway began to collapse. As one-third of the triangle surrounding the mountain of partially-covered woodchips began to come down, the neighboring platforms began to drag downward with the collapse, putting strain on the other two columns.

"Raith! Zane! Little help!" Zoey nodded to one of the other columns.

Neither of them needed an explanation.

Jumping into overdrive—reveling once again in the renewed vitality—Zane cleared the distance in a fraction of a second and began kicking the support beams. Though his vampire strength was enough to warp each of the metal fixtures, it wasn't until Raith caught up and began climbing the structure—putting all of his sizable bodyweight into the weakened system—that the column began to buckle.

Time to call it a show, boys! Zoey called out to them, *This thing's about to come down on Maledictus, and we don't want to be around when he digs his way out!*

Zane roared and glared back, "ARE YOU FUCKING KIDDING ME? WE FINALLY HAVE A CHANCE TO *KILL* HIM AND WE'RE NOT GOING TO—"

Raith growled, throwing his body back and forcing the platform to pitch against the strain—the onslaught forcing it to follow after the collapse of the first and, with two-thirds of the entire structure now dragging on the only intact column, beginning to cave the entire network in on itself—before dropping to his feet and yanking Zane away.

"No! NO! LET ME GO, RAITH! LET ME GO!" Zane fought against Raith's grip, only to have Zoey's aura bind him as the two of them started back towards the entrance of the lumberyard. "STOP! FUCKING STOP IT! PUT ME DOWN! HE'S STILL GOT HER! THAT SON OF A BITCH STILL HAS SERENA! LET ME GO!"

Behind them, the towering structure crashed down, burying Maledictus in a cage of twisted metal, machinery, and sawdust.

They all knew it wasn't enough to kill him—hell, it wouldn't have been enough to kill any one of them with such minimal injuries!—but still they fled. Before Zane could plot his escape from Raith and Zoey's hold and get back to the monster, he felt the familiar tickle of Zoey's aura in his head and the world went dark.

Chapter Nine
Love & Losses

ZOEY SMILED, LEANING INTO HER LOVER'S CHEST as they gazed up into the night sky. She was still catching her breath from their run, and with each ragged breath she inwardly cursed her therion lover's stamina and the pressures it put on her to keep up. Still, it was tough to stay mad at him. She sighed, readjusting herself against Isaac's chest.

She still felt guilty for having to drag Zane away from the lumber yard and the trapped Maledictus, but she'd known that no good could've come from sticking around. Plus, with the new intel that he and Celine had gotten from his informant, she was confident that they'd have another shot at him soon enough.

It *had* been the right thing to do, but it had still hurt like hell to see Zane hurt like that; the hope and eagerness to get Serena back drifting from his eyes after he'd woken up in the car.

"We haven't even gotten naked yet and we're already out of breath," Isaac chuckled, bringing Zoey back from her thoughts.

"Didn't think an auric like me would have what it takes to keep up, hm?" Zoey grinned up at him, turning her sky-blue gaze to his forest-green eyes.

The beauty of nature shone between them.

As a therion—a shapeshifter; what some might call a werewolf—Isaac thrived in this element. He was as much a part of nature as the trees growing beside them. She ran her finger across his broad chest as she remembered their first encounter in that same forest. As a member of the clan of Vail—which had been founded in a troubled time between Serena's parents, a pair of perfect vampires who'd faced a great deal of troubles from Isaac's kind; a complicated time that had resulted in some complicated clan rules—she was forbidden to have any contact with therions. Though set in bigoted claims, the danger to be had was too great to risk any sort of association. Yet, shortly after Zane had brought Serena back to lead the clan, Zoey stumbled across Isaac during a walk—overhearing him play his violin and had been lured to him—everything had changed. He flipped her world completely upside down and she found herself reveling in the feelings Isaac brought out of her.

He was *exactly* what she needed, and with him by her side she knew that she could find a way around any troubles.

"I love you," she whispered against his chest, allowing any negativity to leave her body for the time being.

She felt his hand on her chin as he raised her head to face his own; his green eyes were glowing in the moonlight as he smiled down at her.

"And I love you, Zoe," he leaned in and pressed his lips to hers in a soft kiss.

Zoey felt all of the tender feelings he had for her in that one kiss, and she felt a sudden need for intimacy. Wrapping her arms tightly around his neck, she pulled him down to deepen the kiss. Groaning, he easily sped up the process of undressing them while keeping his lips on hers the entire time. Neither one wanted to part from their kiss, yet neither one could hold back the sudden need to become one.

In a last attempt, Zoey finally allowed her aura to swirl around them, ripping through the remainder of their clothes to feel Isaac's bare skin against her own. The heat he offered her from his natural body temperature set off the already growing warmth she was feeling and she found herself wrapping her legs tightly around his waist. Isaac, still not breaking the kiss, was able to embed himself in her sweet dampness and let out a loud growl into her mouth as she took him.

It was then, under the beauty of the moon and lying in a bed of grass, the two lovers lost themselves and allowed their concerns to melt away from the moment.

After showering together and changing into some fresh clothes, Zoey and Isaac made their way down the halls, headed for the cafeteria. Noticing Zane sitting alone in the community room—staring *far* too intensely at the blank television screen—Zoey had nodded Isaac to go ahead without her and see what was bothering him. As she approached, Zoey grimaced as she got a better look at him and noticed that Zane's injuries had yet to be treated; the multiple wounds and lacerations he'd received still bleeding out as he sat there, staring. She sighed, looking back towards the cafeteria, where Isaac stood, looking back to her.

I need to talk to him about everything that's going on and make sure that he gets to the infirmary. She sensed Isaac thinking that he could go with her and she shook her head, *He's still a man at heart, hun, he won't be able to open up to me with you around. I'll catch up soon, I promise.* She offered a reassuring smile to Isaac who, understanding the friendship she had with Zane, nodded and turned towards the cafeteria.

Zane turned to her, scowling, "You think I can't tell you were just talking about me? Like it's normal to just stare at people for long, silent periods?" He shook his head, "Let me guess, you're hoping some one-on-one time is going to make me cry like a baby over all this?"

Zoey glared and took a seat next to him, "Probably wouldn't hurt to cry. I know I've cried a few times over this already, and I'm sure I'm in for a few more, too. Where's Raith? I thought you two were going to talk."

Zane scoffed, turning away from her, "My pride's been hurt enough by everything that's happened tonight to just let myself start sobbing like a little bitch-boy. As for Raith, I told him what I'll tell you now: that I'm fine on my own and that I don't want to talk."

"Is your pride also the thing that's stopping you from bandaging your wounds?" Zoey pressed her hand to his arm. "You keep all your tears bottled up inside while you let yourself bleed all over the place, is that it? Do you think that putting up a front like this will make you strong enough to save Serena? What happens when the time comes to kill him once and for all and you're passed out from blood-loss? Do you really believe that you're going to be able to defeat Maledictus this way; by letting yourself fall apart at the expense of your emotional constipation?"

Zane raised an eyebrow and turned to face her, "Wait... you want me to take a shit on Maledictus?"

She coughed out, letting out a loud retching sound, "No! Not consti—God! Ew! What the hell's the matter with you?"

Zane paused, shaking his head and looked away, staring off at the blank TV once more, "Plenty, I'm sure..."

Zoey looked over, "Zane? Please, if you won't do it for yourself, do it for *us*—for me and for Serena."

Zane sighed, his shoulders sagging at that. "It's just... that fucking bastard! He dragged me through the ringer; he caught me off guard, beat the ever-loving shit out of me, and then dug into the wounds and planted all the right taunts... just like he always has." He whimpered, leaning forward as he pressed his hand to one of his open wounds. "I mean, I knew he was a sadist with his words...but I've never been the one looking up at him while he was dishing it out. It's even worse than before, 'cause now I can't just tell myself that it's just a voice in my head."

Zoey bit her lip, "What did he say?"

Zane shook his head, "Nothing important."

Zoey set her hand on his shoulder, "Important enough. You know you can tell me, right? I've been beside you through everything that monster's done to you before, and I'd like think I helped on those occasions."

"Zane sighed and nodded, "Yea. Yea, you did. I just... I don't think I'm ready to relive all that right now."

"I understand. Just know that the offer will always be out there," Zoey smiled, "Now, you need to head to the infirmary and get the rest of these wounds bandaged up. My synth blood *may* be strong, but the wounds that are still bleeding *after* you've taken it are the ones that went the deepest. We can talk later." She gave him a stern look then, "And we *will* talk later."

"Alright, alright," Zane sighed and paused for a moment before getting up, "Thanks, Zoe. I really do appreciate... well, everything."

With that, Zane started off towards the infirmary, leaving Zoey to think about the situation. Sighing, she finally stood and was about to make her way to the cafeteria until she noticed an auric shift at the other side of the hall. Turning, she made her way across the room and spotted Celine walking down the hall.

"Were you watching us?" Zoey sneered.

Celine paused, flinching at the sound of her voice, and turned towards her. "N-no... of course not! I was just... just..."

Zoey shook her head. The shift in the shady vampire's aura alerted her once more that something was *not* right with her, and she offered a silent apology to Zane as she extended her aura to probe for some insight to whatever it was she was hiding.

"I can see what you're all about," she sneered, stepping towards Celine as she prepared to enter her mind, "and I'm going to put a stop to it now!"

She let her aura snake into Celine's head, ignoring the growing smirk on the vampire's face as she did.

Whatever it was she had to grin about, Zoey was going to know it soon enou—

The room tilted and faded—colors shifting and melting as Zoey convulsed and dropped to her knees. "N-no… wh-what've y-you… d-d-do…"

"That's one of the perks of having a "psychic firewall"," she smirked. "And that's what you get for digging around where you don't belong, you stupid bitch."

Chapter Ten
The Challenger

~DECEMBER 17TH, 893 AD~
~ARMENIAN OUTSKIRTS; JUST OUTSIDE OF DVIN~
~PALACE OF MELEILZSI SHAYKH NAQSHBAND~
~JUST BEFORE MIDNIGHT~

FOR A LONG TIME THE CREATURE—A TALL, HUNCHED silhouette looming just outside the gates like a vision of Death—did nothing more than chant Meleilzsi Shaykh Naqshband's name and rattle the gates with steady, rhythmic blows that threatened to tear them from the walls.

Meleilzsi… Meleilzsi… Meleilzsi… Meleilzsi…
BA-BANG! BA-BANG! BA-BANG! BA-BANG!

Over and over…

Four informal chants of the great Liche's title followed by a series of strikes against the door: each time coming in two sudden pairings in four successions.

Meleilzsi… Meleilzsi… Meleilzsi… Meleilzsi…
BA-BANG! BA-BANG! BA-BANG! BA-BANG!

At last, Meleilzsi Shaykh Naqshband could stand no more of the incessant pattern, and he ordered his guards to let the creature enter. Though fear shown like the sun's rays at the order, all who served Meleilzsi Shaykh Naqshband knew that there was nothing that could possibly occupy the outside of the palace gates that would be more eager to kill them than their master should his command go unheeded.

Soon after, the great gates opened, and the creature entered. Three of Meleilzsi Shaykh Naqshband's holy men—tasked with purifying any who entered his palace and, as a distant second, offering their guest welcome and promise of hospitality—nervously scuttled forward, their long, black robes offering little concealment for their shaky legs, and offered the creature a bow.

Three heads simultaneously fell across the palace hall, rolling awkwardly like eggs across the marble. Seeing this, the slaves and concubines fell into panic and scattered like scarabs. The creature offered little acknowledgement of the crowd as it pushed past the sagging bodies of the murdered holy men, letting one of its great feet come down on one of the severed heads and let the sound—not unlike that of a melon rolling from a banquet table and meeting its end upon the floor—echo through the halls. The creature did not worry itself with haste as it tracked down Meleilzsi Shaykh Naqshband, but, rather, leisurely strolled—its great robes offering no evidence of a body, let alone legs, and were any of the panicked servants to pause long enough to admire the spectacle they'd have sworn their murderous guest was floating—through the palace. Occasionally, as though simply plucking a particularly pleasant-looking piece of fruit from a low-hanging branch, the creature would lash out and claim another life. In these instances, the slow, casual pace would erupt into a blur of strife and screams—whichever victim he'd chosen suddenly seizing with great tremors; blood frothing from every orifice, as the distorted vision of the creature's gray robes cycled about them like a sandstorm—before returning to the casual pace with which it had begun.

    A concubine running towards Meleilzsi Shaykh Naqshband's chambers in hopes of safety stumbled. Before her flailing body could reach the marble floor, she was swept up in the gray cyclone. The young girl's screams, distorted by the howling of the creature's unnatural swiftness and inhuman shrieks of bloodlust, rolled with the pitching of her body, the sound growing forced with strain and damp with blood. The blur grew denser, hiding the writhing victim entirely, and the panicked servants slowed as terror gripped them to watch on.

    A whimper.

    Snarling… slurping.

    The gut-wrenching sound of bones being snapped like starter kindling.

    Silence.

    Save for the dying howl of the whirlwind the creature

brought with it, not a sound sullied the palace walls.

The gray haze faded...

And a young girl's arm—broken and bent in five spots; two on either side of the still flexing elbow—danced across the floor like a fish out of water.

And, once again, the creature fell into its casual pace as it closed in on Meleilzsi Shaykh Naqshband's chambers.

On the Liche master and his prized concubine, Arezoo.

Meleilzsi Shaykh Naqshband was outraged!

Twelve! Twelve of *his* servants—three holy men, two warriors, six concubines, and an unfortunate chef—had been slaughtered by this monster; a monster that he'd been hospitable enough to *invite* into his home!

Twelv—

One of the guards at his door—one of *four* who had proven himself brave enough to stand his post in the slaughter—met his end.

Meleilzsi Shaykh Naqshband sighed.

Thirteen. *Thirteen* deaths that were not of his own making; *thirteen* deaths that he would become no stronger for.

This guest was stealing more than just his slaves...

It was stealing his source for power!

Bellowing in rage, Meleilzsi Shaykh Naqshband rose from his bed, leaving Arezoo—still naked and spread open in all her glory on his sheets—to smirk at the spectacle.

Her master *finally* had a challenger, and, seeing his dark energies course through his body, she felt pleasured through his exuberance.

The corpses in the walls sprung to action, pounding with a rage that mirrored their master's own. Even with

SCARLET DUSK

the doors to his chambers shut, Meleilzsi Shaykh Naqshband could sense the startled energies of the creature spike in alarm as the din rose all around it.

A great roar shook the palace as the creature slammed itself against the wall. Portions of shattered marble chipped away and fell to the floor, leaving a tremendous hole that the creature thrust a mighty hand into. Meleilzsi Shaykh Naqshband watched through the eyes of one of his risen slaves within the wall as the creature yanked it from the gaping chasm—forcing several of the surrounding bodies to groan in futile protest as they began to topple through the opening—and began using the flailing corpse as a makeshift battering ram against Meleilzsi Shaykh Naqshband's chamber doors.

The sequence had been the same as before:
Meleilzsi... Meleilzsi... Meleilzsi... Meleilzsi...
BA-BANG! BA-BANG! BA-BANG! BA-BANG!
Over and over and...

Meleilzsi Shaykh Naqshband, with a simple flick of his wrist, allowed the barricade on the door to fall free. The chanting and banging ceased.

The door opened, and Meleilzsi Shaykh Naqshband and the creature stared one another down. Behind the Liche master, Arezoo felt the swell of Meleilzsi Shaykh Naqshband's power and she climaxed; writhing on the sheets and mewling in ecstasy. Neither Meleilzsi Shaykh Naqshband nor the creature had to shift their gaze to appreciate the spectacle.

Whatever this monster was, the energies rolling from Meleilzsi Shaykh Naqshband's favorite concubine seemed to have the same effect as all the blood it had consumed.

And Meleilzsi Shaykh Naqshband, having long-since discovered why many referred to the human orgasm as "the little death," felt an equally powerful swell of new vitality as his death-magic absorbed Arezoo's pleasure.

Finally, Arezoo came down from the throes of her vicarious climax and, no more modest in her post-orgasmic clarity, sat up to watch the scene unfold before her. Meleilzsi Shaykh Naqshband, certain that he would not be interrupting his concubine's own "little death," turned his head enough to instruct her to leave the two of them—he and his murderous guest—to their business.

Arezoo protested.

Meleilzsi Shaykh Naqshband, displaying a sternness he'd otherwise reserved for all *but* Arezoo, insisted.

Arezoo left.

The creature, once it was alone with Meleilzsi Shaykh Naqshband in his quarters, slipped free of the hood of its robes before opening the bundle and letting the heap of gray, tattered rags collapse like a dead thing on the floor behind it.

Meleilzsi Shaykh Naqshband fought the urge to sneer at this, finding the act almost more insulting than the butchering of thirteen of his servants.

The creature, beneath its traveling garments, could have easily been mistaken for royalty. Outside of the homely rags, he—there was no questioning the creature's gender at that point—wore a beautiful tunic dyed a deep and luxurious blue and adorned with beads made of gold and jade. Around his neck, along with the long, tightly-woven braid of raven-black hair that was long enough to circle twice around his throat, he wore a thick, golden medallion that Meleilzsi Shaykh Naqshband recognized as Egyptian, and along each ear was a row of solid gold hoops; a pair of gold lion-head earrings—each sporting eyes fashioned from blood-red rubies—weighing down his stretched earlobes. His face—a flawless vision of olive-toned skin and khol-framed eyes that matched the jade beads he wore—though clean-shaven and far from elderly did not take on the infantile features that seemed so common in those that wore beards, and, rather, Meleilzsi Shaykh Naqshband, despite his ongoing years as well as the long, tapered beard he wore, felt shadowed by his visitor in every possible way. Were he to try to guess from appearances alone, Meleilzsi Shaykh Naqshband might have thought this creature nothing more than a young man barely past the throes of a cracked voice, but, trying to ignore his intimidating height, there was an undeniable air of experience; something far more dated; eternal. Tall as he was, there was a regal elegance—unlike others of such size who usually suffered the crippling burden of their own bodies—that gave Meleilzsi Shaykh Naqshband the impression that this visitor was blessed with enough riches to accommodate his health's needs.

And yet, Meleilzsi Shaykh Naqshband could see that this being took to human politics in much the same light a king would consider the struggles of the sand mites outside his kingdom.

Meleilzsi Shaykh Naqshband finally inquired about his guest's name.

He was offered only a title: *Utukku.*

Meleilzsi Shaykh Naqshband demanded to know why he'd come to visit him on that night.

Utukku seemed entertained by that, his shoulders rolling with a silent chuckle as he circled the perimeters of Meleilzsi Shaykh Naqshband's chambers, absently running his blood-stained fingertips across the various sundries that the Liche had acquired through the years. After a long and increasingly uncomfortable silence, Meleilzsi Shaykh Naqshband realized that Utukku had no intention of answering his question.

He asked again, this time shedding all pretenses of pleasantries and formalities.

This drew forth Utukku's chuckles in a much more audible manner; his head pitching back as he erupted with laughter.

The fading glimmer of Meleilzsi Shaykh Naqshband's patience shed its final luster and he released a wave of decay at the still-laughing Utukku. As the spell traveled across the room, the vision of everything between them—arts and antiquities and décor alike—shone through the enchantment as a decayed and destroyed copy of what it would become; when the wave passed, so passed the vision of destruction, leaving the room untouched by the magic until it reached its intended target.

Utukku, still cackling, stumbled back from the force of the spell, and as the liquid-like curtain of death wrapped about him and bled into his body he began to writhe under its magic. His olive-like skin grayed and sagged around his skull; dimming and drooping like melting candlewax. The jade-green eyes, gaping around the pain of the enchantment, dimmed to a pair of murky, pale pools; the dark orbs of his pupils dancing about in their newfound blindness. As Utukku's body befell the effects of Meleilzsi Shaykh Naqshband's magic, it folded over—finally succumbing to the terrible weight of his own frame—and trembled. As the meat and merit of his thinning legs dwindled, his ankle bowed and snapped, toppling his decrepit form and landing him a short distance from the gray rags of his cloak that, like him, lay in a heap like a dead thing.

Meleilzsi Shaykh Naqshband scoffed and approached him, calmly explaining to the heaving mess at his feet that, even for an immortal creature, death and the power of decay eventually claim all things.

Utukku's hair, already thin and gray, began to shrivel and chip away like dried husks after a harvest; the once proud braid that had constricted around his neck beginning to trickle in grotesque clumps around the gangly folds of rotting flesh. Even without full use of his throat, the heaving soon-to-be-corpse lurched and began to cough out a chuckle…

Then, with a wheezing intake and a vulgar expulsion of clotted, black blood across Meleilzsi Shaykh Naqshband's chamber floors, Utukku began to laugh.

Taken aback by this—his victim's exuberant cackles rolling ever-freely despite his nearly totally decayed body—Meleilzsi Shaykh Naqshband took a cautious step back.

Utukku's shattered ankle shifted and *pop*ped back into place, the meat around it beginning to thicken and shift to a healthier shade. Still laughing, the creature stood. Though the effects of the decay spell had taken their irreversible toll on Utukku's tunic—the dye having bled out and what remained of the wool looking tattered and mangy—and the jewelry had all-but rotted and melted out of its original form, the creature was undeniably reversing the effects of Meleilzsi Shaykh Naqshband's spell.

The Liche, overwhelmed by the spectacle, dropped to his knees and begged to know how such a thing was possible.

Utukku's laughter calmed, replaced by an absent chuckle and a condescending and ongoing shaking of his head. He'd called Meleilzsi Shaykh Naqshband a pathetic child then; comparing his magic to a renegade peasant's eager flaunting of a talisman with no clue as to how it worked. Waving an arm towards the door—pointing to the remains of the massacre he'd left in the hall outside the Liche's chambers—he reminded him of all the servants he'd slaughtered just then; all the blood he'd taken into himself. He pointed off towards the side-chamber that Arezoo had retreated to, explaining that her orgasmic energy was *just* as nourishing for his kind. He taunted Meleilzsi Shaykh Naqshband, scoffing at his beloved death-magic and countering that death was, each and every day, trumped and cycled by new life. His laughter doubled over once more as he called attention to the thirteen he'd killed once more.

The blood—the very *life*—of thirteen of Meleilzsi Shaykh Naqshband's servants coursed through his body; the combined energies of their terror *and* Arezoo's climax just as revitalizing.

Chortling, Utukku asked Meleilzsi Shaykh Naqshband how he intended to cast a single death spell when the lives of so many welled within his body.

And, with that, Utukku took a long, gnarled, grayed fingernail and pressed it to his forehead—piercing through the dried, dead husk of skin—and began to drag it straight down, over his nose and bisecting his wicked, grinning lips; down his throat and further past his chest, splitting through wool and flesh alike as he went. The self-inflicted and ever-growing wound widened as the makeshift claw passed, sprouting the same vile, dark fluid he'd vomited earlier, and, as he reached the upper region of his loins, he let out a deep, relieved sigh and withdrew the talon from his grayed flesh. Eyeing the clotted, rancid residue on his fingertip, Utukku sucked the mess into his mouth—smirking at Meleilzsi Shaykh Naqshband's retch at the display—before working his fingertips into either side of the part at his forehead and beginning to peel them apart.

Meleilzsi Shaykh Naqshband's eyes widened in shock as Utukku pulled away the dead, gray flesh that his magic had inflicted upon him to expose, just beneath the surface, his young and vital form; the flesh even more flawless beneath the shedding cocoon of decay. The raven-black hair, not yet braided and shimmering like liquid-night, cascaded down his back and came to sway just above his buttocks. Much like the gray cloak he'd shed upon Meleilzsi Shaykh Naqshband's floor moments earlier, Utukku, finishing his task, left the clotted wool of his tunic and the mangled flesh of his nearly-dead self at his feet before stepping towards Meleilzsi Shaykh Naqshband, the joints and muscles of his naked body rolling like a panther's as he approached the stunned Liche master.

Smirking and running the back of his hand across Meleilzsi Shaykh Naqshband's face, he explained that he was Utukku: son of the great goddess Sekhmet. Raising his hands and making a show of his missing pinkies, he let it be known that, angered by his strength and eagerness to drain the human race, his goddess-mother had come down upon him and taken two of his fingers—one for every kingdom he'd decimated simply out of pleasure. Coming to rest his four-fingered right hand to the quivering Meleilzsi Shaykh Naqshband's chest, he told him that it was *solely* out of respect to his mother and a strong desire to *not* lose more digits that he'd not simply left the Liche master's palace in total ruin, but that, in exchange for his ongoing challenges to the creatures of the night who answered to Utukku, he had chosen to show the brash and arrogant death-wizard what *true* power was.

With Utukku's palm still on his chest, Meleilzsi Shaykh Naqshband had felt a great swell of power grow within his guest's hand and, before he could recoil, was hurtled across the room, where he crashed down on the hardwood frame that housed his mattresses.

The sound of her master's pained cries compelled Arezoo, who'd been eavesdropping just outside the door, to rush to the Liche's side. The young concubine, only slightly taken aback by Utukku's nakedness in her master's chambers, had begun to chant one of the basic death spells Meleilzsi Shaykh Naqshband had taught her in an effort to drive the unwelcome visitor away.

Utukku ignored the young girl's words and kept his gaze on Meleilzsi Shaykh Naqshband, telling him that he was displeased with many things about that night, but none moreso than the disconcerting number of deaths he'd left in his wake.

Meleilzsi Shaykh Naqshband, stunned by the creature's words, gathered enough of himself to demand an explanation.

Once again waving an arm out towards the hall, Utukku told him that he'd been content with the twelve souls he'd stripped from their mortal coils in his efforts to reach him. However, the thirteenth—the bold guard at Meleilzsi Shaykh Naqshband's door—had disturbed the symmetry; the beautiful balance.

Meleilzsi Shaykh Naqshband, listening, remembered the strange behavior that he'd witnessed in Utukku's behavior: four calls of his name, four pairs of impacts on the both the gates and his chamber doors; the breaks in the servant-girl's arm: two on either side of the elbow. Two cycles of his braided hair. Two types of beads adorning his tunic; the perfect symmetry of his jewelry, always in even numbers. The perfectly even split down his face and torso to reveal his renewed body...

And thirteen bodies to his name.

Meleilzsi Shaykh Naqshband stared for a long moment. He was demanding another death; yet another of his servants to be sacrificed in his name to fulfill some personal itch of the mind.

He called him mad.

Utukku started towards him, telling him that he could just as easily claim the Liche himself as the necessary death to offer balance. He pressed that, while he did not care *who* represented the fourteenth body, there *would* be a fourteenth.

Then his eyes fell on Arezoo, and a glimmer passed over the jade-like orbs as he suggested the young concubine, who still chanted her death curse despite an increasingly shaky voice.

Arezoo trembled at the mention.

Utukku swelled and took a step towards her.

Meleilzsi Shaykh Naqshband roared and, for the first time in his life, acted without calculation. Calling once again upon the death-wave, he flung Utukku straight up into the ceiling—destroying the many expensive lanterns and fixtures thereon—and then, issuing forth yet another wave of death-magic, hurling him across the room and through his chamber doors; casting the powerful creature's once-again mangled form amidst the bodies it was responsible for.

The Liche stormed after him, ordering Arezoo to remain within his chambers until he returned, and willed the doors to slam shut behind him as he stepped past the threshold.

Utukku was already reversing the effects of the spells

when Meleilzsi Shaykh Naqshband reached him; pulling himself up on shaky legs and warning the Liche that he would not allow him to claim another attack upon him without grave consequences.

Meleilzsi Shaykh Naqshband nodded, telling him that he could claim any servant *but* Arezoo as his much-needed fourteenth death. With that, the Liche master bellowed for his youngest concubine, Bastet, barely past her first decade, to be given to their guest in exchange for sparing his palace on that night.

Satisfied by their agreement, Utukku retrieved his cloak, offering Arezoo one final leer before starting back down the hall. Meleilzsi Shaykh Naqshband joined the creature at the gates to deliver Bastet, who sobbed and pleaded for mercy. As the girl's panicked cries fell on deaf ears, Utukku let the Meleilzsi Shaykh Naqshband know that their battle of power had only just begun, and that he would soon offer the Liche a more formal demonstration. Confident that his intentions were understood, he turned on Bastet in a sudden and gruesome display; tearing the terrified girl's limbs from her body—snapping each in half like a wishbone—before taking the head under one arm and offering Meleilzsi Shaykh Naqshband the slightest of bows before vanishing into the night.

Chapter Eleven
Distant Dreams

BLONDE.

The color of the sun.

Zane opened his eyes, finding himself facing the sun once more. The familiarity of it all hit him harder than he'd expected, though it had been so long since he'd gazed up at it like this.

It really was as beautiful as he remembered.

The golden orb shimmered and shifted, making him blink

against it, and, when he looked up once more, his gaze fell upon a silhouetted female from; a familiar fantasy from a far-off memory.

He shook his head.

No.

Not a memory.

A dream.

The Dream.

She came to him, pressing her hands to his face as she leaned close to him. The features he'd never been able to make out—features that hid his perfect woman's identity within the rays of the sun—suddenly came into focus; becoming, in the blink of an eye, as clear as day.

Her eyes—those beautiful purple eyes—lit up in front of him as the sun's rays became her hair, falling over her strong-yet-soft face...

And suddenly all the mystery faded into nothingness like the night turning to day.

And Serena was there with him.

His Serena...

The beautiful blonde bombshell he fell in love with was now occupying the previously mysterious silhouette of the woman from the dreams he'd had so many years ago. He smirked at the irony that the dream-woman he had created when he'd been engaged to Celine would turn out to look exactly like Serena.

The exact opposite of Celine in every way possible.

"I've missed you," she whispered, running her hands down his bare chest.

"I've missed you too, Serena," he smiled up at her and her eyes lit up at the mention of her name as though she'd been waiting all that time to hear him admit it.

She ran her lips against his throat, and he groaned at the feeling, wrapping his arms tightly around her waist as she came to rest against him. Leaning up, he pressed his lips to hers. The feeling of her soft lips against his sent a shiver down his spine and

he groaned in the ecstasy that her kiss brought to him.
The memory of her kiss.
A memory he couldn't let go of.
A memory he never wanted to relinquish.
Her lips were the medicine he needed then and pushed against her, eager to take another dose.
"I love you!" she whispered against his lips and he pulled her naked body against his, running his hands down her breasts, teasing her nipples as he continued to kiss her.
"I love you too, Serena. Never leave me again."
He didn't want to break their embrace.
He didn't want to not feel her against him.
He needed this more than anything.
Those beautiful purple eyes of hers shone down at him in need and he smiled, determined to give her exactly what she needed…
Exactly what he needed.
Wrapping her legs around his waist, he pressed inside her, finding comfort within her walls. Groaning loudly, he began to move with everything he had inside her. He loved her so much and he was determined to show her just how much he loved her.
She lifted her eyes to his and he lost himself in those perfect purple pools.
The pleasured gaze she gave him was everything he needed.
Everything he could dream of.
The woman he wanted.
The woman he needed.
She was with him again.
The moment climaxed, and he followed after it; crying out with his release as she cried out simultaneously with her own.
Then the cold air of reality came; a chill he was so familiar with.
The pain and cold that he'd been forced to endure for so many nights now…

"Serena… no. Please don't leave. I can't do this

without you... Serena, NO!"

His eyes shot open and he saw the faint silhouette of his hand reaching out into the lonely darkness.

The cold, lonely darkness.

Falling back against Serena's pillow, he tried to loose himself once more in the fading remnants of her scent; the sweetness of cherry blossoms and the kick of spice on an otherwise bitter cold winter's night.

"Serena..."

~December 28th, 893AD~
~Armenian outskirts; just outside of Dvin~
~Palace of Meleilzsi Shaykh Naqshband~
~Just before midnight~

Arezoo, still naked and wearing the glistening remains of sweat and Meleilzsi Shaykh Naqshband's love on her skin, stood at the open door of her master's chambers. The guards at the door, well aware of the concubine's standing in the Liche's eyes, struggled to keep their ever-alert gazes *anywhere* but the sensual image alluring them to steal a glance. Something that would surely cost them their lives. The challenge was made all the more tolling when, adjusting her posture against the door, her lover's seed—despite being as dead as his magic—found fresh passage and began to trickle down her well-toned thighs.

This fresh stream of lewdness, coupled with the myriad of pearly traces that still adorned her breasts, chin, and portions of her blonde mane—her master, powerful as he was, was notorious for both his virility as well as his copious offerings; something that often demanded the attention of multiple concubines when Arezoo was unavailable—created a visual that the guards mentally cataloged in the hopes of referring to in a more private moment...

Should they live to see such a moment.

Though the other concubines practiced a certain degree of modesty—none so brash as to flaunt their nakedness, let alone the liquid evidence of their exploits—Arezoo had spent too much time in the focus of others as an object of carnal lust to mind the judgments or desires of any that might bear witness to them. Should one be so bold as to stare too blatantly or—gods forbidding—lay a hand upon her, Meleilzsi Shaykh Naqshband would see them personally through to a horrid fate.

And all who served the Liche master knew this.

But temptation, like hunger, can only be tested for so long before...

One of the shakier guards shivered slightly under the weight of his own desires, his linen skirt visibly shifting over his growing erection as his eyes drifted towards the spectacle working its way down Arezoo's inner-thigh.

Not noticing her new spectator, the concubine discovered a lingering pearl over her chin and raked the morsel onto a painted nail before absently sucking her finger clean; never once taking her eyes from the gaping hole that the one called Utukku had left outside her master's chambers.

The guard groaned and pitched, his own seed abandoning his efforts for subtlety.

Arezoo, hearing this, glanced over and giggled at the vision of the guard writhing upon post-orgasmic weakened knees.

As the sound and foreboding chill of Meleilzsi Shaykh Naqshband's approach grew more imminent behind her, she whispered to her admirer that she hoped it was worth it for him.

A shimmering wave of death-magic burst through the threshold and slammed into the guard with enough force to break several of his bones. As his body was thrown into the air, a murky whimper ushered as the magic took hold and he began to decompose before their very eyes.

By the time the unfortunate guard had reached the floor, there was no discerning his remains from the corpses that occupied the palace walls.

Meleilzsi Shaykh Naqshband narrowed his eyes at the other three guards and asked them if they appreciated the show he'd offered them.

Unsure if their master was referring to their comrade's punishment or trying to lure them into a trap of confessing their own stolen glances of his prized concubine, they nervously muttered whatever sequence of words they felt might spare them the same fate.

Satisfied that a point had been made, Meleilzsi Shaykh Naqshband ushered Arezoo back into his chambers.

Arezoo sighed at this, telling him that she enjoyed the spectacle that Utukku had left behind.

Her master pressed her to explain, once again issuing her to return to the privacy of his chambers.

Reluctantly, the concubine obeyed, going on to explain that she'd long awaited a fitting challenger to enter into her beloved master's life; to offer both him and his powers a chance to flex to their full potential.

She offered him a coy smirk to accentuate the last part.

Feeling a fresh wave of vitality in his loins, Meleilzsi Shaykh Naqshband couldn't bring himself to chastise her for her flagrant display.

Still...

He reminded her that her body was his and his alone to enjoy.

Arezoo's grin widened at that, and she made a show of massaging the lingering wetness into her breasts; reminding him, in turn, that she knew full-well that the servants' reactions to such displays made him desire her all the greater.

Meleilzsi Shaykh Naqshband couldn't bring himself to even try to deny this fact, and, instead, pressed the issue of her obsession with Utukku.

Shrugging before allowing herself to drop onto his cloud-like mattresses in a pose that was fit for sculpture, Arezoo repeated that she was excited to see him paired with a worthy adversary; that she knew that her body could stay his boredom only so much.

Meleilzsi Shaykh Naqshband smirked at that, asking her if she'd heard of the prior night's eclipse.

Arezoo's grin betrayed her, and she inquired as to what he planned to do in response.

At nearly that exact time the night before, a great clamor erupted that the moon was being swallowed by the heavens. Intrigued by these claims, Meleilzsi Shaykh Naqshband had hurried to witness the spectacle for himself.

Sure enough, almost half of the moon had been rendered unseen, and, with every passing moment, more and more of the silver orb vanished. Squinting against the shadowy cloak of night, Meleilzsi Shaykh Naqshband was certain that it looked like...

Blood?

Curiosity flared in the Liche then as his suspicion gave way to certainty, and he focused his powers—honing his magic senses to confirm that there was, indeed, an unprecedented amount of human blood saturating the very air—and traced the source to a neighboring hill not far from the palace.

Though his eyes were, tragically, still quite human, Meleilzsi Shaykh Naqshband could see beyond the veil of death that Utukku was behind the phenomenon. The blood-creature was *somehow* sending so much blood into the sky as to totally block out the moon!

And, as this fact dawned upon Meleilzsi Shaykh Naqshband, his rival's voice boomed within his mind, telling him that no display by a mere death-wizard could counter such a visceral vision of power.

Unable to curse the creature from such a great distance, Meleilzsi Shaykh Naqshband was forced to endure the inescapable taunts as he watched the moon vanish behind a massive curtain of blood.

Arezoo crawled across the mattresses towards her master, tugging lightly on his tunic and, once again, inquiring to his plans in responding to Utukku's challenge. Clearly unsettled by Meleilzsi Shaykh Naqshband's silence, she—rolling onto her back to look up at him—added that such a large amount of blood must have cost many people their lives, and she casually began reciting and correcting a series of rhetorical estimates.

Meleilzsi Shaykh Naqshband, not a fool by any stretch of the imagination, could see that his prized concubine was pushing him to counter the prior night's "eclipse" with a display not only for the sake of meeting Utukku's challenge, but for her amusement as well.

Were she but any of his other servants, he'd have

executed her for such brash efforts at manipulating him.

But this *was* Arezoo, and under the weight of her insistence he couldn't bring himself to feel anything other than the thrill of the challenge.

Finally nodding to her, he issued her to his balcony.

She eagerly obliged.

From the vantage point of Meleilzsi Shaykh Naqshband's personal balcony, he could overlook the lights of the city Dvin in the distance. There were so many of them down there, and he absently uttered this aloud for Arezoo to hear.

Intrigued, she asked if he meant the people.

Shaking his head and smirking, he motioned to the great land before them and explained that so many years of death and burial had created an unseen and often ignored *foundation* of death beneath the feet of those going about their lives.

So many corpses.

So many dead.

And the dead *were* his power.

A display of power.

The thought rolled with Meleilzsi Shaykh Naqshband over and over until it became auditory. And while he knew that Arezoo was audience to his ongoing mantra, he was somehow certain that Utukku was not far and just as privy to the chant.

Then he acted...

Willing them—all of them; each and every corpse dwelling beneath the lands before him—to awaken and make their might known.

The hour of midnight came and went as Meleilzsi Shaykh Naqshband continued to usher new life into everything dead; commanding them to rise.

So Utukku wanted to hide the moon?

Meleilzsi Shaykh Naqshband would shake the very earth!

The sands began to shiver.

The wail of frightened livestock grew.

Startled cries and shouted warnings grew…

As did the tremors.

Until all of Dvin and its surrounding lands shook with the combined rising of the dead.

Buildings toppled, burying entire families and communities.

More and more deaths; more and more fuel for Meleilzsi Shaykh Naqshband to will into action.

For every body that fell, a new minion arose to follow the Liche's command.

Soon, excluding the corpses that had been dead prior to Meleilzsi Shaykh Naqshband's display, he'd accrued over thirty-thousand new playthings.

Arezoo's eyes—unblinking and awestruck—took in the spectacle as she absently dipped a hand between her thighs.

More than thirty-thousand deaths…

Meleilzsi Shaykh Naqshband smirked, beckoning to Utukku and demanding to know how a mere eclipse could fair in comparison to a being that could make the very earth quake with the dead beneath it.

Utukku answered.

The air shimmered with grayish-blue strands of light, like glowing lengths of thread that arched over Meleilzsi Shaykh Naqshband's balcony and wavered before his chest; tickling the marble length of the railing. Then the strands began to vibrate with such ferocity as to drive both the Liche and his prized concubine back several steps…

And, as though he'd been there all along, Utukku was

there; crouched like a lion on the railing and glaring.

He roared; declaring him a greater fool than he ever could have fathomed. His mouth gaped far wider than any man's should, his teeth quivering like the sands of Dvin and growing—two dagger-like pairs of fangs along either side of the upper row and another pair like them from either side of the bottom—and his eyes glowing like a pair of green suns. The bluish strands emerged once again, though Arezoo seemed unaware of them this time, and shot from Utukku's shoulders; lashing at Meleilzsi Shaykh Naqshband's palace. Utukku moved then, though Meleilzsi Shaykh Naqshband could not trace the motion and only saw the powerful creature—once perched on his railing—suddenly standing before him.

How could he move so quickly?

What was happening?

Meleilzsi Shaykh Naqshband ordered Arezoo back into the chambers; demanding that she warn the guards and have them prepare for battle once and for all against this monster.

His concubine offered none of her typical, playful resistance, and fled with such haste as to inspire some meek hope in the Liche. Confident that his beloved was at a safe distance, he worked a death-wave into his palm and prepared to strike. Though the attacks had not been fatal for the creature before, he was confident that he could cripple its onslaught long enough to grow his forces and, perhaps, call the thirty-thousand lumbering minions he'd ushered into being to his aid.

If he could only hold this blood-and-soul-sucking monster at bay long enough…

His powers welled and he moved to hurl the attack…

Only to find his left arm no longer attached to his

body.

Eyes widening as the sudden rush of pain and horror struck him, he looked up at Utukku, realizing that this creature had severed one of his limbs with such speed that neither pain nor motion had registered in any sense to him.

He was still so very, very human…

And Utukku…

What a monster earns in challenging another…

You're no monster, Meleilzsi Shaykh Naqshband, Utukku snarled again, and the strange strands began to rip the walls of his palace down, *But you can bring them down upon this world with such recklessness.*

Meleilzsi Shaykh Naqshband abandoned his severed arm *and* his lingering hope then; turning on shaky feet and sprinting back into his chambers as the outer walls of his palace crashed down and began to pelt the balcony behind him.

He didn't need to look to know that Utukku was no longer occupying that space; somehow he was already inside, laying waste to all that Meleilzsi Shaykh Naqshband had worked to build.

The screams of his servants began to echo through the chaos—new ones birthing before the old had even had a chance to fall silent with their impending demises.

Utukku was a *true* monster, and a far more effective being at bringing death.

The eclipse hadn't been a full display of power!

It had been a display of control!

A blood-red sign that *true* power wasn't in breaking the dam and letting the full capacity of destruction consume all in its path, but in letting a small river destroy enough lives to *show* what potential awaited *should* the dam be broken…

Arezoo lay sobbing on the floor, the vision of the three guards' dead bodies outside the chamber doors—the fruit of their stolen glances at Arezoo's body never to offer them a moment of comfort—giving Meleilzsi Shaykh Naqshband a sudden awareness that the murderous monster had spared his prized concubine long enough to offer him some chance at atonement before death came to them.

A rage welled within the Liche; a destructive hatred and wicked perverseness that consumed everything he was.

Utukku had humiliated him and destroyed his legacy.

And he had only a great quake within the destroyed city of Dvin in response to an awe-inspiring eclipse to show the world what he'd been worth.

He wanted to maim!

He wanted to rape!

He wanted to claim every bit of terror and pain and destruction that was coming down upon him; to multiply all of it upon the world as the greatest destructive force both man and monster would ever witness.

A great curse upon the world.

A *maledictionem* of destruction and despair.

But his body wouldn't survive that night, not with Utukku's tirade taking everything at such a rate. He wasn't strong enough…

Not as he was.

Pulling Arezoo to her feet, he told her that they were about to die, and that, in their deaths, he would see his final act as the Liche master Meleilzsi Shaykh Naqshband offered them a new potential when the time came.

His beloved concubine's eyes showed that she did not understand, and he didn't expect her to.

Offering Arezoo one final kiss, Meleilzsi Shaykh Naqshband spotted his coveted chalice—the perfect relic to fulfill his needs—and he scooped it up into his remaining arm; pressing his lips against its polished surface.

Carry us, great treasure, he could feel Utukku's presence at the chamber door, and he turned to see the creature closing in on Arezoo. *Carry us, and find us our new body… our Maledictus!*

Throwing the chalice into the air, he aimed his open palm at his beloved, howling his magical command.

Arezoo's body seized, and Utukku paused to watch as the blonde-haired beauty rose into the air like a holy creature. A light grew behind her eyes, increasing in luminosity until it erupted and bathed the room in a blinding wave that forced Utukku to shield his eyes.

When, at last, the light died down, Utukku watched the broken and decayed bodies of Arezoo and Meleilzsi Shaykh Naqshband collapse to the floor along with a hunk of metal; as black and festered as the blood that he, himself, had shed upon those very floors over ten nights ago. Lifting the strange trinket, he felt a dark and horrible energy coursing through it, and instantly thought of a warped chalice teeming with something evil…

The Liche had done *something* with this abominable relic, but, with the palace of Meleilzsi Shaykh Naqshband coming down and all of its inhabitants dead, Utukku cared little for whatever the late Meleilzsi Shaykh Naqshband had planned for it.

He could only hope that The Council would recognize his efforts in keeping their kind hidden from the humans and spare him the indignity of taking more of his fingers…

SCARLET DUSK

May the world never have to suffer another moment from that awful wretch!

Chapter Twelve
"A Necessary Tragedy"

"FUC-FUCKING P-PUNKS! BUNCH OF BLIND—AH! Dammit!—blindsiding assholes!" Maledictus groaned, pulling a warped crossbeam that had wedged a large portion of one of the wood chippers on top of his legs. Freeing his right leg, he kicked at the pile until enough had fallen free for him to pick away the remains with his hands and exhume his mangled left leg from the pile of twisted metal. "Gah! That *does not* fucking look good! Motherfuckers…" he grumbled as he pushed himself up and took a labored, painful step out of the wreckage.

Still cursing Zane and the others, he faltered on his

broken left leg, and his body—the lizard brain beginning to overwhelm his own logic and telling him over and over again to simply *eat* the crippled appendage—let out an instinctive hiss as he glared down at the three predominant breaks traveling the length of the leg. His femur—*thankfully*—hadn't suffered any breaks when he'd been buried in all that collapsing hardware. Had he not been cunning enough to shield himself under an overturned portion of the platform, he might not have gotten out of it with such minimal injuries.

Still...

The leg bent forward at an aggressive and unnatural angle just below the knee—break number one—before suddenly shooting inward with a compound fracture that left the exposed portion of sharp bone pointing down in a morbid mockery of where the leg *should've* led—break number two—and, finally, "righting" itself with a nearly ninety-degree bend that, by some strange fate, *hadn't* pierced the skin despite its jagged appearances—and that one made the hat trick.

Maledictus growled. The ongoing streams of witless, sarcastic nonsense in his head making him wish that Serena actually *had* struck his brain when she'd attacked him with one of his horns.

All thanks to Zane, he groused to himself, *him and his friends and his infernal obsession with sporting events.*

Hat trick, indeed.

The real trick would be collecting all those hockey player's testicles and stuffing them in a hat!

He laughed at the thought and, trying to take another step out of the lumber yard, heard something snap in his leg and toppled over on himself.

"SON OF A FUCKING WHORE!" he hissed and writhed, struggling against phantom opponents as the pain overwhelmed his body; his mind succumbing to the illusion of battles that weren't there.

The logical part of him didn't care.

Let the body have its moment; let the stupid animal exhaust itself and go into some hibernation in the back of his mind so that he could, for once, not be forced to warp his perception with its carnal contributions.

Then something caught *both* their minds—animal and monster alike.

Flashing lights.

The familiar shrieking, two-note melody.

Maledictus grinned.

"Lights and music?" he mused, sitting up, "Looks like Christmas came early this year."

Police *and* fire units. No doubt in response to the collapsed machinery that he'd just dug himself out of. The three cop cars—screaming a brightly-lit path for the two fire trucks taking up the rear—ground to a halt just beyond the entrance to the lumber yard, their tires squealing like excited children rushing to their stockings and kicking up a blizzard of dirt and sawdust. Six doors swung open like the flaps of holiday packaging being yanked open, and twelve eyes fell on Maledictus.

"Oh? Is it *my* turn to open a present?" he leered, rolling onto all fours—letting his broken left leg drag beside his tail—and taking a scuttling advance towards the response team. Three sets of high-powered spotlights came to life—each mounted over the driver's side mirror of the squad cars—and came to focus on Maledictus, momentarily blinding him.

He hissed and scuttled back, the body once again going into pain-fueled fits and rolling about on the ground, kicking up dust and debris.

"Sweet mother of—what is that? Some kind of body

armor?"

"Shut it, Ians, we ain't got—"

"POLICE! DROP TO YOUR BELLY WITH YOUR HANDS BEHIND YOUR HEAD OR WE *WILL* OPEN FIRE!"

As the trucks came to a stop behind the police cars, several of the firemen occupying them poked their heads out to get a look at what was going on.

"Is that thing even *human*?"

"What the hell else would it be?"

"I dunno. Looks like a damn croco—OH SHIT! LEWIS!"

Even down one leg and exhausted from his battle, Maledictus had enough strength to launch himself across the space between him and the nearest cop. Gunfire erupted around him as the other five officers came to their colleagues' aid. The bullets that found their mark stung Maledictus, but few actually punctured his still-scaly body. The sudden uproar of screams and gunshots set off a primal rage in *both* Maledictus and the ykali, and the first cop cried out as a giant clawed hand came down on his shoulder—breaking his collarbone—and forced his head into the doorframe of his squad car.

Maledictus slammed the door.

"Oh god! Oh sweet holy mother Mary and baby Jesu—"

"SHUT THE FUCK UP!" Maledictus roared, yanking the headless body of Lewis from the warped car door and flinging it over the hood and into his panicking partner. "If you're gonna pray, pig, you pray to *me*!"

The other cops rushed from their cars to help pull the body of their late comrade from the shrieking, blood-covered officer beneath him.

"Backup!" one shouted over the chaos, "Call for

backup! We need SWAT in here YESTERDAY!"

"O-officer down. I-I… I repeat: we have an—oh god, please n-no—we've got an officer down! Lewis… they got Lewis!"

"Idiot! Give them the damn location, rookie!"

"Ah, uh… right. L-location… uh, officer down at… uh, the Willsbury Lumber and Logging Pla—AH!"

"HEADS UP, FUCKER!" Maledictus retrieved Lewis' decapitated head and pitched it with all his might at the stammering cop, grinning at the sight of the right-half of his head caving in under the force of the collision.

The four cops turned towards Maledictus at once, pistols drawn.

"TAKE 'IM OUT, BOYS!"

Maledictus chortled as he ducked behind the frame of the car—the windows shattering and raining down glittering reflections of blood-splattered moonlight all over the ground—as the officer's on the other side peppered the vehicle.

"Keep 'im down! Keep 'im hiding 'til we can get Ians out of here! Just keep 'im—"

"Fuckin' dumbasses!" Maledictus laughed to himself, hooking his talons under the frame of the tortured police car and flipping onto its side, "Can't you brain-dead pork-chops see that Ians is already dead?"

"Did that thing just ta—"

"GET OUT OF THE WAY! MOVE!"

Maledictus tipped the police car, letting it roll onto its roof and, in the process, onto two of the cops that weren't quick enough to jump free of it.

One of the pinned cops, still alive as he tried to pull himself from the overturned car, let out a startled cry as Maledictus' foot came down on his skull.

The two remaining cops let loose another storm of bullets, forcing Maledictus to drop to all fours once again and scuttle behind the closest police car for cover.

Coming face-to-face with a fireman as he did.

Though clearly terrified, the fireman—having seen the fate the other cops had been met with—pulled a serrated hatchet from a sheathed pouch at his hip and brandished it as a weapon against him. Laughing at the sight, Maledictus grabbed the fireman's arm in his left hand and struck forward with his right, forcing the hand holding the weapon to slam back into its owner's face and embedding the steel pick opposite the axe blade into the fireman's skull. The body slumped—the helmet crashing loudly against the reinforced back window of the cop car—and fell to the ground before Maledictus made a note of tossing it back towards the fire trucks as a warning.

All those dead humans—five in less than two minutes—and he could *feel* the death inside him; could feel his body responding to their lost essence as he soaked it up. It made him stronger. It made the pain from their bullets and the haze of their noise fade away. It numbed his leg; hell, he could *feel* the broken bones trying to heal with the death-energy.

"Oh yes," he chuckled, kneeling down and beginning the painful-yet-somehow-pleasant process of manually resetting his leg.

Bones ground together and scraped against the splintered sections of their once unified counterparts—the vibrations traveling the length of the bones and tickling his kneecap—as he worked to marry them back together.

He laughed.

The compound fracture ripped more of his flesh as

he jammed it back into his body and wormed it past the torn muscle and ligaments.

He roared.

A pair of cops flanked the car, one on either side, as they came around to get the drop on him. Maledictus yanked the spotlight over his head and cast its beam into the face of the front-side cop, who howled at blinding light and began firing blindly in a panic. The rear-side cop charged Maledictus from behind, the sound of metal snapping against metal and the sharp intake of a trained fighter—Maledictus' residual memory from being trapped inside Zane told him that the cop had pulled a switchblade—as he closed in. Maledictus scoffed, glancing back and, with a quick pass of his tail, took the cop's right leg off above the knee. The policeman hissed in pain, keeping his teeth clenched to avoid screaming and keeping his eyes trained on his target. Maledictus smirked and turned to face him, letting his already blood-splattered tail blindly eviscerate the blinded cop at the front of the car.

"You're a soldier?" Maledictus sneered.

"So," the cop's voice came out in a pained rasp, "it can talk."

Maledictus growled. "It?"

The cop laughed at his reaction, nodding. "Ain't gotten a good look at yourself lately? You look like I ate a desert toad in a drunken bet and took a bloody shit on one of my kid's dinosaur toys," he scoffed. "I can't say what you are exactly, it-man, but I've read enough—"

"Enough *what?*" Maledictus glared, "Enough of the Bible to—"

"To answer your first question, it-man: I was a *marine*, and, before I answer your next one"—he lunched forward on his remaining leg, plunging the switchblade just above the gaping wound that Serena had given him—"*that* should teach you not to interrupt."

Maledictus hissed in pain and rage, staggering back and clawing at his face in a blind scramble to rid his jaw of the second thing to get stabbed into his face that night. "FUCKING SHIT-SUCKER!"

The switchblade clattered to the ground and Maledictus lunged at the one-legged marine, jumping into overdrive and positioning himself behind the man.

The marine didn't bat an eyelash at the giant monster suddenly vanishing, but, rather, turned his head knowingly.

"Before I kill you, man-pig," Maledictus planted a clawed hand at his throat, "I want to know what it is you've read... and what you think it's taught you about me."

"Comic books," the marine said flatly. "Things like you are a dime a dozen in those stories. And, in all the best comics, there are those just as strong and powerful as the things like you, and they *always* win."

Maledictus scoffed, "Oh? Comic books, eh? So what, in this disgustingly two-dimensional world of make-believe that you jerk off to, would you be?"

"Us?" the marine looked around at the dead policemen and the terrified firemen, who were, at that moment, radioing for backup. "We're fallen heroes; those brave enough to fall trying to stop the likes of you and prove to the readers that you're an evil monster in *desperate* need of whoever's going to kick your ass to do *just* that." He smirked and shrugged, "We're a necessary tragedy, and I gladly take that role knowing that my boy will remember me as a hero... and *knowing* that, when whatever superhero you've gone and pissed off catches up to you, you're going to get what's coming. And on *that* day, it-man, I'll be watching, and I'll be cheering!"

Maledictus couldn't think of any vulgar retaliation to the marine's words. He couldn't bring himself to think or say anything as he smashed the marine's head repeatedly into the side of the police car until there was nothing left of the mouth that had spoken those cold, defeating words to him; *him*! The marine hadn't been afraid of him, hadn't cowered or groveled or begged, hadn't even screamed when he'd finally been slaughtered. The damage had been done—his typical confidence, vicious and unwavering, had been tamed and skewed. Even when he'd killed the rest of the police and the firemen—even after ripping through the SWAT that had shown up in response to the last officer's call—he couldn't bring himself to taunt or laugh; he couldn't do anything but slaughter the lot of them and soak in the energy of their deaths.

"Hero?" Maledictus spat the name like a bitter taste, "Is *that* what the gods want to see Zane as?" He shook his head and glared up at the night sky, "Let me *show* you—once and for all—that there are no more heroes!"

Chapter Thirteen
Past Regrets & Present Secrets

"DAMMIT, SERENA, WHERE ARE YOU?" ZANE SHOOK his head, "So much for the hero always winning," he snarled as he slammed his fist into the wall as he stormed out of the infirmary, stopping in time before colliding with Celine.

He watched as Celine's eyes widened at his fury and he shook his head, not wanting to startle her any further. Her emotional trauma was the *last* thing he needed added to his laundry list of reasons to go insane.

Besides, he wasn't about to make more of a scene within the walls of the Vail Clan with all the chaos already plaguing them.

It just wasn't fair to everyone else.

He remembered past instances when he'd taken his rage out by punching the walls. Gregori, when he'd still been alive, would've complained about the costs of fixing all his damages when he got like this, and the fear of his mentor-slash-father figure's rants about repair costs had been enough to stay his hand… most of the time.

Glowering, Zane desperately wished for the strength his Gregori had possessed; he needed it now more than ever before.

You're NOTHING *without me, Zaney-boy. Face it!*

Shaking his head, he let out another growl and slammed yet another hole into the wall, ignoring Celine as she yelped and jumped back.

Maledictus…

That smug, arrogant beast! He wasn't his only strength! He couldn't be!

Dammit, he felt his blood boil and, without the threat of his curse to force him to fight against it, he threw a few more punches into the wall for good measure. *Fuck the cost!*

He needed Serena's warmth!

He needed Zoey's guidance!

And, instead, he got Celine's vacant doe-eyes shimmering in fear at his rage.

He sighed, *Figures*.

Though they *still* hadn't found any sign of what was wrong, Zoey was, thankfully, in stable condition in the infirmary. Their medical staff had told him that it was some sort of seizure—something that shut down all but her most basic functions—and, without any clues as to *how* she'd been put in such a state, any attempts at reversing it were a risk.

"Z-Zane?" Celine's nervous whisper brought him back from his thoughts and he turned to her.

"What is it?" he grumbled.

He watched as she stepped back and let out a deep sigh. Growing impatient with the prolonged display, he ran a hand through his hair, wincing as his fingers caught a tangled patch of dried blood.

Suddenly he was painfully aware that, in Serena's absence, he'd barely changed his clothes or taken any steps to keep up with his appearances.

He was certain he looked like hell.

And, coupled with his exposed temper, he figured that's what had Celine so tongue-tied.

"Sorry. I'm just going through some shit." Zane sighed and rolled his eyes, "As I'm sure you've noticed by now."

"We can talk if you'd like," Celine smiled.

"I-I'd really rather not," Zane shook his head, still not fully trusting her, even if he didn't have a real reason not to, somewhere inside of him didn't want to trust her. "Look, don't take this the wrong way, but the two people I trust most to talk to about this sort of shit are now *both* out of my reach. Talking to you is just…" he shook his head, "I just can't. I just don't know *how* to talk to you after all these years."

"Come on, don't you remember what we used to have?"

~*Fall, 2001*~

It had been a month since Zane had met Celine and while their time was brief in comparison to many other couples Zane had encountered, he felt a strong connection to her. She was kind and sweet, not to mention beautiful. Despite this, he continually found himself craving something—*somebody*—but not feeling instinctively drawn to *her*.

And while he'd felt guilty about this, he often found himself turning down her offers for pleasure out of a natural lack of interest.

Though that wasn't to say that his new vampire body wasn't lusting for *something*.

Something Zane didn't recognize at its core.

Something that he only felt close to in his dreams…

Zane opened his eyes to a familiar brightness. Cautiously, he squinted against it and, realizing it was the sun, began to step back in fear of being burned.

Crying out in fear of the pain and potential death that he'd been warned of, he'd waited—held in the throes of panic—for the agony of the sun to take him.

But nothing happened.

He shook his head; finding the courage to open his eyes once more and was met with a feminine silhouette with features hidden from the sun's rays. He stared at her, watching as she stepped forward and her long hair swayed around her, the golden hues of the sun radiating off her and giving her a golden halo.

He smirked, somehow knowing that the woman in front of him was someone special; someone no other could take the place of for him.

Someone he'd take on the devil to stand beside.

"You came," her sultry lips let out a hungry purr as she took the last step to reach him.

"You were waiting for me?" he tilted his head; confused at the familiarity she presented him with.

"Of course, you created me after all, Zane," she grinned teasingly.

"I did?" he asked.

"Don't act so surprised. Your innermost desires created me," she smirked as one of her hands caressed down his bare chest.

He tilted his head, noticing that he was now as naked as she was and he watched her mouth open to reveal a pair of fangs extending past her lips.

"I'm so parched," she whimpered, leaning forward. "Can I take a bite?"

He groaned, his shaft instantly hardening at the idea of her feeding from him. He somehow felt if she didn't bite him soon, he'd go out of his mind from need. Wrapping his arms around her waist, he pulled her into him, arching his neck enough for her to leave her mark. The sharp pain was quickly remedied by an intense pleasure as she began to drink from him. His hands found her golden orbs and relished in the heat she seemed to radiate with. As she went to pull away, he felt her lick around the puncture marks.

"So beautiful," he leaned down, "I think I should return the favor."

"Mm, what are you waiting for?" she shivered and pulled him down to her neck. "Just do it!"

Taken aback by her forwardness, he quickly went to work and pierced her with his new fangs as his cock throbbed with a need to pierce her in much the same way. Seeming to know what he was thinking, the female ran her hands across his shaft and pressed it to her entrance. In one quick motion, she wrapped her legs around his waist and slid his entire length inside her. He cried out as he was met with her heated tightness as he drank her hot blood.

"Zane! Don't stop!" she cried out, "don't leave me now!"

He bit his lip, not understanding the last part as he went to thrust inside her more, continuing to drink her sweet blood. He shivered at the sudden chill that ran down his spine and the emptiness that came with it. The woman he was holding dissipated into a chilled mist and he looked around, desperate to find her.

He turned, hoping to find her in the sun and frowned, watching as a black inky liquid began to slide across it. The air turned frigid as the sun was completely encased in blackness and Zane fell to his knees.

His body felt just as cold as his surroundings and he screamed out as he begged for the woman in the sun to return.

"No!" Zane cried out, jumping up from the bed, still sporting an erection.

"Zane? What's wrong?" Celine cried out as she hopped from the bed to make her way to him, "What happened?"

He frowned, catching his breath and turned, noticing her eyes falling on his crotch and he bit back the sudden need to cover up. Coughing into his hand, she looked up and he watched as she paled from the knowledge of being caught by him.

"I had a crazy dream," Zane admitted.

"I bet," she whispered. "Do you want to tell me about it?"

About me fucking a sun goddess? Or about the fact that I've never felt that kind of pleasure with you? Zane bit his lip, guilty at the thoughts.

"I… I can't really remember. I just felt…" he sighed and shook his head. "I'm sorry. I can't remember. If I do, I *will* let you know…"

"That's fine," Celine offered him a soft smile.

The moment was interrupted as three familiar knocks sounded at the door, and Zane silently thanked Raith for his timing.

"I take it you are going out with *him* again?" Celine sighed.

"I am, but it won't be long and I'm also picking you up a surprise," Zane smiled and watched her eyes light up. He had gone into town a few days ago and picked out a ring to get her. While it had only been a month and he'd hoped to use the intended promise ring as a sign of his thanks for her patience and support, he had a feeling he'd be forced to treat it as something more.

"Well, I *do* like surprises," she sighed. "Just be careful, please?"

"I will!" With that, he forced himself to kiss her cheek and hurried to get ready.

~Present Day~

Zane rubbed the back of his neck as Celine proceeded to move closer to him and shook his head, pulling away from her.

"I..." he sighed and pulled away, starting down the hall, "I need to go check on Zoey!"

He sighed, trying to shake the chill he got from Celine's advances and barely noticed Raith in front of him as he walked headlong into his friend.

"Raith! Sorry about that," he sighed. "I-I must not have been paying attention."

"Seems pretty common around here, mate. You alright?" Raith frowned, "You look... I don't know, *more* worked up than usual."

"Just all the same shit *and* the added discomfort of Celine's nonstop advances," Zane shook his head. "I fucking can't do this on my own, Raith."

"Then I guess it's a good thing you're *not* on your own, bud. I certainly won't be going anywhere—heaven help the dumbass that tries to move me—and, once we wake Zoey up and get Serena back, then we'll have the whole gang together again," Raith smirked.

Zane stared at him, "How can you sound so certain?"

"It's called 'hope,' mate. Try it sometime," Raith smirked.

Zane nodded and smirked, "Alright. Just know I won't be putting any hope into any jobs you bring my way. They never end well."

Raith chuckled, "Well, you can't say that it was boring, can ya?"

"That's one way to put it," Zane smirked, feeling relaxed with Raith's comforting attitude.

"Come on, let's go check on Zoey," Raith grinned, turning towards the infirmary.

"Yeah, I need some distance from Celine," Zane sighed, "She's getting clingy again. It's like the past twelve years never even happened and she just expects us to pick up *exactly* where we left off."

"Well, honestly, she'd always seemed like a psychotic twat in my eyes," Raith looked over at him.

Zane paused at the comment for a moment and finally let out a laugh, "I think that's the most accurate description I've ever heard."

Celine narrowed her eyes, watching Zane and Raith chatting, keeping her distance as they walked towards the infirmary. While she couldn't hear the conversation, she suspected that at least partly, it was about her. Pausing as they closed in on the infirmary, she began chewing on her nails. If Zane's mangy friend got in her way, she would do what should've done in the first place and killed the dog.

She sneered as Zane let out a laugh at something Raith said.
I should've killed that dog before he'd even lifted a leg near Zane.

Isaac lifted his head and let out a snarl at the sound of the door opening, the sound only relaxing and stopping when he saw Zane and Raith stepping through the door. Then, as though nothing had happened, he rested his forehead back on Zoey's bedside by her unconscious body; holding her hand and talking inaudibly to her.

"How's she doing?" Zane tilted his head, "Any changes?"

"Nothing at all," Isaac sighed. "They have no idea what could've done this to her. One minute she was awake and fine and then this? It makes no sense!"

"We will find out what happened to her, Isaac. Make no mistake of that," Zane nodded to him. "For now, we have to hold hope." He smiled over at Raith, who gave him a nod. "That's what Zoey would want."

Isaac bit his lip, nodding slowly. He'd refused to move, even threatened to bite any of the med-staff who tried to remove him from the room, and Zane knew that, if he had to, he'd wait by her side forever.

The doorknob turned again, and the same tension grew along with another growl from Isaac until Nikki emerged, then, just like before, his growls and tension settled.

"Isaac, are you going to be alright?" Raith asked, "If you need to breathe, we'll be in here for Zoey. Maybe it would help clear your head."

"No, I won't leave her. I won't leave her side until she is awake," Isaac shook his head. "Zoey is my life, before her the only enjoyment I got in life was my music. She gave me somebody to *play* for," he shook his head, "That might not make sense to you, but it's the world to me. I won't leave her!" He let out a deep breath and bit his lip, looking back up at them, "Thank you for the offer, but this is where I belong right now."

The others nodded—none understanding his convictions more at that moment than Zane—and took in the sight of Zoey's peaceful face as the machines around her beeped and buzzed. Finally, unable to stand the heart wrenching sight a moment longer, Zane turned and left the room, fighting the well of tears he knew Zoey would want him to shed.

Chapter Fourteen
Tracking Down Maledictus

SPOTTING ZANE SITTING ALONE IN THE CORNER of the munitions storage, Raith couldn't help but roll his eyes. His old friend, though he was certain that his footsteps had been heard, made no move to acknowledge his presence as he ran the banded tuft of Serena's hair between his fingers. A silent moment passed as Raith watched Zane pinch the base of the blonde-mass between each of his fingertips and slowly let the strands slip through to the tip. Again and again and again.

"She's still alive," Zane finally said, though Raith had no guarantee it was meant for him to hear.

Still, despite this uncertainty, he stepped towards him before settling in beside him. "Nobody thinks she isn't. In fact, everyone seems pretty surprised that Maledictus has lasted this long."

Though Zane noticeably flinched at the mention of Maledictus' name, he didn't advertise his shaken nerves.

Raith looked over, "I was sure you'd've passed out by now, or at the very least punched a few walls down."

Zane chuckled and shook his head, "You'd be surprised how hard it is to punch a wall now that I haven't got *him* to blame for the damage."

"Ah hah! So our boy *does* have a conscious, after all?" Raith smiled, "Well then, that leaves the question of why you aren't sleeping then."

Zane shrugged and looked away, "Couldn't sleep."

Raith leaned forward, "Bad dreams?"

Zane turned back to him, eyes studying him for a moment before he shook his head. "No. No, just… just dreams."

"I see," Raith leaned back against the wall, looking around at the rows of guns and blades and bullets surrounding them. "Couldn't just watch TV like a normal insomniac, eh?"

Zane laughed, "Nah, man. Television'll rot your brain; shit *kills* ya!"

Raith rolled his eyes, "Yup. And all *this?*"—he nodded towards the weaponry—"is much safer lounge material, I take it?"

"I've been living for *years* as a living A-bomb, Raith, I'm not really—"

"*We*," Raith corrected him. "*We've* been living for *years* as a living A-bomb. I was there, too; don't forget that. I had to watch *everything* without even having the benefit of a say in *any* matters. But I saw something else while I was in there—and I hope beyond hope that you don't punch my teeth in for reminding you of this—you and Serena."

Zane looked up at him.

Raith sighed, "Look, at risk of sounding like a Peeping Tom or something, I *was* able to *see* everything you saw, but I feel like you missed something crucial in that girl, Zane."

Zane leaned forward, seeming more intrigued than angry; something Raith was thankful for. "What?"

"You."

Zane frowned, "Is that supposed to be some kinda dirty joke, 'cause I am *seriously* not in the mood, man!"

Raith chuckled and shook his head, "No, though I should've picked my words more carefully." He sighed, "What I meant to say is that *you* have done something to that girl, something powerful. She was a fighter her entire life—you said so yourself—and fighting for *that* long all on your own takes a toll. Just look at us; we've been shackled with that fucking psycho for *years* and now we can't keep our bodies from shivering like a damn bobble-head toy every time we hear his name!"

"What do you mean... about Serena?" Zane leaned forward, returning the length of Serena's hair to his pocket.

"The point is that *you* have given Serena the ability to take the weight of the world off her shoulders; you've offered her a companion in you. Sure, she's a fighter through-and-through—always was and always will be—but she's stronger *with* you. Now I'm sure that she'd be tickled pink—and, no, that's not a dirty joke, either—to know that you're out there beating the shit out of club-goers and whatnot trying to track her down, but your little stunt earlier was... well, fuck, Zane, it was damn-near suicide! If Zoey and I hadn't gotten there when we did, Maledictus"—Zane shifted uncomfortably and Raith, though he didn't falter, felt himself squirm as well—"*would* have killed you. That would've been you: dead; gone; bye-bye, brave-but-stupid Zane!" Raith took a deep breath, "And then where would Serena be? No closer to being saved and condemned to a world *without* the man who's made this major impact in her life."

Zane frowned and looked over at him, "You sound like Zoey right now."

Raith shrugged a shoulder, avoiding eye contact with his friend. "So we *might've* talked a bit in the car while you were unconscious."

"Thought so," Zane rolled his eyes. "I bet Celine *loved* being a part of that conversation."

"I wouldn't say she was a part of the conversation, mate; more like, an awkward, pouty lump in the corner."

The two laughed.

"So you're here on Zoey's behalf to chastise me for almost getting myself killed, is that it?" Zane finally asked when the laughter had subsided.

Raith gave him a look, "Like I'm too stupid to chastise you on my own, dipshit?" He gave a playful-yet-solid punch to Zane's hip, "I'm here 'cause, both *before* we got you into the car and *after* we got back, you cursed us out pretty bad, and I—this is *me*, with my own brain and everything—think you needed a reality check."

Zane sneered at him, "And what reality are you going to check me into that I'm not already aware of."

Raith glared at him, his voice turning serious. "The one that you proved to me just a little bit ago, mate: that you *are not* the only one who wants to see that psychopath dead and gone; that you're not the only person who's suffered because of him!"

Zane shook his head, "I *never* said that—"

"You don't need to say *shit* to send a message, Zane," Raith's tone was low-but-powerful, rumbling through the room like an earthquake. "You throw yourself into an impossible fight and then think you have a right to bark orders at the friends who show up to drag your ass out of the grinder—friends who are *every* bit as eager to see this chapter of their lives added to the 'executed' pile—just because they have sense enough to *not* get themselves killed? And what if we *had* killed him back there, Zane? Were you planning on punching the hideous corpse until it—what?—*belched* out Serena's location? Or did it not even occur to you that you could've left us with *no* way of finding her?"

Zane's face turned red as the truth sank in and he looked away. "We could've found her some other way."

"Says the dipshit who didn't have sense enough to consider it *before* getting his ass kicked," Raith sighed. "Did you even get a single hit in on him?"

Zane shrugged, "Not really; ugly bastard kinda caught me off guard with everything." He smiled then, "Though I *did* piss him off. Like, *big time!*"

Raith smirked, "Oh?"

"Mmhm," Zane beamed, "Just like Serena."

Saying her name brought the sadness back to his face, and Raith saw his hand start to drift back towards his pocket.

"So let's go find her," Raith said.

Zane looked up. "Huh?" His eyes narrowed, "Like it's *that* easy? Like I haven't been combing the whole fucking city for a week? Besides, with Zoey out of commission we've lost our best source for finding her."

Raith groaned and let his head fall back against the wall, "You must *really* think I'm an idiot. Come on, asshole, let's track this fucker down."

"An atlas?" Zane laughed, "Really? We have *millions* of dollars of top-of-the-line computer equipment *literally* right behind you and you're using an *atlas*?"

Raith sighed, "Let me start by remarking that it's *because* of things like this atlas that the information on *those* computers exist. I'd also like to add that, with Zoey unconscious, nobody seems to know how to *work* the millions of dollars of top-of-the-line computer equipment short of logging onto Facebook or watching porn."

Zane frowned, "I thought I cleared the history…"

Raith chuckled, "Busted."

Zane rolled his eyes, "Moving right along to Raith's ancient map of wonders."

Raith laughed at that, "Fair enough." He pulled out the file that Zane had gotten from the club and flipped it open; Zane saw that a bunch of the pages had been highlighted and scribbled on. "These are all of the various events that your informant felt had *something* to do with Maledictus, and, in that, he wasn't wrong. Mind you, yes, *some* of these are unrelated—either having some connection to other clan cases that have been wrapped up since then or random on-goings and a few pranks—but, for the most part, these all outright *stink* of that asshole." Raith pushed five of the pages—all of them with a red X scribed in the upper-right of each page—off the table.

Zane stared at him. "Really?" he nodded to the pages

that now littered the floor, "Was *that* necessary? You could've just—"

"It was for effect, asshole," Raith sighed, "an effect, I'd like to point out, that *you* just deflated." He shook his head and spread out the remaining pages before taking out a Sharpie. "I was looking through these before I came to get you, because I *genuinely* think I've narrowed in on his hideout," he shook his head, looking over at Zane, "but I don't know the area well enough to determine *where* exactly." He opened the atlas to their city—Zane already seeing a few marks from Raith's Sharpie—and pointed the tip of the marker to Ben's club on the map. "This is where you first spotted him before he led you to the lumber yard"—he dragged the capped tip across the map in the direction they'd taken—"which actually tells us something."

Zane frowned, "What? That the asshole likes wood?"

Raith cupped his face in his free palm. "Sometimes I just *cannot* believe that I actually went on missions with you. No, you dunce! It has *nothing* to do with the lumber yard, it's the *direction*!"

Zane looked back at the map and frowned, shaking his head, "What about it?"

Raith retraced the path from the club to the lumber yard several more times as he spoke. "A lot of animals—birds especially—will, when the threat of a nearby predator is felt, travel *away* from their nest or burrow. It's an instinct—a baser one—to lead the threat *away* from their home; to protect their families."

Zane's eyes widened, looking at the map. "Then that son of a bitch high-tailed it to the lumber yard because…"

Raith was already nodding.

Zane studied the map harder, taking in the various

marks that Raith had already applied. "So wherever he's stowing Serena must be around…"—he circled his finger roughly around a site on the map as he looked at the pages from Ben's file—"But where? Where?" he chanted to himself as he looked at the documents with a renewed hope.

Raith nodded, "That's where I got snagged, too. So I figured I'd come find you; see if you couldn't figure out something I was missing."

Then Zane spotted the police report on the body at the cemetery.

"Bringing the dead back to…"

Raith leaned forward, "What? You're mumbling, mate."

Zane motioned to the page. "That report; they found that body dug up and lying a few feet from its grave."

Raith nodded, "Yea. Pretty sick shit. It definitely stinks of our boy's MO, but I couldn't figure out *how* exactly? I mean, I have a few guesses, but nothing I want to think about too long, y'know?"

Zane shook his head, "No, he wasn't digging up corpses to *fuck* them, Raith, he wasn't digging them up at all! He told me earlier that he could bring the dead back to life; that he'd been able to do this way back before he was him. This body *did* dig itself up—just like those kids in the report said!—but it was *because* that son-of-a-bitch brought it back to life!"

"What? Like a Leiche or something?" Raith looked up at him.

"A what?" Zane looked back.

Raith's palm met his face again, "Don't you Council-appointed warriors have, like, homework or something that you have to do before they give you a bunch of weapons and turn you loose on the world? A *Leiche* is a… well, it's like a zombie."

It was Zane's turn to cup his face in his palm, "You can't be asking me to believe in zombies right now, Raith. You really can't."

"Just bear with me here," Raith sighed. "A Leiche is *like* a zombie—the whole walking dead thing—except that they're *not* all brain-dead and dull-witted and such. They're like auric vampires—all that energy and aura-manipulation and whatnot—except that they gain their energy from *killing*; they are *human* magic users who, through magic, have locked their own essence into their bodies and *purposefully* died so that they could come back to life as one of these things. They're like… like anti-aurics, in a way. They *absorb* the auras of the dead and use that power to manipulate death and decay." He pointed to the picture of the corpse in the police report, "Like that! You told me he said he could raise the dead! When is the *only* other time shit like that happens?"

Zane sighed, still not believing what he was hearing; his entire life—his existence!—was set in the foundation that *nothing* that was dead could *also* be alive. It was why the growing zombie craze had become such a joke within the mythos community. "Raith, do you *really* believe that—"

"C'mon, Zane! I *know* you know this much! *When* can a *dead* body—gone, *not* a vampire in the midst of the change, *not* an enchantment; a true, blue *dead* body—come back to life?"

Zane sighed, "Only situation I can think of is if an aura winds up possessing it somehow."

Raith nodded. "Exactly! An aura! Auric energy! We've seen it before; aurics are *always* taking control of minds to control them. The truly sinister ones outright *control* the people themselves!"

Zane nodded, "Right, but whenever they do the brain can't take it. Humans under the control of an auric end up—"

"—dying," both Zane and Raith finished the sentence; Raith nodding his point.

"See? A *living* body isn't equipped to handle *that* much strain. An auric can't keep those they control alive because, without the human's aura in control of body—in control of the brain—it loses hold and passes. And a body without an aura is a *dead* body! If Maledictus was…" he shook his head, "If he *is* a Leiche—a death wizard—then he *could* have control over something like that; he *could* raise the dead. And it would sure-as-hell explain why he's such a murder-happy bastard!"

Zane frowned and nodded, looking down at the file. "A sang needs blood, an auric needs life-energy…"

Raith nodded, "And a Leiche needs *death*-energy."

"Fuck me sideways…" Zane shook his head, looking back at the map. "He said he's got something big planned, Raith; something that could change the world. He said that it wouldn't be long until he was strong enough to do it."

"There's nothing more certain in this world than death, man," he looked over, biting his lip. "That's *a lot* of fuel for something like that if it wants to start some shit."

Zane groaned, wiping his brow. It was so much easier to want Maledictus dead when he was just a dangerous psychopath who'd made him and his loved ones suffer, but this was turning out to be something *far* greater than he ever could've imagined. "Okay, this is serious. He's gotta die. Like, *really* gotta die; like, him… or *all* of us—*that* kinda serious."

Raith nodded, "You're not exactly a poet, mate, but

you don't hear me arguing. So where the hell is he?"

Zane looked at the area on the map that Raith had determined to be the likely region Maledictus was in, but it was still over fifty square miles of city. There had to be more...

He looked at the files again. Risen corpse at the cemetery. Spooked patients at the old folks' home. Creepy shadows scattered about the region. Missing college kids. Murdered rape victims near the hospital.

"Like an animal," Zane muttered to himself.

"What's that, mate?" Raith looked up.

"You'd said that he'd been like an animal earlier tonight when he tried to lead me away from his 'nest,'" he nodded to himself. "What if that's how he's acting now?"

"How do you mean?" Raith's heart rate sped up in Zane's ears, and he knew his friend could tell he was on to something.

Zane scratched the back of his neck, "I mean, he's *in* an ykali body now. We moved that thing inside the corpse and Nikki replicated the curse's markings on his scales to transfer the essence into that thing; figured we could just dispose of it later."

Raith nodded, "Yea. And?"

Zane shook his head, "It's still an ykali, though. It's not like we replaced its brain or swapped out all the old parts of what it *had* been; we just *added* a crazy psychopath *into* a dumb animal. Albeit, a seven-foot, ravenous *mythos* animal, but an animal none the less."

"So you think that the ykali brain is still calling some of the shots?" Raith asked.

Zane nodded, "Why not? I always thought that he was such a vulgar, perverted fucker because *that* was how the taroe created him, but he wasn't created; not like that, anyway. What if the bulk of what made up the personality of the *Maledictus* we know was how the essence of whatever he'd once been perceived itself through *our* vulgar, perverted minds. However old that thing is, I'm sure that it wasn't words like 'fuck' or 'cunt' or the whole mess of porno-words he loves to play with; all that had to have been learned after we were cursed with it. And think of who he targeted when *we* were the hosts: all those close to us. It fooled me into thinking we'd killed Celine, and every time after that it was always local incidents. It never transformed and then went on some road trip to take revenge on somebody from a past life. It was *always* acting through *our* filter; it was those close to us."

"So who's close to an ykali?" Raith shook his head.

Zane smirked, "That's the thing. *Nobody*! He's got no modern filter *except* that of a blood-thirsty lizard. No connections or focuses; it's probably why he's even beginning to remember his old self."

Raith nodded, "He's got no other distractions from the ykali's brain."

"Exactly! All that's there is basic animal instincts. And that pretentious cocksucker is so certain he's on top of everyone and everything that he'd *never* suspect that his actions were being dictated by a 'stupid animal,' so he's casually acting on 'stupid animal' logic thinking it's his own. Which is *why* he went to such great lengths to lead me *away* from this area," Zane motioned to the area on the map.

"So where would Maledictus, driven by an animal brain, think to go?" Raith finally asked.

Zane's eyes moved around the map once more. "A stupid animal would want to stay close to its shelter"— he pushed a few pages off the table—"A stupid animal wouldn't stray far from what it knew"—he 'X'ed out a few areas on the map—"And a stupid animal would *always* seek out the perfect home to suit its personality…"

Honing in on a spot on the map, Zane smirked and drew a circle around the location of Maledictus and Serena.

"An abandoned loony bin? Are you kidding me?" Celine frowned, looking at the map while everyone suited up around her.

Zane nodded, fastening the last of the buckles on his boots before he hurried to begin arming himself. "Absolutely! That son-of-a-bitch has proven time and time again that he's nothing more than a psychotic, misery-seeking asshole. He'd seek out someplace private, someplace that nobody would dare go poking around, and someplace *teeming* with pain and suffering."

"He's right," Nikki offered, zipping up her leathers and securing her bright red hair in a tight ponytail. "If he *is* a Leiche—and all evidence points to it—then he'd be innately drawn to places where many had died."

"And, though the records are a bit sketchy, this place has seen more localized death than *any* other site for the next hundred miles *at least*," Raith, wearing minimal layers to allow for a quick transformation when the time called for it, didn't bother looking up. "All irony set aside, there's no better place for something like him to hide out, and almost every event we can tie him to took place within twenty-five miles of there."

Isaac, like Raith, was wearing simple street clothes for the ease of transforming when the time called for it, and, like Zane, he was impatient. He'd initially refused the request to help them track down Maledictus, taking Zoey's hand in his and telling them he wouldn't leave her side for *anything* until she woke up. Both Zane and Raith—having their own lover to weigh their situations against—couldn't argue with the loyal therion's convictions, but they'd known that they needed as many on their side as they could get, and the few Vail warriors they'd been able to muster weren't going to be enough. It had been Raith, having an understanding of *both* Zane's desperation and Isaac's focus on Zoey's wellbeing, to convince him.

"Serena is the most powerful psychic this clan has," he'd said, "Second *only* to Zoey. If *anybody* could get through whatever was clouding her mind and bring her back, it's her."

Sighing impatiently, Isaac glared at the others. "We gonna take all night, or are we going to kick some ass?"

Zane couldn't help but smirk at that as he slipped his favorite katana into a sheathe on his back. "I'm with Dick-zilla, guys! Let's get a move on!"

It was just after four in the morning when Zane's entourage—two non-matching cars and Isaac on his motorcycle—took to the streets and started towards Sacred Gates, what had once been an asylum for the psychotic and criminally insane. Back when the Gates had been open, psychiatry had been more of a series of torturous experiments and counterproductive practices that typically did more harm than good. As time passed and studies into psychotherapy advanced beyond scheduling near-drowning sessions or drilling holes into patients' skulls, the treatments that the doctors at Sacred Gates began to fall under scrutiny. As more and more media attention fell on the hospital and more and more people began protesting the inhumane treatment of their patients, the Gates found themselves forced to hide most of the horror stories they'd created before everyone working there faced criminal charges. Many doctors had reportedly killed themselves on Sacred grounds, while others suffered nervous breakdowns that moved them from the staff files to those of the patients. Several reports of a few patients who'd only suffered of minor mental afflictions being killed to keep what they'd seen quiet bubbled to the public's attention, and, practically overnight, Sacred Gates was turned into a vacant site that served as nothing more than a reminder of far too many horror stories.

Ever since then, the unholy gates of Sacred Gates Asylum were locked to the public.

The property, being as massive as it was, represented too great a financial burden to simply destroy, and any hopes of selling the land were soon after dashed when a prospective buyer learned of the history. Even those without superstitious reservations felt unnerved with the idea of having any investment in a place with such a terrible history. As the years passed, the building—like the stories it contained—faded into a sweet oblivion; falling victim to disrepair and neglect and, though fewer chose to admit it, shame—the sheer abundance of dark energies that had been pounded and saturated and shocked and drilled into the very foundation turning it into a festering place of self-destructive magic cast by an unknowing many.

Zane, riding shotgun next to Raith in a dark blue SUV, pulled back the slide on his pistol—feeding a round from the magazine into the chamber—before setting the safety and holstering it before beginning with the next gun.

"Are those going to do you any good if Maledictus can now move in overdrive, as well?" Nikki leaned in from the back seat.

Zane shook his head, but still worked to load the second gun. "Probably not, but I've seen enough zombie movies to know that having *lots* of guns is never a bad thing."

Raith rolled his eyes, "I'd like to go on record and point out that at no point did I *ever* say there would be zombies."

Zane shrugged, drawing back the slide and letting it slap back into place. "No, you didn't. But *he* said that he can bring the dead back to life; that is to say that he can *control* a bunch of walking dead people, right?"

Nobody answered.

Zane holstered the other gun and sighed, "Right?"

Nikki chuckled, "Well, sure, but that doesn't mean—"

"I rest my case," Zane crossed his arms in front of his chest and watched as they pulled into the run-down parking lot of the once the proud Sacred Gates. "And remember: shoot 'em in the head."

Raith sighed, "Damn you, Romero!"

Zane led the team of nine—himself, Isaac and Raith, Nikki, four of the Vail clan's warriors, and, though he still wasn't quite sure *why*, Celine—around to the front of the building.

"Yea... he's *definitely* in there; I can sense him!" Zane paused and looked back, "What are the chances he hasn't noticed us yet?"

Nikki scoffed, "Are you serious?"

Raith frowned and shook his head, "Not that I agree with her *means* of response, Zane, I've got to agree with her on this one."

Zane rolled his eyes, "Uh huh, I'm sure if it has *nothing* to do with your history."

Raith sighed, "I can say with confidence, old friend, that even if you *were* fucking me I'd *still* have to agree with Nikki on this one; there's no chance Maledictus hasn't noticed *two* cars and an *extremely* loud motorcycle"—he shot Isaac a glare—"pulling into *his* hideout."

Isaac cursed under his breath.

Zane did the same. While he'd certainly been *hoping* for stealth, he also knew better than to expect it. After letting another stream of vulgarity fly under his breath, he nodded—more to himself than the others—and signaled them to enter, falling back long enough to step in beside Raith.

"Just for the record, buddy, I wouldn't fuck you if you were the last warm hole on Earth."

Raith chuckled, "I'll just have to try and contain my heartache 'til this is over, I guess."

Chapter Fifteen
The Dragon's Den

MALEDICTUS ROARED AND SLAMMED DOWN THE HALL. The previous night, coming back from all the hell of Zane and his buddy-bunch dropping an entire wood chipping plant on top of him and *then* having to deal with the cops—that *damned* marine!—and the firefighters, he'd found Serena struggling to escape. In his haste to get out and lure Zane away from his lair, he hadn't bothered to check Serena's cell. As it turned out, the warped doorframe that he'd been slammed into—the foundation and source of the enchantment he'd placed on the room to keep her locked in—hadn't closed properly, and, as a result, the spell had never reset.

By the time he'd gotten back, the blonde vampire—though rendered as weak as a human from starvation—had nearly ripped her binds from the wall.

If he'd showed up ten minutes later…

Enraged at the events he'd endured and the discovery of his soon-to-be bride trying to get back to the one *thing* he hated most in the world, he'd gone a bit overboard with forcing her into a new room and recasting the containment spell on the new cell; testing the crippling shock spell on Serena until her hair started to fizzle and burn.

Fuck it, he'd thought as he kept the current passing through the shrieking blonde vampire until he'd had his fill, *I've always preferred short hair, anyway.*

Now, however—even in hindsight to the torture he'd put her through the night before—it suddenly didn't seem like enough.

Roaring, he hauled back and kicked through the new door, the aged and unused hinges screaming from the strain and startling Serena, who instantly began to shiver at the sight of him. Maledictus, still growling, cleared the distance between them in two massive steps and dragged her to her feet.

"You *called* to them, didn't you; used one of your insipid mind tricks to tell them where you are, *didn't* you? Deceitful, fucking slag! I should've *lobotomized* you the moment I dropped your disgusting carcass in here! You're *mine*—MINE!—and until you realize and *accept* this I will be certain to rip *everyone* who tries to claim you to pieces and *shit* on what's left!"

Serena stared at him—confusion and fear dulling her eyes until she realized why he was so angry—and, mustering some hidden reserve of strength, she smirked at him. "Oh? I didn't have to contact *anybody*, komodo-cock! I'm sure they could *smell* your scaly crotch-rot the next town over"—she spit in his face—"and now that they've found me, we'll see who's shitting on who! If I know Zane—and, trust me, I do—he'll have—"

Maledictus slammed a fist through the wall a few inches from Serena's head, cutting her rant off and causing her to flinch. "DO YOU FORGET WHO KNOWS HIM BEST, YOU FERMETED TWAT-SCAB?" he snickered and shook his head, holding out his arms in a mock-crucifixion pose. "Your little boyfriend and I *were* one and the same until recently." He raked his elongated pinky talon—which, in the process of the previous night's "renovations," he'd allowed to grow to just over eight inches; keeping his other claws at only two—just beneath her chin and pushed up just enough to draw a bead of blood. Her whimper motivated an excited shiver from him, and his tongue snaked out and threatened to graze her cheek, "And if I know him—and, trust *me*, I do!—he'll be too busy cowering in my shadow to offer you even the *slightest* thought!" He scoffed and shook his head, turning away, "When I get back, buttercup baby, I'll be wearing your friends' skins as a robe and Zane's head as a new codpiece. Perhaps you'll be more compliant towards behaving as the slut we *know* you to be once you see his dead eyes gazing up at you from my loins!"

With that, he slammed the door, making sure to check the seal on it *twice*.

They'd barely made it halfway through the main

entrance before the stink of rot dropped the entire group to their knees. In a single step, the sheer *density* of the putrid odor overwhelmed their senses, seeming to swallow all the air in their lungs and refusing to let any fresh air in to dissipate it. As they squirmed and fought for air—one of the warriors and Celine trying to crawl back for the door in hopes of reversing the effects by reversing the direction—Nikki, grimacing and forcing herself to take slow, steady breaths, rose to her feet. Seeing this, the others stared, unable to speak, and pleaded with their teary eyes for the secret that was allowing her to breathe.

"Re-relax…" she said, seeming to grow more comfortable with the air with every passing second. "It's a trick; a sensory illusion. The Leiche is trying to—hey, no!" she hurried towards the center of the group, where one of the warriors—Charles, an auric with an affinity for psychology and auric manipulations of psychotic minds who Zane had hoped would prove a valuable asset on this mission—had begun to panic. "Stop! Stop it! Get a grip! It's in your mi—AGH!"

Charles' frantic mind started lashing out, and though Zane couldn't see his aura he couldn't deny the effects it was having; the closest warriors to him suddenly flying in every direction as the wave hurled them back.

Raith, seeing Nikki get flung across the room, was the first to get control of his senses—suddenly filling his lungs with air and letting out an enraged howl—as his body began to change. Still howling, Zane saw his friend's jaw dislocate and roll about as his muscles reformed and took new shape before yanking his jaw—now jutting several inches past his upper lip—back into place; his skull warping and reshaping around the misshapen lower-half. Though the transformation was causing his arms and legs to break and reform, Raith was still able to scramble to his feet and begin a long-winded sprint as he took either side of his yellow, button-up shirt into his hands—a human left and a therion right—and ripping the material from his body. With his back to Zane, the still heaving vampire could see his friend's spine rolling and reforming under his already sweat-drenched back. The howl continued to roll from Raith's bestial throat, the sound echoing down the halls and throughout the asylum, as the change completed in time for him to spring into the air and catch Nikki in midair and snag hold of an old, dusty chandelier.

Zane struggled to stand, repeating to himself that the air *was* breathable and, with each cycle of the mantra, finding the stench less and less foreboding until he couldn't smell anything. Satisfied that he was no longer under the manipulation, he gave Nikki—still clutched in her therion lover's arms—a quick once-over; though her magic and combat made her a valuable ally, she was, at least in body, still human. While something like being struck by an auric wave might've been a painful, if not crippling ordeal, with somebody like her it was very much a fatal risk. Spotting a trail of blood traveling down the dusty crystal segments, Zane shifted his gaze upward and spotted one of the warriors impaled on one of the spires adorning the side of the fixture.

"Oh no…" Zane bit his lip.

So much for non-lethal…

Looking back at the group, where Charles' renegade aura continued its onslaught. Isaac, not far from the panicking auric, had also transformed into his therion form to anchor himself to the floor with his claws. Though he looked strained and was clearly struggling with his own mental uprising against Maledictus' illusion,

Zane could see that—with the auric whirlwind dying down—he had himself handled and knew better than to embarrass the proud therion by asking. Past Isaac, already suffocated by the illusion, was the bug-eyed body of Charles; a thick, bloody foam beginning to creep from his gaping mouth and nostrils. The others that had been caught in the chaos, except for the one who had met his end on the chandelier, lay dead, having, like Charles, succumbed to the suffocating illusion.

"Jesus-fucking-Christ…" Zane groaned, looking around the room. "Barely in and the shit's already hit the fan."

"Ma-maybe… maybe we should go; let's just go!" pleaded Celine, who was still wheezing with every breath as she wavered beside the warrior, an auric combat specialist, who'd tried retreating towards the door with her when the illusion had struck them.

Zane ignored her, and instead focused on the auric beside her. Though he was young—both in appearance and in years—he wore a great deal of scarring on his face and neck, the left side of his jaw somewhat offset by some prior injury that hadn't quite healed right. Past this, however, Zane saw a maturity and rigidity in his posture and in his expression that gave away his maturity. His light-brown hair was short and even, a traditional and nondescript style that left his stoic features and wise eyes to hint towards the sort of person he was.

Something about this young auric vampire demanded respect.

"You hurt?" Zane asked.

The auric shook his head.

"Did you keep her safe during all that?" he nodded towards Celine.

The auric nodded.

Zane fought the urge to roll his eyes, then felt suddenly guilty for it. "Good to go then?"

Another nod.

Seeing a pattern, Zane raised an eyebrow, "Can you speak?"

Not out loud, sir, the auric's voice chimed in his head, and, from the way the others around him shifted, he could tell everyone could "hear" him. *Therion crime lord tore my tongue out when I was on assignment.*

"Yeesh," Zane frowned and looked back at Isaac, who stood not far between them, and Raith, who finally let go of the chandelier and set Nikki on her feet. "You gonna be alright working with these two? I don't need some checkered history with their kind impacting your willingness to—"

If I may be so bold, sir, I'd like to admit a lie.

Zane raised an eyebrow, "Oh?"

It wasn't a therion that took my tongue, sir. It was you—well, that thing that was inside you.

Zane stared. For a long moment he couldn't bring himself to respond, unsure of even *how* to respond to such a confession. Finally, knowing that he still had the mission ahead of him and a team to lead, he sighed and nodded. "Not that it'll make much of a difference, but I'm sorry. And I'm sorry I don't remember… all that. If you don't want to continue—"

If I may be so bold yet again, sir; I was aware of the details of this assignment when I agreed to suit up. I knew who we were going after, and I knew who would be leading us.

Zane felt himself smile at that. "You going to be alright taking orders then?"

The auric gave the first hint of a smile. *To be blunt, sir, I wouldn't trust anybody else with leading me into taking my revenge on this twisted shit.*

"I like your style, kid," Zane offered, "What's your name?"

Michael Johnson, but my friends all call me 'Long-John Silver.'

Raith and Isaac both let out a set of stifled chuckles that sounded like dogs choking on a Milk-Bone.

Zane fought the urge to laugh with them. "Why in the hell would they call you that?"

Michael laughed, a strange-yet-musical sound coming from a mouth with no tongue. *I came in second place holding my breath in training.*

"That," Zane chuckled and nodded, "is probably the coolest nickname story I've ever heard." He nodded towards Celine, "Probably helped to keep her in one piece, too, didn't it?"

Michael nodded.

Zane nodded back and looked at Celine, "You owe that kid your life."

Celine didn't offer any response.

Zane rolled his eyes and turned away. "Now the only question is—"

Looks like a certain crusty nutsack and his pube-posse have gone and tracked me down! Maledictus cackled in his head, causing him to double over in shock and agony. *Like my little trick, Zaney-boy? I appreciate you bringing all the added backup for me to twist and mangle—kinda like the red shirts from Star Trek, right?*

Zane growled, shaking with rage, "You bastard! Those were *warriors*! They had—"

Blah blah blah. Spare me your inflated conscience; you just got through having a tender moment with somebody covered in evidence in what we *did to him—poor fucker can't even talk because of us!—and you want to spout about how important each one of those warriors were? The only reason I'm sad to see them go so easy is knowing that the numbers just got whittled down to you fucking clowns. Still... WHOO! Who knew that a head-shrinker auric would go ballistic and... well, look who I'm telling; you were there!* Maledictus' auditory cackles echoed about the building, bringing all the warriors to square themselves against any possible attacks.

"Oh no... oh no... oh no..." Celine's panicked chanting picked up in volume as her wheezing breathes grew more frantic. "Wh-where is he? Where is—What do we do? What's going to happen? I don't wanna die! I don't wanna—"

A strangely peaceful sigh sounded in everyone's heads. *Why did you bring her, exactly?* Michael asked.

"She insisted," Zane shook his head, his right hand clasping the still-sheathed katana—ready to draw the sword at any moment—while his left hand held his Glock at the ready. "And, quite frankly, I didn't care enough to tell her 'no.'"

Celine's eyes went wide at that, "Zane? H-how could you say that? You... you don't care? What does that even mean? Are you saying—"

Zane groaned, "Michael, could you do the honors?"

Gladly.

Celine, still in mid-rant, suddenly went silent as Michael's aura snaked into her head and put her to sleep. As her body went loose and fell back, the auric vampire caught her and set her gently down against the entrance to the asylum.

Both therions nodded their thanks.

Nikki smirked at him, "I'd kiss you, sugar, but..." she motioned to Raith, who curled his lip at the idea.

Michael smirked and held up a hand, *I'm honored, but your boyfriend's bigger than me.*

The air went cold and dead; as though anything of

vitality floating on the particles had suddenly been slaughtered all at once.

Why did you bring her, Zaney-boy? Hoping to butter me up with a bribe; trade one piece of pussy for another, is that it? You're gonna have to do better than that, though. I'm sitting on some pretty fucking choice merchandise here—or, should I say, she's sitting on me.

Zane sneered and shook his head, reminding himself that it was all a lie.

I have a feeling I tickled a nerve with that one, bitch, Maledictus' internal rant pressed on. *It could all be over in an instant if you turned that pretty little pea-shooter of yours inward. I'm sure a single bullet or two won't do much to kill you, but if you just keep pulling the trigger and pumping all the bullets into your heart I'm sure the fates will see fit to finally bury you!*

"Shut the fuck up," Zane growled, hoping the others couldn't hear him.

No? Well then I guess the show must go on then, eh? Here... we... go!

Six streams of breath came out in thick, frigid plumes.

"COWARD," Nikki screamed, yanking her twin sais from the sheathes at her hip and spinning the forked daggers in her grip, "STOP HIDING BEHIND YOUR TRICKS AND FACE YOUR FINAL MOMENTS WITH HONOR!"

The group turned at once as a wet, rattling hiss of laughter erupted in the neighboring room. "Honor? Are you hearing this shit, Zaney-boy? The stupid slag talks of *honor!*"

Raith growled, starting to take a step towards the voice only to have Nikki hold her arm across his stomach to stop him. Whimpering, he looked down at her, curiosity glistening across his features.

"Trust her, buddy," Zane sighed, his left leg twitching with his own eagerness to advance. "She's going to help keep us both alive," he glanced back at her, remembering their checkered history and biting his lip, "Right?"

Nikki flashed a coy grin, but finally nodded. "You've grown on me, and my man seems to like you. You're not gonna die on my watch."

Zane nodded, smiling. "Thanks, Nikki."

"Isn't that just fucking *adorable*? Like a goddam buddy movie or something! Oh! I like the one with the talking toaster and all his little friends—each and every one of them a hobbling, chattering piece of household shit!—something about seeing all those cold, *dead* appliances hopping around…"

All around them was the sound of new life. As though an entire colony of rats had awoken in the ancient building's foundation, the frantic, scrambling noises of *something* grew; scuttling and scratching in the walls and the ceiling…

And even in the floor beneath their feet.

"Look alive, team," Zane warned the others, who'd all prepared for whatever was coming.

Maledictus laughed again. "Strange choice of words, Zaney-boy."

The walls began to chip away as the bony, rotting limbs of every creature that had ever called the dilapidated halls of Sacred Gates "home" began to come to life and crawl their way free of their insulated tombs.

A hissing possum missing half its head and dragging a skeletal leg beside its rat-like tail worked to scurry through the tight opening it had made in the walls—baring its incisors at the group and rattling like a cheap toy—before it slipped free and tumbled to the floor, its reanimated body erupting under the pressure and falling apart.

"While this rancid, undead Disney army gets its bearings"—the group continued to watch as more and more risen creatures fought and clawed, sacrificing limb *and* new-life, in a frantic effort to follow their Leiche-lord's command—"I'd like to readdress that subject that the taroe-cunt brought up: *honor*! Bleh! The fucking word itself just rolls like something weak and pathetic; something destined to fail and leave anybody believing in it cast into the void... hey! Maybe we should call *you* 'honor,' Zaney-boy!" he cackled again. The risen creatures started breaking free of their confines and started to close in on the group. Maledictus, wherever he was, offered a rumbling applause at the turn of events. "Anyways, as I was saying, I can't help but question the whole honor shtick. It seems to me that it's the sort of concept that *weak* people who favored themselves as warriors would cook up in an effort to keep from getting *too* fucked up in battle. Like, 'No hitting below the belt' or 'Don't stab your opponent in the back' or 'Let's declare napalm a global war crime'"—he laughed again—"'War crimes'... yea, *there's* a dumb-fuck notion if ever there was one. A bunch of people declare war—sweet, glorious, death-bringing war—and then politely sit around and discuss what's *not* alright? Is that the sort of *honor* your little spell-casting tramp is preaching about? 'Cause it all sounds like the sort of stupid, pussy shit that a dumb bitch would cook up while she's ragging."

Nikki sneered, "You disgusting monster."

"Oh please, honey! You wanna talk disgusting, let's talk about a few of the things I've gathered that I'm gonna *stuff* you with. I wanna see how much I can fit inside you before your V rips through your—"

Raith had had enough, and he let that fact be known by letting loose a roar that silenced Maledictus, the mumbling group, *and* the scuttling horde of risen creatures.

The therion dropped to all fours, the blondish-brown hackles around its neck and shoulders standing on end as he sprinted off in the direction of Maledictus' voice.

Nikki held her arm out to try to stop him, but Zane held her back.

"If you want to help him, clear him a path," he said, looking back at Michael. "You too, Long-John! We need every creep-tastic creepy-crawly out of our way."

One snow-blower special coming up, sir, Michael nodded.

Nikki grinned at him. "I like the way you think."

The cold, dead air went alive then as Nikki's taroe tattoos began to glow—the enchanted ink preparing to focus her peoples' natural magical abilities—and Michael began to work his aura.

Zane finally drew the katana and started after Raith. Though he considered jumping into overdrive, Zane held back, remembering what had happened when he'd been brash enough to deplete his energy the previous night when he'd fought Maledictus. As the two of them came up towards an ever-growing wall of dead vermin—the mass converging as a single mind and working to assemble their tiny, rotting parts into something larger—Nikki and Michael acted.

Zane and Raith could feel something brush past them, like the tug of air one would feel when a car passes nearby…

Then an invisible truck slammed into the horde.

Snow-blower special, indeed! Zane thought with a smirk.

As he and Raith charged towards Maledictus—the rest of the crew not far behind—everything in their path was blown away by the enchanted force that Nikki and Michael had produced. A few times, one of the festering animals would leap at them, trying to get past the unseen force, only to burst against an invisible barrier—Michael's aura, Zane guessed—before it could reach them. Coming around a corner, they found themselves facing down a massive *thing* that was, at one time, a dog—now a snarling, three-legged mess with no lower jaw and a lolling tongue that garbled its growls—and Michael, not needing an order, put a bullet into its restarted brain.

"Now you've done it, asshole," Zane grumbled, certain Maledictus could hear him, "I *like* dogs!"

Like you needed any more reason, shit-sucker! Maledictus cackled.

"Stairs!" Zane ordered, tracing the sound of the laughter; the growing sense of Maledictus' presence growing stronger as they approached.

The team took to the wide stairway, bolting past an overturned, rusty folding chair and a sign on the wall—dented, twisted, and hanging from a single tortured nail—that read CHECK IN WITH SECURITY.

Around the bend, second flight...

A blur of movement caught Raith and Zane off guard as Maledictus came in from the side, jumping from the second-floor and tackling the pair.

Raith whimpered as he took the full force of the monster's attack, the two of them crashing into Zane, who fought through the pain and leveled his Glock—aiming around Raith's shoulders and straight for Maledictus' leering face—and squeezed off three rounds before he was sandwiched between the wall and over six-hundred pounds of therion fury.

Not a single bullet found its mark.

Gritting his teeth against the pain, Zane called out to Isaac.

The second therion—a dark-amber bullet—vaulted the railing, dropping in behind Maledictus and bringing its powerful arms around the monster.

Raith pulled free as Maledictus fell back, giving enough room for him to free himself and Zane. Roaring in their opponent's face, Raith pulled back one of his cinderblock-sized fists and drove it into Maledictus' chest. The Leiche-lizard heaved under the force, its inhale coming in ragged as it sneered in Raith's face. Still growling, Raith prepared for another punch.

Sucking in a loud breath of air, Maledictus belched a rancid cloud of mist into Raith's face before following with a head-butt that toppled Raith, whimpering and clawing at his face, down the steps.

"Raith!" Nikki cried out in a panic, seeing her lover collapse in front of her.

"Help him," Zane ordered, lunging forward and driving his elbow into Maledictus' stomach. Above him, the still-pinned monster leered—struggling against Isaac's hold—and opened his mouth to deliver the same toxic mist at him. Spinning the Glock on his trigger finger and gripping the still-hot barrel, he drove the grip of pistol into Maledictus' jaw, forcing it to slam shut.

A writhing, forked tongue fell onto one of the steps.

"Good," Zane growled, delivering another vicious pistol whip to Maledictus' throat. "Maybe now you won't talk so damn much."

Maledictus' laughter burst in Zane's head like fireworks. *Or maybe I'll just do this...*

His mouth opened again, and Zane watched as the bloody stump of his tongue writhed and stretched for a brief moment before suddenly shooting out at him like an angry snake and wrapping around his throat and beginning to burn into his flesh.

You don't know much about reptiles, do you, Zane? he taunted.

Zane's pained cries were throttled as the elongated tongue constricted around his throat.

Isaac growled, sacrificing his hold on Maledictus' arms in an attempt to punch him in the side of the head, only to have the monster rocket his head back—driving the horned surface of his skull into Isaac's bestial face—and worm free of his grip.

Drop to your knees on three! Michael's psychic warning buzzed in Zane's dazed head.

Zane struggled to understand what the words meant in his oxygen-starved, pain-flooded mind, but somehow was able to bring himself to remember how to count to three. On faith alone, he let his legs drop beneath him.

One of Nikki's sais screamed through the air, slicing through exposed length of Maledictus' tongue and letting Zane's fall *not* end in a hanging.

Isaac, also having heard Michael's warning, jumped back over the railing to the first floor.

With the two safely out of range, Zane watched Michael move his arm in a wide arc, directing his aura like he'd seen many aurics do in the past. Maledictus saw the auric's movements, but was too late to react as the attack caught him and threw him.

Maledictus howled in agony.

The group felt a swell of glee at the sound.

Zane, yanking the acidic length of tongue from his throat, hurried to Raith and Nikki, who was just finishing an enchantment on her still-whimpering lover.

"Is he going to be okay?" Zane asked.

Nikki nodded, "Things might not smell right for him

for the next few days, but I neutralized the toxins before they could do any damage."

Zane nodded, "Good. Wouldn't want to have to find him *another* new face."

Nikki forced a smile, "I know. I just started liking this one."

Zane stood and gave Michael a pat on the shoulder. "You did good, soldier."

"Did… good?" Maledictus growled.

Both therions dragged themselves to their feet and exposed their teeth to the monster.

Nikki's tattoos flared as she retrieved the sai she'd thrown; catching it as it flew back to her.

Both Zane and Michael drew their guns.

"Where's Serena, you twisted fuck?" Zane demanded.

"YOU THINK I'LL GIVE HER BACK TO YOU, MOTHERFUCKER?" Maledictus roared, dragging himself to his feet and clutching a dripping stump that remained of his left arm.

Zane gave Michael a smirk without taking his eyes off their enemy. "You took off his arm?"

Michael shrugged, also keeping his focus on Maledictus. *Figured you'd want a trophy.*

Maledictus' voice echoed in their heads: *I got your trophy right here, fuckers!*

The severed arm shook with spasms before twisting and beginning to drag itself down the stairs with its fingers.

"Oh for fuck's sake!" Maledictus rolled his eyes, "This is going to take forever!"

Kicking the scuttling limb towards the group, everyone shifted their focus towards the animated arm coming their way.

Only to have Maledictus' tail swing around at them...
Seeing the attack coming at them, Zane jumped into overdrive.

Time stopped.

The arm, with its clutching talons, froze in midair. The incoming tail, its razor-sharp barbs positioned to slice the entire group in half, stopped a short distance from Isaac's side.

Maledictus' face, a horrific, inhuman mask of murderous gluttony and rage, was captured in the moment like a wax museum tribute to the worst things the world had ever known.

Zane had to put a stop to it all!

Lunging for the impending threat of Maledictus' tail, he passed the blade of his katana through the wide hunk of bone, meat, and scales; kicking the severed mass away from the group so that its momentum wouldn't finish its intended purpose after he dropped back out of overdrive. Turning back, he snatched one of Nikki's sai from her hand and stapled the airborne arm to the wall with it. Then he sprinted towards Maledictus...

I imagine that's *going to sting when we get back to real time,* the monster's voice chimed in Zane's head as he followed him into overdrive, his body starting to creep to life as his muscles and mind caught up with Zane's pace. *I'll have to repay you for that... and that fuck-wad of a muted auric for my arm.*

Zane didn't have any way to respond, and, at that moment, he didn't want one. Brandishing the katana, he started at Maledictus. Seeing the glistening blade—his time-frozen blood still caking the blade—Maledictus sprinted up the stairs, forcing Zane to chase after him. As they reached the second floor, Zane threw himself after Maledictus in a hail-Mary attack to bring the monster down. Once off his feet, the laws of physics began to take hold; the sounds of the world beginning to creep more and more into focus as his midair dive lost its superhuman momentum and took root in gravity...

Then Zane slammed into Maledictus. Realizing the tackle had worked, Zane scrambled to bring his enemy down before he could shake free and kill him in overdrive. The distorted outline of Maledictus took shape as he buckled. Zane howled and drove a fist into what he guessed was Maledictus' knee. A blur became a shimmer of focus, and the two crashed to the floor.

Behind him, Zane heard the wet, loud sound of the severed tail as it landed on the floor—the shocked and then relieved sounds of his allies as they realized what had happened—and a brief bout of barking laughter from the therions as they spotted what Zane had done with the severed arm.

"—top of the stairs!" Nikki called out.

They were close; very close.

Zane could hear the cavalry coming up the stairs. So close.

He kept punching Maledictus, trying to keep the monster that had plagued his life from getting up; trying to keep him from getting another chance at whatever else he had in his new bag of tricks.

So close. So very, very—

"Zane," Celine's voice rang from the base of the stairs.

He ignored her. He was too close to finishing this; he couldn't allow himself to lose focus. Celine was a liability now; she'd woken up inside Maledictus' lair alone and, more than likely, with no idea of *how* she'd passed out in the first place. With nobody around to protect her and no idea if the monster they'd come to kill might be back for her, she'd be frantic—desperate—and, in her desperation, she'd be a hindrance.

A hindrance at the one moment when they needed *none*.

Please, Zane pleaded to himself, throwing more and more weakening punches into the back of Maledictus' head, *just let this nightmare end!*

"The nightmare," Maledictus forced his head to turn towards Zane, "has only just begun!"

"Zane? Zane!" Celine's voice rose above the sound of the others as they all reached the top of the stairs.

And suddenly Zane couldn't contain his anger towards her; his *hatred* of her.

Zane growled and stood, turning towards the group—towards Celine—and jabbed a finger towards her.

Nikki's eyes widened, "Zane, what are you—"

"You!" Zane bared his fangs at Celine and started towards her, "It's not bad enough that your chicken-shit ass had to turn up *now*, when everything was actually working out for me, but that you have to be an ongoing fucking *plague* to my life—tagging along on my outings, begging for things to be like they were, interfering with my missions—just because you're too fucking weak—too fucking *pathetic*—to watch out for yourself? Or is it that you're just too eager to jump on my dick after all these years that you've gone stupid and can't see that I've moved on like you *should* have *years* ago when you fucking *lied* and made me think I'd killed you!"

Celine gaped at him. "Z-Zane?"

The therions started to shift back, but, as their hulking, bestial bodies deflated into frail, pink human bodies, their growls remained.

Isaac turned on Nikki. "You said that if I joined this

joke of a team that we'd get Serena back! You *told* me that coming here would give us what we needed to bring Zoey back from—"

Raith snarled, "Don't you fucking talk to her like that, savage! There's no way that she could've—"

"God dammit, Raith, I don't need your protection," Nikki pushed him away. "If this arrogant *child* wants to start throwing blame then I'd like to ask him where he was when Zoey first—"

"DON'T YOU FUCKING SAY HER NAME!"

Michael looked around the group, sneering and glaring at each one until his eyes fell on Zane. *You… it's all your fault! All of it! If you'd have been decent enough to just kill yourself years ago when her wretched tribe*—he threw an accusatory finger towards Nikki—*decided to curse you with that… that thing, then maybe none of this would've happened!*

Nikki glared, "My tribe…" she stopped and looked down.

Raith growled and took a step towards Michael. "You want a piece of this, you muted mind-fucker?"

Try it, Cujo! I'll turn you inside out before you can lay tooth or claw on me! Michael took a fighting stance.

Nikki shook her head, "Stop…"

Zane scoffed. "Do it, Raith! Rip him apart! Smear him across the fucking walls! Do what Maledictus *should've* done!"

Nikki took a deep breath and sheathed her sais. "Guys… stop."

Michael glared, *Yea? You gonna do something now that you can actually control yourself, freak? Good luck with that! You couldn't control that pathetic blonde loser we have to call our leader now*—*not that it matters, since Maledictus is going to*—

"SHUT THE FUCK UP!" Zane roared at him.

"No," Celine sneered, "He's right, Zane! That

monster is going to rape and murder that stupid bimbo, and she *deserves* it! She shouldn't have involved herself in *any* of this—shouldn't have gotten involved with *you!*—but she's too dense to know what's good for her! Her and her loser father, who couldn't have just *left* you to rot in self-loathing when he had to walk into the same bar as you and fuck up *everything* we had planned! If I'd have just done what I was told from the very beginning and *killed* you and that stupid mutt of yours"—she glared at Raith—"then Maledictus would still be inside the chalice and—"

"STOP!" Nikki threw out a blast of magic, her tattoos glowing bright enough to illuminate the entire floor in an eerie reddish light.

Everybody slammed into the ground.

Then, as they started to collect themselves, everybody—teary eyed and confused—began to apologize to one another.

Zane groaned, clutching his head. "What… what in the hell just happened to us?"

Nikki was shivering, hugging her arms around her upper-body. "It was him; it was Maledictus," she whimpered. "He did to us what that… that *thing*—that relic of his—did to my tribe." She shivered and slid down the wall, looking up at Zane and Raith, "That… that fucking thing turned everyone in my tribe—my *family*—into furious, blame-filled, monsters. It made them hate everyone," she shivered and looked away. "Every day in my home was like that: everyone yelling and tormenting everyone else—using anything and everything they knew about one another to spread hate and pain—until the day you two showed up and gave them a single direction to point *all* their rage. That thing was *designed* to cause enough hatred for whoever found it to do the unspeakable..."

Zane frowned, looking around. "Maledictus?"

Gone, sir, Michael's "voice" was noticeably upset by that. *And I can't sense Serena's aura anywhere in the building, either.*

Zane growled, punching the wall and turning away as the damage spread and rained down chunks all over the floor. "Motherfucker! He *saw* we had the drop on him and he fucking *cast* that bullshit spell on us to keep us distracted long enough to get away..." he turned and drove his boot into the wall, sending more debris scattering across the floor. As his pounding heart settled, he looked back at Nikki, "Are you going to be alright? I know that the memory of that thing can—" he stopped himself, "The relic..." He looked back at Celine, narrowing his eyes, "You..."

Celine shook and backed away, "N-no, Zane. I'm sorry... I didn't mean what I said. You heard her! Just like she said! It was just... just blind hate; crazy talk! That's all!"

Zane shook his head, walking towards her. "Crazy talk," he narrowed his eyes, "Crazy talk motivated by *truths*." He pointed back to Nikki, "I heard what she said: anything and everything a person knew, right? What about the relic? You called it a chalice. You *knew* about it?" He shook his head, "*That* wasn't crazy talk. So what was all that about doing what you were told? What was all that about *killing* me and Raith? What reason would you have to kill us, Celine?"

Celine backed away with each advance Zane took. "Please, no. I didn't mean it. It's nothing. I wasn't thinking."

Zane shook his head and cocked his head back. "Hey, Michael, you know all that shit I said was a part of *his* magic, right?"

Michael nodded, *Of course, sir. No harm done.*

Zane motioned towards Celine, "So what do you think about what *she* said?"

I think you've caught on to something she doesn't want you to know, sir.

Zane smirked and nodded. "Yea. I think so, too. Maybe I'm not so dumb, after all." He started towards Celine again, "You going to start talking?"

Celine shook her head, "Please, Zane, I *swear*! I don't know anything!"

"Good," Zane waved Michael towards them, "Then you won't mind letting us have a look inside your head, will you?"

Celine's eyes widened, "N-no! You can't! Don't! Why can't you trust me, Zane? Why can't you—"

"Oh I'd say the trust-train has long-since left the station, doll." Zane nodded to Michael, "Do it. I want to know *everything* that she's hiding."

Michael nodded and started towards Celine, who took another two steps back before her body froze within the auric's hold.

"P-please… don't," Celine whimpered. "Y-you can't look inside my—"

"We can," Zane said flatly. "We can, we will, and we are."

Michael's eyes went glassy as he probed into Celine's head, his pupils shifting as he navigated her mind. As his efforts progressed, his eyes grew wider—his face more and more horrified—until his body suddenly seized and he dropped to the floor in convulsions.

"Oh shit!" Zane hurried to the auric's side, dropping onto his knees and trying to keep Michael from hurting himself in his seizure. "Nikki! Help me!"

The others hurried to Zane's side, trying to see what had happened. Nikki's tattoos glowed as she chanted spell after spell, but nothing stilled Michael's tremors.

"I... I can't. I don't know what's happening to him, but I can't stop it!" Nikki told him.

"God dammit!" Zane growled and stood, "What did you do to him, you bi—"

But Celine was already gone...

Chapter Sixteen
The Miller Family's Morning

"WELCOME BACK, PEACHES. DID you have a good run?" Mister Miller looked up from his morning paper as his wife of fifteen years—breathing heavily and glistening with a fine sheen of sweat from her exercise—stepped through the door.

Missus Miller, though winded, felt a fresh swell of happiness at the sight of her husband's freshly shaven face, and she nodded to him as she started towards the table, where he'd already set out a glass of OJ for her. Already prepared for another day at the office, he looked somewhat silly in his undershirt tucked into his dress pants. This, however, Missus Miller understood, spotting her husband's button-up white dress shirt draped over the back of his chair, the two of them having learned from past mistakes not to trust the morning routine to keep his piping hot coffee from spilling on his work clothes.

Gulping down the juice and relishing in the bliss that was her post-run, pre-breakfast moment, Missus Miller toweled off her face and hair before taking a seat across from her husband.

"Did you see that Bill and Sarah got a new dog?" she asked, starting to relax her breathing.

"They did?" Mister Miller looked up again and, deciding against finishing the Sports column, folded the newspaper and set it aside. "Did you happen to see what kind?"

She nodded, "A poodle, I think. Maybe some sort of a mix. It looked like it might have had a bit of collie in it."

"Collie, eh? That's a fine dog. Not sure why anyone would want to go and muck up something like that with a poodle-mix, but"—he shrugged—"live and let live, I suppose."

Missus Miller giggled and nodded, "It *did* look a little silly, to be honest."

"Now now, dear," Mister Miller fought the smirk growing from her comment, "one man's trash…"

"… is another man's treasure. You're right, dear." Missus Miller smiled. "Are the kids up yet?"

Mister Miller considered this a moment and glanced over his shoulder. "I was certain I heard *somebody*…" he spotted his elderly mother—still wearing her light-blue robe and matching slippers—pouring herself a cup of decaf by the entrance to the kitchen. "Morning, Mom. Did you sleep well?"

"Oh my, yes," Grandma shuffled in, her feet barely lifting from the floor as she blew some of the steam from the mouth of the mug. Slowly, with the calculation and forethought of her years, she set the coffee down—making a small noise as she let the corner of the mug touch the tablecloth without a coaster before retrieving one from the center of the table and remedying the problem—and pulled her chair back inch-by-shaky-inch before carefully settling in and scooting herself forward. Once comfortably set at the table with her son and daughter-in-law, she picked up the mug in both hands, letting the warmth melt into her arthritic palms, and took another sip. "That new mattress you bought was just lovely, dear. Not a toss or turn to be had all night."

"Grams," Missus Miller smiled over at her mother-in-law, "you didn't happen to see the kids on your way down, did you?"

Grandma considered the question for a moment before shaking her head, "No, I don't reckon so. Should I have woken them?"

Mister Miller smiled and stood, giving his mother a kiss on the top of her bluish-gray hair, "No, Mom, we've already discussed this; you're a guest in this home. We didn't move you in here to treat you like some sort of darned nanny. Now drink your coffee. I'm going to go get the kids ready for breakfast."

Grandma smiled at that and nodded. "Such a dear boy," she offered before taking another sip of coffee.

Missus Miller smiled and, after topping off the last of her OJ, stood and started towards the kitchen. "Bacon and eggs sound good for breakfast?" she called out to her husband.

"Sounds like a million-dollar breakfast, dear," Mister Miller called back before he started up the stairs.

"No. No, I *know* your parents are douchebags too, Marie, but hear me out: it's like they're damn carbon copies from Little House on the Prairie or something! It's driving me insane! I mean, my dad used to be some strung out loser—probably sucked dick in alleys just to get high—and my mom was a *hooker* that he met in rehab! Yea, yea… Yea, I *get* that it's great that they turned themselves around and found Jesus or whatever, but I just wish they'd cut it out with this whole 'perfect Miller family' bullshit; Dad manages a SubWay and Mom—what? No! Not like the train station, Marie; a goddam *sandwich* store! My dad, the 'sub artist'—god, what a tool! And, y'know what's worse, he acts like he's a goddam executive for it. Like if Mom *weren't* giving piano lessons on the side he'd actually stand a chance of keeping this house. And now that they've gone and moved my grandmother in—which I'm *so* sure has *nothing* to do with the fact that Grandpa just died and that will-money is starting to look pretty damn close, by the way—they're just *slathering* the act all the harder. The old broad's, like, this hardcore ol'-skool type—probably lost her virginity to a guy who traded two pigs and a cow for her—and if she had any idea that I was conceived before they even went down the aisle she'd probably White-Out their names from her inheritance and donate it all to the KKK or something classy like that. I swear to god, Marie, running away and joining the circus is looking like fucking *Heave*—"

"Tiffany," Tiff's father knocked on her door and she

quickly held her breath to see if he showed any sign of overhearing her phone call. "Tiff, hun? You awake?"

"H-huh? Oh, oh yea. Sorry, Dad. Did I oversleep again?" Tiff faked an alerted yawn and grumbled sleepily, rolling her eyes to herself and stifling her laughter in response to her friend's cackles over the line.

"No, no. It's just time to rise-and-shine, love. Mom's making bacon and eggs, so shake a tail-feather unless you want to miss out."

"Mmm! Sounds great, Dad. Be right down," she faked the upbeat inflection and waited until her father's footsteps started past her door. "Choke me with a big black dick, Marie, the man acts like we don't eat bacon and eggs *every-fucking-morning*! Anyway, I gotta go. I'll text your ass when I'm leaving, so don't be late in that new VW Bug, bitch! Bysies!"

Between an eight-PM bedtime *after* the nightly "Merry Miller Pray-O-Rama" and a six-AM door-to-door wakeup call, Jeremy hardly ever had any time to jerk off. His parents insisted that he was still too young for a cell phone, and with a mandatory lights-out rule at bedtime he'd been forced to hunker under his covers with a flashlight and whatever porno mag he'd blindly scored from under his mattress. The other day, however, he'd gotten to trade a pair of his mom's used panties, four weeks' worth of allowance—adding up to a whopping twenty bucks—and a jumbo Ziploc bag full of his grandma's chocolate chip cookies for an issue of Penthouse. This being a special occasion and all, he'd set an alarm for five-thirty to get a few loads out before his dad came knocking.

He'd woken up at five-seventeen.

Four loads later, Jeremy knew he was pressing his luck with pushing for a fifth before the "wakeup" knock, but he'd fallen particularly in love with a shot on page one-twenty-three that demanded just a few more pumps to get the perfect morning started.

From down the hall he could already hear his dad's voice by his sister's door, and he fought to keep his mind from abandoning the fantasy of coming on the sexy blonde's heaving breasts.

Tiff was already awake, anyway; he knew it.

She woke up early *every* morning to call her friend, Marie—a senior who'd just gotten her license—about how much she hated her life and how much she wanted to run off to fuck black circus performers.

She sees Cirque du Soleil *one time and suddenly she wants to be a runaway*, he thought to himself, pausing long enough to turn the page of his masturbatory aid to enact the final stretch of his fantasy. *She's such a whiny bit*—OH GOD! AM I THINKING OF HER WHILE I—*gross gross gross gross gro—*

His father's knock came at the door then. "Hey, J-man! Time to get up, buddy! I've got a few crispy strips of bacon downstairs with your name—"

"GAH!" Jeremy started hating himself as the first string of climax emerged, the overwhelming sensation tarnished by the past three seconds of his life. "S-so-sorry, Dad. I… I just had a nightmare; a really, *really* bad nightmare."

"Oh," his father's voice faltered; never having a response for any news that *wasn't* perfect, "Well, hurry on downstairs. I'll get you some Sunny-D. That'll cheer

you right up!"
    And then his footsteps moved on.
    "Yea," Jeremy sighed to himself, reaching under the bible in his bedside drawer to retrieve his trusty-yet-crusty tube sock. "Thanks for the pep-talk, needle-dick!"

    The razor glided across little Mary's thigh, and the preteen shivered as a fresh trail of blood seeped to the surface and started rolling over the side of her leg. Not wanting to let the blood stain her bedspread and give her away. Snatching up a stolen roll of toilet paper, she ripped free a piece and let it drop onto the fresh wound; marveling with a morbid appreciation as the pristine white material soaked in the deep, rich red of the blood—drawing the makeshift bandage closer as it did. Recalculating her next cut, she placed the razor several inches inward to keep the blood from moving too quickly for her to appreciate. Then, when she was certain that she had the placement right, she made another pass across her leg; groaning at the bitter-sweet sensation of the release.
    This was the only moment when she could *genuinely* let the tension of her life ooze from her body, and while she understood that wasn't the healthiest of relaxation techniques, her mother had seemed rather disinterested and, even more upsetting, belittling of the sort of troubles a nine year old girl like her could have.
However, between the hideous dresses that her parents insisted on sending her to school in—the sort of outfits that looked more appropriate on the porcelain dolls of

the antiques shop her family often visited on Sundays after church—and the fact that all of her classmates used both the outfits *and* her forced lifestyle habits as a constant fuel to tease and berate her, she'd come to this method as her only potential solace. Even the fact that she preferred reading over playing Angry Birds or Tweeting or Tumbling or any of the other activities that her classmates insisted were "normal"; her one escape, books, becoming just another reason for her to be sent home crying day after day after day.

"Bookworm."

"Dweeb."

"Dyke."

The last word she'd been unfamiliar with the first time it had been used against her, and, being cursed with an inquisitive nature, she'd made the mistake of asking her teacher what it meant. Not pleased with the question and misunderstanding the reason behind it, her teacher had called her a "stupid little bitch" and sent her to the corner for saying a bad word.

And while "dyke" had not come up in any of Mary's books, the young girl had read enough over the years to see the event as a cruel irony.

The kids all said that she should kill herself and gone to great lengths in describing the different ways she could do it. During recess, many even cornered her with their cell phones opened to internet pictures of kids who had committed suicide, telling her that *their* chosen method would be the best for her.

Mary didn't want to die, though. Not by any stretch of the imagination. It just had become too much for her to handle; all the pain and ridicule that her peers subjected her to had become too much to simply let accumulate in her mind. And so, during a trip to the library—after getting away from her mother long enough to use one of the facility's computers in private—she'd looked up bullying on the internet, and soon thereafter discovered that others like her had turned to cutting as a means of venting the inner pain with outer pain. Intrigued by the notion, Mary had tucked it away as something to explore later and, still curious about what had gotten her into so much trouble, searched "dyke."

The computer had blocked her access then, and the head librarian had pulled her away from the computer and back to her mother, explaining that she'd caught her daughter attempting to look up pornography on their system.

And so, though she was no closer to knowing what a "dyke" was—though she was certain it had some connotation to a crocodile in much the same way a "bitch" was a female dog—she began cutting. It had been an easy enough task retrieving one of her father's razorblades; though she was not quite tall enough to reach them in the medicine cabinet, she'd been able to use the ceramic crucifix adorning the bathroom sink to pull it into her waiting grasp. Several months later, the stolen razor wasn't quite as sharp as it had been—the more recent efforts stinging a great deal more than before and the wounds not healing as quickly or as cleanly—but, as she'd been clever enough to read the secrets of cutters, mostly how to hide the wounds by avoiding commonly seen parts of the body like the wrists and arms, she'd never had to worry about being caught.

She was in the process of her sixth cut that morning—three already on her right leg and into the third on her left—when her father's typical wakeup call came upon her door. Startled, she'd yanked the blade a bit too quickly and, in doing so, cut a bit too deep and a bit longer than she'd intended. Working quickly to bandage the wound with more and more toilet paper, she worked to mask the sound of pain on her voice by assuring her father that she'd be down in "two shakes of a lamb's tail."

"That's my perfect little pumpkin," her father had beamed from the other side of the door before moving back down the stairs.

Still working to stop the bleeding, little Mary had stifled her morbid literary mind's eagerness to point out that people carved pumpkins, as well.

Not even five minutes later the entire Miller crew was seated at the table and happily sharing their morning breakfast.

"Mary," Missus Miller chimed in after swallowing a mouthful of eggs, "Where's that pretty yellow ribbon I got for your hair?"

Mary poked a strip of bacon with her fork before looking at her mother. "I wanted to wear my hair down today, Mother."

"Oh nonsense!" Missus Miller waved her hand at the suggestion, "A pretty little girl should have a pretty ribbon in her hair. It's how the world can see she's so happy."

"Now you mind your mother, Mary," Mister Miller chimed, not looking away from his paper. "Your mother spent good, hard-earned money on that ribbon to make you happy, so you be a good little girl and wear it, you hear?"

Mary poked at the bacon again. "Happy. Right," she nodded and smiled to her mother, "I'll put it in after breakfast."

"That'a girl," Mister Miller turned the page of his paper. "J-man, how's that Sunny-D working for you, m'boy? Helped you forget all about that nightmare, didn't it?"

Jeremy shook his head, "Not really, Dad. It was a pretty—"

"Darn it, boy," Mister Miller set down his paper and locked his steely gaze on his son, "I'm trying very hard to have a pleasant morning before I go off to work so that I can keep putting bacon on this table for you. I'd like to think that my work is appreciated, and I'd like to have the last thing I see every morning be a happy family that I can feel proud to come back to. Now I'll thank you to stop complaining about your stupid nightmare and be pleasant. For cripe's sake, boy, your grandmother's here! Try to show her some happiness!"

Jeremy sighed and nodded, finally smiling and taking a bite of his bacon. "Right, Dad," he said with half a strip of meat between his teeth.

"Don't talk with your mouth full, son. It'll give you lockjaw. And, Tiffany, stop stirring your food and eat it. You're never going to get a quarterback boyfriend if you're all skin and bones."

Tiff looked up and bit her lip, finally putting down her fork and clearing your throat. "Actually, Mom and Dad, I wanted to talk to you about that? I was really hoping you'd allow me to ask the captain of the sports team out on a da—"

Mister Miller perked up, letting his gaze pierce the rim of his lowered newspaper. "The captain of the football team? My my, Tiff, I've been waiting for some time to hear you say th—"

"Umm, no, Dad... the captain of the *basketball* team?" Tiff corrected him.

The room went deathly silent.

"Oh, baby... no." Missus Miller cupped her hand over her mouth, fighting a wave of tears.

Grandma leaned towards little Mary—the closest to her—and whispered. "Did she say the 'basketballs' team?"

Mister Miller frowned and shook his head, setting down his paper calmly, "Now, Tiff, I thought we talked about this sort of thing. Football's a good, clean *American* sport, like baseball *used* to be. But basketball..."

Tiff shook her head, cupping her hands on the side of her head, "No, Dad, don't say it. Don't give me a reason to—"

"Sports like basketball are sullied and unholy; dirtied up by all those *minorities*!"

"That's it, Dad," Tiff threw her napkin on the plate and stood up, "This... I don't know what it is, this *act* has got to change! You and Mom pretend that we're in some TV Land rerun while you tote Grandma around like some sort of *novelty*. Meanwhile, one of your teenaged kids can't even own a cell phone like every other person in this country—I practically had to move Heaven and Earth to convince you I should have one!—and, to make matters worse, you refuse to let him date and tell me who I *should* date based on your dated racist bullshit!"

Missus Miller gasped, "Oh my... Tiffany Frank Miller!"

"Oh please, Mom, we both know that you've had dirtier things come out of *and* go into your mouth!" She planted her hands on the table and stared down her enraged father, "And while we're on the subject on dating, I think it says something that the fact that Jeremy—without any outlet for his budding curiosities—has become a chronic masturbator who's honestly liable to sell the living room TV if he could get his hands on a decent porno DVD."

Jeremy's eyes widened. "Shut up, Tiff."

"It's fine, Jeremy," Tiff assured him, "It's not like it's not obvious—and, quite frankly, it's perfectly normal; though you wouldn't know it to ask our parents, even though Mom caught me when I was your age, as well."

Missus Miller gasped, "Tiffany! A lady doesn't talk about—"

"And a lady shouldn't sell anal sex to truckers who could film it and leak it to the internet, Mom! But a few clicks on my friend's laptop and—OOP!—there it is; the picture-perfect Missus Miller getting spit-roasted for fifty bucks. Now be quiet or I'll tell Dad the URL to find out for himself what sort of woman he married."

Mister Miller's eyes widened as his wife of fifteen years promptly sat down at her daughter's command, shivering like an autumn leaf.

"Tilly?" Mister Miller looked at his wife.

She didn't respond.

"She's coming to grips with her mistakes, Dad. Maybe you should take a hint from her. Maybe you should abandon the ongoing charade of *pretending* to be the perfect family—telling people you're the perfect parents—and actually try *proving* it for once." Tiff nodded to little Mary, "Let's talk about Mary, for example. You're both so blinded by the stories you're hiding behind, that you're actually *neglecting* a genius! Did you know that Mary can read at a college level, Dad; that she's actually helped *me* with my book reports? Hell, she's practically a child-prodigy—a self-made one, I should point out, 'cause you've certainly nurtured *none* of it—and she could go on to do great things. Don't remember any of this, do you? Or about how she's come home with *multiple* notices from the school asking for your permission to move her into a higher grade. If you don't remember *any* of those I can shed some light on the mystery: see, the *first* notice she brought home—singing and dancing the entire way, I might add—she had the pleasure of watching *you* rip up right in front of her. And why? Because you didn't listen to your daughter *or* read anything on the page! You just shredded it and kept saying how you wouldn't be signing a permission slip to have some 'godless fool teaching your god-fearing kids about premarital sex.' After that little show, she'd never bothered showing you the rest. I've seen her ripping them up and telling herself that Daddy doesn't care enough to see her go places." Tiffany shook her head. "You're so eager to convince yourself and others that you've freed yourself from your dark pasts that you're oblivious to the fact that your children are being forced into their own dark present just to let you feel comfortable in your charade. But I can't sit by and let you fuck up our lives just so you don't need to feel a moment of shame at how *truly* fucked up yours was!"

"Young lady," Mister Miller was shaking mad, already in the process of rolling up his newspaper, "I ask for very little in return for all I do for you kids, but when my eldest starts spewing the devil's poison at the breakfast table, I can't help but—"

Somebody pounded on the front door.

Mister Miller stammered in mid-rant, glancing at the door for a moment. "Who in the blazes?" he grumbled, looking back at the grandfather clock at the end of the room and shaking his head. "Six-thirty in the morning? What sort of business does anybody have knocking on a man's door at…" He retrieved his dress shirt from the back of his chair and slipped into it, sloppily working to button it up as he hurried to the door, "Give them a piece of mind, I will. Interrupt a family at breakfast!"

Missus Miller bit her lip, "Dear, your blood-pressure."

"Blood-pressure?" Tiff scoffed, "Dad doesn't have any health problems, short of being clinically *insane*! What's with you people? Do you just get high every morning and make up what character from The Jeffersons you want to be?"

"Listen to me, you little bitch! The mistakes your father and I made in the past will *pale* in comparison to the one you're making right now! Now you *will* shut your nigger-loving mouth and sit the fuck down or I will do what I should've done sixteen years and *end* you!"

Tiffany narrowed her eyes, "You use the N-word around me again, and I'll show you how *real* badasses roll in this century. And if you think that I—or *any* of us—are going to stick around in this house with a delusional druggie and his gaping anal-whore of a trophy wife, then you must *really* be high."

"Son of a—" Mister Miller stared at the empty front yard, shaking his head. "Doesn't make any sense! I was certain I heard—"

Another knock. This time from the back patio.

"The *backyard*?" Mister Miller heaved, "These assholes are starting to get on my last fucking nerve! *Now* they're trespassing!"

Mister Miller continued to mumble as he stormed across the hall and disappeared into the living room—his irate rant, though muffled, still audible—as he worked his way towards the back of the house. "—and if I catch that little bastard sneaking any more of the pulled pork during his shift, I'm going to cut his—HOLY SHIT!"

The rest of the Miller family—with the exception of a very startled Grandma—jumped away from the table as the sound of something crashing through the sliding back door thundered throughout the house.

"Oh my—D-dad?" Tiff, despite their heated argument, was the first to start towards the sound.

"To hell with this!" Missus Miller shook her head, already bolting for the front door. "It's not worth it to die for this shit!"

"Mommy?" Mary's eyes were already welling with tears as she watched her mother running away.

Missus Miller yanked open the door, already preparing to sprint for her new life, and fell back in an effort to distance herself from the creature occupying the front porch.

"Pardon the intrusion, madam, but do you have a moment to discuss our dark lord and master, Satan?"

Tiffany turned, hurrying back to her brother and sister at the sound of their mother's terrified cries, and fell back at the sight of what had just stepped inside:

The creature, forced to duck under the door frame, must have been about eight feet tall. It stood, seeming somewhat unbalanced—perhaps drunk?—over their mother, looking around at the rest of them before kicking the door shut. As she got a better look at the intruder's legs, she saw that he was wearing some sort of alligator or synthetic lizard-like pants that, when coupled with his humongous reptile-replica boots, gave the appearance that he had dinosaur legs. None of this, however, seemed too strange as she took in the rest of the sight. Twin trails of dark blood followed him; the first coming from his left arm, which, though there was some sort of growth that somewhat resembled a little arm jutting from the center, looked to have been freshly severed. The second trail of blood, one that Tiffany was content *not* learning any more about, seemed to be coming from the intruder's backside. His face—if it could even be called that—looked like something from a horror movie. A bunch of bony horns sticking out from the top of his head above a dark-red, leering face with burning eyes and a wide, jagged sneer; all of which was tattooed—or engraved?—with pale-yellow designs that looked like claw-marks carved into the skin.

And as though the entire vision wasn't enough of a nightmare on its own, he had a woman—an unconscious, nearly naked blonde—tucked under his one good arm.

"Jesus Christ…" Tiffany gaped.

"Not quite, doll," the intruder offered, "But we get mixed up all the time."

The Miller kids ran, sweat and tears pouring down their faces, until they couldn't bring their bodies to run any further. They'd easily put three miles between themselves and their home—no, not theirs; not anymore; not by any stretch of the imagination—and they still had a few miles left before they reached their uncle's house.

"Do you really think Uncle Howard is going to let us stay with him?" Jeremy asked, still breathing heavily from their sprint.

Tiffany, now carrying a whimpering and very tired Mary on her shoulders, shook her head. "I don't know; I hope so. He seemed pretty annoyed by Mom and Dad's bullshit the last time we visited, so I'm sure he'll understand why we finally had to leave."

"Wh-what was that thing?" Mary sobbed.

"Looked like one of the bad guys in my friend's fighting game." Jeremy offered. "Maybe he was some kind of psychotic cosplayer or something."

"Yea… maybe," Tiffany mumbled, not believing it. Something in the things he'd said; the way he moved.

Their mother hadn't lasted too long. As soon as the intruder had gotten a quick look around he'd dropped the naked woman he'd come in with and snatched up their mother, taking her by the throat in his one arm and stabbing her through the back on the coat rack, leaving her shrieking and flailing in an effort to free herself.

"Stay there, darling," the intruder had laughed, stepping past her. "I left your husband in the living room underneath your grill. You prefer medium or medium-rare?"

Grandma had finally gotten to her feet by that point, though she, like Tiffany, didn't seem to know what good that was going to do any of them.

With the intruder in the living room, Tiffany had hoped to help her mother down, but found the task of lifting her bodyweight enough to ease her off the slight incline of the coat rack's jutting hook proved too difficult. In her effort to get her thrashing mother down, the coat rack had tipped and sent the two toppling over. Tiffany had hit the floor hard enough to numb her elbow and twist her ankle, but her mother—almost six inches taller while stuck to the rack—slammed into the front door, the fake crystal doorknob breaking against the force of her forehead and spilling a torrent of blood down on Tiffany, who screamed as her dead-eyed mother crashed to the floor in front of her.

"God-fucking-dammit!" the intruder had roared from the living room, where a series of grunts and metallic squeals were emanating. "You bitches better not be dyking it out in there! I'm pretty sure mother-daughter incest is still a taboo in this day-and-age."

Their father's body, what was left of it, had flown into the hall at that moment—moving like it had been shot from a cannon—and slammed into the wall by the door, rolling onto their mother. He hadn't been dead, not just then, at least, and through what remained of his mouth he'd rambled about the golden years of black tar and Osbourne and complained that he didn't want to be remembered that way.

Fighting to distance herself from the horror, Tiffany had caught sight of her father's severed arm protruding from the shredded remains of his work pants, and she fought to keep from vomiting as she took her brother and sister's hands in each of her own.

She'd told them that they had to run.

She'd told them that the crazy man would hurt them—*kill* them—if they stayed.

She'd told them that she was sorry for not speaking up for them sooner; for always acting like a dumb bitch and wasting her time talking like the cast of Jersey Shore.

She'd told them that she loved them, and that she'd make sure that they'd be okay.

And she'd meant it.

They'd left Grandma behind, not that the crazy intruder gave them much choice when, as they bolted out through the shattered back door, they'd spotted him dragging the old woman to the floor where he'd begun ripping her skin off.

Then they'd ran; the lingering words of their murderous intruder pushing them every step for three miles:

"Run along now, kiddies. Tell the world that the devil stole your house."

"Was that man really the devil?" Mary whimpered after a long silence.

Tiffany shook her head, patting her sister's leg. "No, Mary, that wasn't the devil. That was just a crazy person. And he *did* give us a reason to finally leave." She gave Jeremy a gentle nudge, "Now you can get that girlfriend you so desperately need."

Her brother smiled at that, though he was still clearly pretty shaken from everything he'd seen. Looking over at her, he caught sight of her hand and frowned, "You're bleeding."

Tiffany looked at her palm and caught sight of the fresh blood. Confused, she began looking for a source and, in doing so, caught sight of a trail of blood running down Mary's leg.

Tearing up, their little sister confessed to her habit—much to the shock the two of them, who only saw it as more evidence that they'd needed to get away from that house—and that she hadn't meant to go so deep.

When she was finished, Mary looked—on top of the already hefty emotional burden that morning had put on the three of them—nervous that her brother and sister might judge her in much the same way her classmates did.

"Firstly," Tiff held up her pointer finger, "this needs to stop. I'll help get you a counselor to talk to, but you've gotta promise us that you'll never do this again."

Whimpering, Mary agreed.

"Secondly," Tiff added her middle finger to the already extended pointer, "I'm going to teach you how to throw a punch."

"To throw a punch?" Mary asked.

"Mmhm," Tiff nodded, "So the next time one of those little shits wants to tease you, you know how to knock them right on their ass. But all of this is going to cost you."

Mary flinched. "It is? H-how much?"

Tiff smirked, "You gotta agree to not make fun of Jeremy too much when you skip a few grades and wind up in the same class as him."

Chapter Seventeen
Hope Awakened

SERENA COULD BARELY LIFT HER EYELIDS AS she pressed herself against the bathroom's tile floor. She couldn't handle much more and she could no longer hide her fear from Maledictus. The cold tile helped numb the pain she was feeling and she pressed against it more as she let the tears flow.

How much more could she take before breaking?

She needed Zane.

She needed Zoey.

She needed everyone that she had always taken for granted.

She bit her lip, silently promising to change her ways

if she got out of this. She whimpered as her stomach began to cramp and she folded over, the intensity of her hunger sending a tremor through her body.

Serena?

She looked up at the voice.

It couldn't be!

Zoey? She responded through her auric abilities.

Serena! Is it really you? Oh thank—I've been scrambling about the astral plane for what feels like years!

How? I mean, you're back at the clan, aren't you? Serena bit her lip.

I am...I'm unconscious, I think. Something... something must've done a number on me, because I can't find my way back to my body.

Serena looked up as Zoey appeared in a ghostly wisp, and she smiled softly at the sight. Zoey's concerned eyes looked her over at the state she was in.

Serena...you're so thin! Have you been eating?

I haven't... Serena frowned, *He tried to give me rats, but I kept refusing them and eventually the offerings stopped.*

Well, if he does it again, put your pride to rest and take it, Serena! We need you to live! Zoey shook her head, *We all need you. Zane needs you!*

I know, it's just so hard, Zoey... Serena looked down as the tears began to fall.

She didn't have the strength to stop them from coming. She didn't think she could if she wanted to anyway, they were the only release she had of any emotions.

Serena, we'll be there soon... Zoey's voice began to fade. *I promise. I'll find a way back to my body and we'll find you!*

Zoey? Zoe! Please, no! Don't leave me! Serena whimpered, holding out her hand. *Please!*

Hold on, Serena... Zoey smiled warmly, *you are surviving for two now.*

Serena gasped, waking up again on the cold floor. Biting her lip, she pressed her hand to her stomach.

S-surviving... for two?

Zoey's eyes widened as she sat up, gasping in air as the fog began to clear from her mind. She was just talking with...

Serena?

She shook her head, trying to get a clear view of exactly what she saw through Serena's point of view. It was a residential house; Serena had been taken there with Maledictus and thrown into the bathroom. Zoey closed her eyes for a moment more and took a deep breath, realizing they had the beginnings of a location.

They could make it there!

"Zoey?" Isaac's voice brought her back to the present.

She smiled, facing her lover and wrapped her arms tightly around his neck, "Isaac! Oh my... I was so scared. I missed you so much!"

"I was so worried!" Isaac moved over her, pressing his lips to hers. "Do you need anything? Can I get you anything?"

Zoey nodded, "The others. I need to talk to them. I think I know where we can find Serena."

Zoey knew what had to happen next.

"I was so worried about you, Zoe..." Isaac whispered.

"It's okay now," Zoey looked down, biting her lip, "I was able to chat with Serena."

"Serena?" Isaac bit his lip, "How?"

"Somehow through my unconscious mind, I was able to pinpoint Serena's auric signature; I *found* her and was able to talk to her; able to *see* her." Zoey bit her lip. "She looked so sick…"

"You could see her?" Isaac asked.

"Sort of. It wasn't with my eyes… but I could—I don't know how to describe it—visualize her through her aura," Zoey shook her head. "I need to get to the communications center, can you get Zane for me?"

"I think we should get him—"

"No. I need you to go get Zane, Isaac. I need to help him *and* Serena, and I'm the only one who can," Zoey shook her head, grabbing a pile of clothes and beginning to dress. "Please, trust me."

"You know I always will," Isaac nodded.

She watched as her lover stepped out of the room and took a deep breath, summing up the courage to do what she had to. There was something off about Celine, something that she felt routed directly from Serena's brother, Keith.

A conspiracy of this multitude could not be taken lightly.

She ran a hand through her short hair, heading into the room and making sure it was locked behind her. She knew both Isaac and Zane knew the code, so she had no worries of them getting in…

But she couldn't afford any unwanted visitors.

She shivered, remembering Celine's last words to her before she'd blacked out.

A auric firewall?

She knew a simple auric couldn't work that kind of energy on a sang, but if she *was* involved with Keith in *any* way, then perhaps…

Shaking the thoughts away, Zoey set up a secure line

and sent an urgent call to The Council's direct line.

"Yes, hello. This is Zoey—"

"Yes, yes. I know, my dear; not many from the Vail Clan would be using this line. To what do I owe the pleasure for this call?" Jade, one of the Council's operators purred into the line.

Zoey knew if anyone could help her, it would be Jade, a powerful auric with a nose for conspiracy and an eagerness to sniff it out. In the past, when Zoey had worked with Jade, the results had been nearly instantaneous.

"Jade, I'm glad I got you," Zoey sighed. "Do you remember the case we had with Keith Vailean?"

"I do. I believe he was sentenced to be placed in an auric-induced coma if I'm not mistaken," Jade replied.

"That's correct. I've brought up his file here, but I think there may be more to the case; *a lot* more. We need to get a mind sweep on him, pronto," Zoey bit her lip. "There is more than what we thought going on, and the only way to get the info I need is through Keith's mind."

"Ooh, I *knew* there was something about that slippery little bastard," the scowl could be heard on Jade's voice. "Alright, Zoey, since I trust your judgment—and because I'm eager to see if you're right about this—I'm going to put a flash call on this, and, by that, I mean I'm going to *personally* dig through that eel's noggin," Zoey heard Jade call out for a moment through an intercom before returning to the phone, "any info you want directly searched for?"

"Search for anything you can find to do with somebody named Celine with direct connections to our clan warrior, Zane Murdoch." Zoey frowned, thinking more about everything. Then, as an afterthought, "And, while you're at it, anything to do with a Kristine, as well."

"Alright, I'm on it. Shouldn't be more than ten minutes," Jade chuckled over the line. "I'm a fast worker."

"Thank you so much, Jade!" Zoey smiled, "You're a life-saver."

"You got it, Zoey. You owe me for this, you hear?"

"Alright, next time you're in the area, drinks are on me," she chuckled.

"I like the way you think," Jade laughed. "Talk soon."

"The same," Zoey sighed, disconnecting the line and turning at the sound of the door's locks disengaging.

Zane rushed forward then, scooping Zoey up and holding her in a tight bear-hug.

Zoey laughed, coughing a bit as he pulled away.

"Too tight?" he grinned.

"What gave it away?" Zoey smiled, "Good to see you."

"I should be saying that to you," Zane bit his lip, rubbing the back of his neck for a moment, before sighing. "Anyway, what info do you have for me? What the hell happened back there?"

"When I was out, I was somehow able to channel Serena's aura," Zoey told him.

"You... you talked to Serena? Is she okay? Did Maledictus hur—"

"Whoa!" Zoey held up her hands, nodding, "She's fine; alive at least. But she *does* need our help, and I think I finally know how we can do it. I don't know the specifics, but when I was unconscious a lot of things came to light," Zoey sighed. "Not just with Serena."

"What then?" Zane narrowed his eyes.

"It's *everything*, Zane," she said, "I think that *all* of it has been a part of—" She stopped and frowned, "Celine? Where is she? Has she—"

Zane shook his head, "She hightailed it after a spell Maledictus cast drove her to blurt out some rather unpleasant things."

Zoey raised an eyebrow, "Oh? Like what?"

"Like how I fucked up some plan, and how if she'd killed me and Raith like she'd been ordered to then the relic—she called it a 'chalice'—wouldn't have ended up with me and such. Bunch of psycho-babble, but there was some truth behind it; no doubt about that."

"So what happened?" Zoey asked, chewing her lip.

"So I tried to have one of our auric warriors look inside her head to find out what, and he—"

"Oh no…" Zoey looked up, sadness washing over her face, "Are they…?"

Zane nodded, "Something in Celine's head must've been booby-trapped or something, 'cause the moment he started digging he was flailing around and, before long, his heart had stopped." His eyes widened as he thought back to it, "Holy fu—Is that what happened to you? Did Celine do that to you?"

Zoey frowned and nodded, "She called it a 'psychic firewall.' I guess somebody cared enough about keeping her memories a secret to make sure that no prying psychics ever caught on about what she'd—"

The computer monitor began to glow with a red warning icon and Zoey turned, punching in her credentials to receive the restricted information and gesturing to the screen as a data stream began to scroll in life-time from Jade's system.

"What? The Council?" Zane looked over at her inquisitively, "What would they have to do with this?"

"I had them do a mind-sweep on Keith," she stuck

her finger out before Zane asked her another question. "Now, I'd had my suspicions for a while, but all this business with Celine was just bugging the hell out of me. The events with Keith seemed to lead almost *too* quickly to Kristine's attack on you, and then her new clan shortly after that. It just didn't seem right; how could she have known everything that was happening so soon after it had happened? And how would somebody like her be able to afford a full clan construction in such a short time, let alone sway The Council into giving her her own clan credentials in such an unprecedented amount of time? And then, literally a few days after we got Maledictus out of you, the sudden appearance of your *dead* ex-fiancé—"

"Hours," Zane's eyes had gone wide as she'd explained her theory to him.

Zoey looked up at him, "What?"

"Remember when you took me out to the gas station for junk food after Maledictus was taken out of me? How I'd suddenly freaked out and told you to stop the car?"

"Yea?" Zoey frowned.

"It was Celine," Zane confessed. "I could've *sworn* I'd seen her watching us from the sidewalk, but by the time I'd gotten out she was gone."

Zoey shook her head, "So soon after…? How could she possibly have known?"

"So, are those the results of what they found then? What do they say?" Zane narrowed his eyes, feeling more than enough suspicion now from Zoey's rundown.

He *had* felt something off with Celine.

"I can't believe it…" Zoey gasped, "It was worse than we'd ever expected…"

"What is it?" Zane asked.

"Everything...*everything* has been connected, Zane. Keith, your turning, Maledictus, EVERYTHING." Zoey shook her head, "Celine and Kristine had been working for Keith since the beginning; since he'd caught Celine feeding from and siring a human," she looked at him, biting her lip. "You, Zane; she was caught with a group of other vampires feeding from *you*. It says here that Keith used this to blackmail her and Kristine into working for him—helping him climb to power—and..." Zoey shook her head, "And she's the one that warned the taroe tribe that you and Raith were coming; she *planned* to have you two killed up there! Zane, this is bad! Very, very bad! We need to get the others and get them up to speed, but first..."

Zane's face had paled under the onslaught of the news, but he'd nodded, knowing what Zoey was thinking. "First we have to save Serena."

Chapter Eighteen
"Growing in Nicety"

"JUST LOOK AT THAT; JUST FUCKING *LOOK* AT that," Maledictus chuckled, not noticing in his self-satisfied stupor that Serena hadn't laid her eyes on him since she'd come to in the house.

She had no idea *where* they were, or *whose* house it had been, but the alluring scent of blood was everywhere and that was evidence enough of what had happened to them. When she'd come to, she was already shackled in the bathroom, Maledictus explaining that, since she refused to feed, running water and a toilet was all she'd need until she decided to comply to his wishes.

The circumstances hadn't seemed quite so bad until Maledictus had decided that he needed a shower.

"Hells-fucking-yes, bitch! It's all growing in nicely," he mused further, admiring his new tail, which, judging from the nub it had been several hours earlier when Serena had woken up, meant that his abilities to change his shape and regrow missing limbs were growing stronger. He'd also, after seeing how much he liked his new left arm, decided to tear his right one off so that he could grow another new one just like it.

Though she didn't want to give him the satisfaction of looking, Serena could see through her peripheral vision that the new arm was already half-formed.

"For the life of me, I don't see how you can resist all of *this* and continually hold out some fucking hope about Zane," Maledictus' voice was getting more irritated as he engineered the path of his mood from manic and malicious to enraged and murderous. Yet, no matter where his seemingly bipolar delusions took him, he seemed intent on harboring the ongoing delusions that he was, in any conceivable fashion, desirable. "Fuckwads like Zane and all those little shits are a dime-a-fucking-dozen, but those like you and me, buttercup baby, *we're* golden; we're the cream of the fucking crop; we're out-fucking-standing!" he filled his mouth with water from the shower head and spit it across the distance between them, making Serena retch and struggle to move out of his range while keeping her breasts hidden by the hand towel that he'd left for her. "And *that's* why I'm so certain that our spawn will be *perfect!*"

Serena couldn't hold in her disgust by that point, and,

thankful for the toilet, threw open the lid and vomited.

Just hold on, she thought to herself *and* her unborn child. *They found us once already, and your dad's too damn persistent to just give up. You and I just gotta hold on just a little bit longer. You hear me, kiddo? Just put up with this cocksucker for a little bit longer, and we'll be home free and making Daddy's life miserable. I swear it.*

"You know, you seem different suddenly," Maledictus said, his voice low and curious. Turning towards her, Serena could hear the talons of this feet clacking against the bottom of the tub. "The puking thing I'll accept—it's hard to be in the presence of all *this* without feeling nauseated by the reality that everybody else is a total shit-pile by comparison—but you've barely said a word since you woke up, and you seem awful bashful 'bout shaking those titties all of a sudden. What's gone and turned you into a stoic fucking prude, huh? One close call with Zaney-boy and suddenly you're a changed woman?" He leaned in closer, sniffing at the air, "Or is it something else?"

"Maybe I just don't feel like talking," Serena let her voice reverberate in the toilet bowl, not caring if Maledictus could understand her or not. "Maybe I've just got nothing else to say."

"Well fuck me up the ass with a squeak-toy and call me a clown car!" Maledictus spat and turned back to his shower, "Pardon the fuck outta me for thinking I'd never see the day that the relentless snarky backlash and bitchiness from the *queen* of snarky bitches would ever turn to bitter silence. Seriously! I've heard pussy-farts with more lip than you right now, and I was so certain that the change in scenery would spark some fresh wit from you."

"Change in scenery?" Serena heaved again, shaking

her head, "Do you *seriously* think that girls are at home flicking the bean to fantasies of a mutant Kermit the frog bathing their festering body modifications in a poorly ventilated bathroom?"

Maledictus laughed. "Now *that's* the snarky bitchiness I was expecting. Certainly took you fucking long enough, you tease-happy bitch!"

"Sorry to disappoint," Serena rolled into a sitting position and rested her head against the wall. "I'd hate to think that, when Zane finally fucks you up, your last memory of me would be *anything* but me reminding you how fucking much I hate you."

Just a little longer, baby. Just hold on a little bit longer.

"And the chase is back on," Maledictus laughed, finally shutting off the shower and stepping out of the tub. "I hope you don't mind me saying so, buttercup baby—not that I particularly care if you *do* mind—but I'm pretty sure it's *because* of Zane that you've gotten so soft."

Serena glared at him, offering him the first eye contact since she'd woken up. "I'll admit that Zane's changed me, you disgusting fuck, but believe me… it's *only* been for the better!"

Chapter Nineteen
Fast Forward

ZOEY FOLLOWED ZANE TOWARDS RAITH and Nikki's room. She could feel the tension rising off her friend's aura, and she rested a hand on his shoulder and gently squeezed it, stopping him from walking any further.

"We need to stay focused right now," she shook her head. "Which means you *need* to let go of the past *and*

Celine for now to do that."

"I'm not worried about *Celine* right now," Zane sneered, "That conniving little bitch can rot in whatever fresh hell she's planted herself in for all I care! It's Serena I'm worried about!"

Zoey nodded, "And we're going to save her now. No more waiting."

"'No more waiting,'" Zane smirked, "I like that. It feels a lot more satisfying to hear than 'have hope.'"

Zoey laughed, "Well, let's just agree that both are good in their own ways, shall we?"

"Fair enough. I just hope that Raith was able to work more of his atlas-magic to figure out where Maledictus is hiding out now," Zane sighed.

"I don't think we're going to need much magic—either real *or* atlas-related—" Zoey smirked at him, "Or have you *not* been hearing the buzz?"

Zane frowned, "What buzz?"

"Word on the street is there was a *massive* attack on a small neighborhood house. Family was terrorized—most of them killed—and an auric who had been nearby called in a report that said that 'the devil had stolen their house.'"

"Holy fucking shit," Zane shook his head, "That psychopath doesn't believe in subtlety anymore, does he?"

"It would certainly appear not. Oh, and there's one more thing," Zoey smiled, her eyes lighting up.

"And what's that?" Zane raised an eyebrow.

"Call this an incentive—I won't give away any details—but Serena's got some big news waiting for you," Zoey winked.

"What do you mea—"

"Zane? What's going on?" Raith's voice interrupted

their conversation as he stepped up behind them.

"Come find me when you two are finished," Zoey grinned.

Sighing, he watched his blue-haired friend skip away as he turned to Raith, who looked just as curious as Zane was feeling. He shook his head, preparing to tell Raith *exactly* what he'd just found out himself.

"That's fucked up, man," Raith sighed. "Nikki will be glad to know though. She was starting to think that the entire curse-thing was her fault."

"Why would she even think that?" Zane shook his head.

Raith looked up at him, "Do you really think you're in a position to judge the unnecessary burdens people put on themselves?"

Zane frowned at that, looking down. "You're right…"

Raith shrugged, "No worries. That's what best buddies do; they bust each other's balls when balls need to busted. So consider your balls busted and know that I've got your back, mate."

"Thanks, Raith," Zane smiled. "I really can't tell you how much I appreciate that." He sighed, turning to press his head against the wall. "So Zoey said that there was a bunch of talk about an attack on a residential home that's obviously Maledictus. You heard about that?"

"You're joking, right? There might not be too many people wandering the halls of the clan right now, but it's kinda hard to miss the chatter. The address is everywhere if somebody knows what they're looking for, but nobody has the balls to go near there after what they've heard."

Zane smirked, "Well I guess I should thank you again for busting my balls, 'cause now I don't need 'em to just mosey on in, I suppose."

Raith laughed, "I'm not sure it works that way, but I still love the way you think."

"So I take it you're in?" Zane looked over, hopeful.

"Fuckin' A, mate! You helped bring Nikki and me back together, the least I can do it return the favor. Besides, I owe Serena a *major* debt of gratitude."

Zane frowned, cocking an eyebrow towards him, "You do?"

"You know it! See, that girl went and turned the mopey asshole that my best friend had become into a total badass hellion," Raith winked.

"Total badass hellion, huh?"—he smirked as Raith nodded—"I like the sound of that, I guess I owe Serena a pretty major debt too, then."

Raith smirked and slapped his shoulder, "Glad to hear you talking some sense. Now, let's go get the others and save your woman!"

Chapter Twenty
Reunited

ZANE AND ZOEY FELL INTO PACE BEHIND RAITH and Isaac, the four of them hidden from any potential onlookers as they crossed over two sets of lawns—having parked the car two streets over to avoid tipping off Maledictus with their arrival. Zoey had told Nikki to stay back for this mission to keep an eye on any other activity in their surveillance center...

As well as to have an eager and able-bodied fighter

perched back at the clan if Celine dared to show her face.

Though Nikki had looked like she was ready to argue with everything up until that point, the mention of Celine and the potential that she might get to sink her sais into one of the manipulative deceivers behind *all* of their past tragedies was too good a chance to turn down.

As they came up to the house—a plain-looking, nondescript two-story white home with blue shutters and a matching door—Zoey held up her hand for them to hold their positions while she scanned inside to get an idea of the area.

Letting her aura probe the inside of the house, Zoey shivered from the uncomfortable frigidness; an unnatural chill that ran over her body causing her to shiver. Noticing this, the others turned towards her, Isaac—already in his therion form along with Raith—stepped over to her and cocked his head, offering a sympathetic whimper.

Offering him a smile, she nodded that she was okay and motioned towards the house, meeting Zane's nervous gaze as the others awaited her response.

She's in there, she nodded. *Once we're in, I'm going to her get to her first to set up a shield around her and give her some synth-blood. The shield will offer some protection, but if Maledictus is as strong as I think he is it won't be enough if he attacks us directly.*

Zane nodded, clearly eager to kick some ass.

So cold; she was so cold…

Serena could barely pry her eyes open, let alone lift herself from the corner of the bathroom. Maledictus had thrown her into the bathtub days ago…

No… not days. How long had she been there? Minutes felt like hours; hours like weeks; and days… She couldn't wait any longer.

The only thing keeping her breathing was the hope that Zoey and the others might be able to track her down again…

And she'd get to see Zane again.

To hold him again.

To see their child…

Just a little longer, baby…

The house shook as though in response to her silent mantra, and her eyes fluttered open.

"Z-Zane…" she whimpered, blinking at her own voice.

What made her so certain it was…

But even then, in a moment of clarity, she couldn't shake the feeling that…

She smiled, hearing Maledictus curse somewhere in the house.

"Th-they got you… you fuck-stain!" she groaned.

Serena, mustering the strength to get to her hands and knees and crawl towards the door—to crawl as far as the chains would allow her—and she struggled to offer voice or aura enough to call out to them

Then the bathroom's door was torn from its hinges, and there, on the other side—like a picture of an angel— was Zoey.

"You're… you're here," Serena cried out, tears streaming down her face. "Zoey! Y-you really made it! Thank you…"

"We're all here, hun. All of us, and we're getting you out of here! We're taking you home!" Zoey whispered, pulling Serena against her and flooding her body with a wave of warm energies as she threw up an auric barrier at the door and pulled a flask of synth-blood from one of her pockets. "Here. It might taste like—"

Serena snatched the flask and scrambled with the cap, her shaky fingers refusing to close tightly enough to offer any grip. As the desperation to get to the contents grew, she began to whimper and sob again.

"Oh god, Zoey... I though-I thought I was going to die. I kept... kept fighting and fighting him—the things he said; the things he tried to do!—b-but he never got me, Zoe," Serena looked her in the eye and she shook her head. "H-he beat me a-a-and tortured me... b-but I never let him have me, Zoe."

Zoey nodded, smiling and holding her friend; reaching out with her aura and helping her unscrew the flask. "I believe you, Serena. You're a total badass, and you held out for just as long as you had to."

Serena started to choke down the synth-blood, coughing as the first wave of liquid reached her parched throat. Just as quickly as her starved body tried to reject the horrible-tasting substance, however, it was just as quick to see it for what it was and drive her to gulp the rest of the contents.

As the magic and science began to take effect on her battered and starved system, Serena's eyes began to spark back to their normal vitality.

"Where's Zane?" she finally asked.

"Kicking Maledictus' ass, probably going to kill him." Zoey smiled at the thought.

Serena smiled as well, nodding to herself. "Then we'll get out of here."

"That's right," Zoey agreed. "Then we'll get out of here."

Serena sighed, looking up at her. "I... I want to

apologize."

Zoey frowned at that, "What do you mean? You don't have to—"

Serena shook her head, "Please. I had a lot of time to think about this, and I really need to say it." She took a deep breath, "I've always tried to be the big bad bitch—putting up this mask to keep others from getting too close to me"—she let the breath out slowly—"But I don't want to be that girl anymore, Zoe. I needed you all more than I ever realized, and, even *unconscious* you came to me and promised you'd save me... and here you are." She let her head fall into Zoey's chest, exhaustion taking her then, "I'm so sorry if I ever made you feel like I didn't care or that I didn't need you; nothing could be further from the truth."

Zoey stroked her hair, keeping the warm, positive energies flowing "It's okay, Serena," she reassured her, "I know; I knew all along. And everyone else knows, too." She smirked, "You're a badass, Serena, not an actress."

"Thank you, Zoe," Serena smiled and snuggled closer to her friend as the sounds of chaos grew.

She felt safe now, safer than she had in so long. Her friends had come, Zane had come! She would make it!

We did it, baby. We made *it!*

Zane wanted nothing more than to run to Serena; to run to her and to hold her and to never let her go.

But first, there was the little matter of the creature responsible for the hell they'd all been through.

Maledictus leered in front of him and the two therions, "How nice of you and your wretched *bloodhounds* to stop by."

Raith and Isaac started to advance, but a vicious snarl from Zane stayed them.

"Let me have him," Zane pushed past the two, surprising them and himself with how easily he knocked both of the towering beasts off balance.

Maledictus chuckled, "Oh *this* should be fucking rich! Is this your act of vengeance again—FUCK!"

Zane snarled, not letting the monster finish as he jumped into overdrive, dropping in on Maledictus with enough force to throw both of them across the living room and into the kitchen. All the while, Zane, roaring and cursing every day he'd ever been burdened by Maledictus, continuously threw punch after punch into the shocked monster's face. Zane didn't even *give* Maledictus the chance to say *or* do anything.

When his mouth opened to offer an obscenity, Zane punched it shut and punished him for trying with another five to his face.

When he tried to move to block or counterstrike, Zane would break the bone of whatever moved and punished him for trying by breaking another two.

Finally, battered, broken, and bleeding all over the place, Maledictus was able to pull himself free from Zane's attacks. Starting to move away, the lumbering monster stumbled—time and time again losing his footing and crashing into something that impacted a broken bone or scraped an open wound—and drove Zane to seek *more*.

Zane, however, had grown addicted to the feel of the monster's body breaking under his skin, and as he started to slip into sudden withdrawals he let out a low growl as he lunged, snatching a grease-caked frying pan that was waiting on the stovetop and bring it down hard again and again on Maledictus.

"YOU DARED TO TOUCH HER, YOU PIECE OF SHIT! YOU PUT HER THROUGH HELL AND THOUGHT I *WOULDN'T* RIP YOU TO PIECES? DUMB MOTHERFUCKER!"

He couldn't lose this one again.

He would finally kill the bastard!

For everything he had done.

To him!

To Serena!

To anyone who'd *ever* been hurt by him!

Zane pushed forward, barely registering his body's growing exhaustion at all the energy he'd used. However, as the fire in his muscles began to hinder his blows, the chances of finishing the task…

Maledictus let out a roar—something, then several things, roaring back—and Zane froze under the unexpected response to the monster. The pause, though brief, was long enough to allow Maledictus a chance to turn and begin his retreat.

"No you don't, fucker!" Zane growled, jumping after him and grabbing the base of his tail before driving a powerful kick to his lower back.

With a loud, wet, meat-tearing sound, the second tail was torn free from Maledictus, leaving a partially exposed tailbone that wagged furiously as its owner howled in pain.

Maledictus' pained hollers were music to Zane's ears as he unsheathed his katana, raising it above his head for the kill shot.

As he moved to slice, he was thrown back by *something* that dove in to defend Maledictus, and, stumbling back, Zane watched as his target vanished into overdrive and fled.

"Son of a fucking bitch!" Zane growled, turning to face whatever had distracted him, narrowing his eyes in the creature's direction. "Oh fuck…"

Perched on all fours on the dining room table was a pale-faced, partially-skinned naked body of an elderly woman.

Zane groaned.

It was a step up from vermin.

Maledictus was *officially* raising the dead!

He retched at the sight, imagining an army of naked grannies missing chunks of skin scuttling around.

"And I thought he was disgusting, *before*…"

The old-corpse chattered at him before finally bellowing a strange, gyrating growl.

Two sets of twin vocals replied behind him.

Turning, Zane watched as several more dead bodies lumbered towards him, and he finally turned to Raith and Isaac, whose faces—ones of disgust and disappointment—mirrored his own.

"Destroy them," he ordered, shaking his head and feeling no pride in what had to be done. "They are already dead!"

The two therions quickly snatched up one body each and went to work dismembering them in their own, personal preference.

Zane, sighing—again—turned to Golem impersonating elderly corpse, "Sorry, Granny, it ain't personal."

None of the three could take any pride in what they'd

accomplished, still burdened with the awareness that Maledictus *had* escaped. Zane, however, wiping the blood from his katana and sheathing it, was already beginning to think of—

Zane, the others are taken care of! Get up here and he—

Before Zoey even finished her auric message to him, Zane had already rushed up the stairs—ignoring his body's screaming muscles and burning exhaustion—to the bathroom, where he scooped up Serena in his arms and held her so close to him it hurt.

"Serena! I'm so sorry… I tried; I tried to find you. I looked every—"

Serena ran her fingers across his face, smiling as her fingertips met warm flesh and blood. "Shut up and kiss me, Zane… I've waited too long and fought too hard for more misery."

He didn't need to be told twice.

Leaning down, he pressed his lips to hers.

As the kiss parted, the two of them seeming suddenly lighter with the passing of the act, Serena smiled up at him. "I was so afraid. I was… I was worried we would die without you finding out."

"Find out? W-wait… did you say 'we'?" Zane blushed.

"I'm pregnant, Zane," Serena beamed. "You're going to be a father."

Chapter Twenty-One
Love You to Death

~ONE WEEK LATER~

"SERENA, SHOULD WE REALLY BE DOING this with your condition?" Zane called out as he fought to catch up to her.

"Just *try* to stop me!" Serena grinned, jumping off another rooftop and scaling up the ladder before hurling her body onto the neighboring rooftop. Still hauling in a full sprint and using the momentum of her consecutive jumps to propel her further and further to each new rooftop.

She was free!

Truly free!

Jumping on the ledge of a building, she paused to let Zane catch up and took a deep breath of the crisp night air. As Zane jumped to the ledge beside her, she smiled over at her lover. He grinned at her, shaking his head as he sat back against the edge of the building's roof and let his legs dangle over the edge.

"You know, this parkour thing… I *am* still getting used to it," he shook his head, chuckling. "You think that *maybe* you can cut me a break and—you know?—*not* move so fucking fast?"

She smirked, winking at him, "You'll never learn that way, baby; you gotta feel *forced* to keep up, or else you'll never feel driven to even try. Trust me, it'll come eventually."

"Uh-huh," he sighed, shaking his head, "This coming from a natural who was trained by a parkour-pro rogue, my confidence is an overflowing cup. Hoo-fucking-ray!"

Serena smirked, "You know, *technically* it was *your* aura inside that parkour-pro's body at the time."

"Now that's not fair," Zane scowled. "It's obviously the body! Just look at Raith! This parkour shit wasn't a thing—least I don't think it was—when he was in his original body, but the moment you put him in Mister Parkour-pro he's bouncing around the walls like fucking Spider-Man! It's obviously not the driver in this case, it's the vehicle. And, while we're on the subject, are you sure it's alright to be doing all this bouncing and running when you're pregnant?"

"The baby is fine, Zane! He's barely a bump in my

belly yet," Serena sighed, absently rubbing her still-flat stomach, "The only condition I should be worried about is a lover who can't keep up!"

"He?" Zane grinned, "Were you hiding something from me?"

"I *may* have been," Serena smirked, "Damn! I was hoping to surprise you with that!"

"How long have you known?" Zane raised an eyebrow.

"A few days now. I don't know, I can just sort of *feel* it, y'know?" Serena smiled.

He nodded and scooched closer to her, wrapping his arm around her.

"I'm so happy to have you back," he whispered. "I was a total fucking wreck without you. I swear, I was so close to just starting an all-out assault on the city; kicking in every door and ripping everyone inside-out until I found you."

She giggled at that, "Only you could make mass genocide sound romantic."

"I doubt that," Zane confessed. "Plenty of charming-yet-sick fucks out there. We have our own union and everything."

Serena laughed, "Don't make it sound *that* easy. Maledictus certainly can't woo me with his filthy mouth."

"I'd fucking hope not," Zane faked a gag.

Serena smirked over at him, "You wanna know something *else* I can still do in my 'condition'?"

Zane looked over at her, raising an eyebrow. "I have a few guesses."

Serena winked, "The first few don't count."

Her lips slammed against his then, and suddenly free running across rooftops sounded like the *least* painful

activity of the night.
This, however, was a contact sport he was *more* than apt at participating in.
He groaned, loving the taste of her and relishing in them being together once more and pulled her tighter to him.
Finally.
Things were finally coming together.
She ran her hands down his chest, and Zane groaned, looking down at her and grinned. "You want to do it right here, huh?"
"No one can see us," she smirked, then immediately faked a pout. "Plus, it's been too long, Zane!"
"Too long? It's been less than three hours!" Zane chuckled, looking over, "Do you realize that you use something to the tune of 'here's a nice pregnant activity' or 'I'm not too bloated to do this one' or 'Wanna know something else I can still do?'" he said with a laugh. "You being pregnant has made you hornier than ever! You almost fucked me in the car the night we brought you back to the clan."
Serena raised an eyebrow, "Are you complaining?"
"Hell-fucking-no!" Zane shook his head, "I actually am loving every minute of it and hope to see if it's possible to double-impregnate somebody."
"Oh?" Serena chuckled.
Zane nodded, "Yup. I just wanted it recognized that you playing this 'it's been far too long'-game won't hold up; that is perjury, and it is *wrong!*"
Serena sighed, "Will you shut the hell up and fuck me on this rooftop already?"
"Yes, ma'am!" Zane pulled her to him then and kissed her again.
She moaned, loving the feeling of him against her

and the urgency began to grow.

Using her aura, she ripped Zane's shirt off and he looked down at her, his eyes blazing with just as much passion as she felt.

"That was one of my favorite shirts," he smirked.

"I'm not sorry," she smirked, pulling him across her body as he reached up and began to rub her breasts through her shirt. She moaned, arching up more against his touch and he groaned in her mouth as she wrapped her legs tightly around his waist.

Zane groaned and began to pull the remainder of their clothes off with just as much urgency as she'd ripped off his shirt. She ran her hands across his chest, taking more attention with his tattoos, his now-*normal* tattoos.

She smiled running her hand down his torso, following the "landing strip" where his torso met his thighs to guide her hand to his shaft and smirked, wrapping her hand around him.

Caught in the addictive rhythm, she lost track of time as she played.

"F-Fuck! Serena!" Zane clenched his teeth, "If you stroke me anymore I'm going to lose it!"

"Then lose it inside of me," she moaned, directing his shaft to her entrance. "I can't wait any longer, Zane!" She pushed up, pushing his length inside her. "Now make love to me, or I swear I'm going to just tie you up and take all reins!"

"That doesn't sound *so* bad," he groaned as she began to slide down, taking all of him into her.

Serena cried out and arched back, letting herself become one with her lover.

Together, the two were unstoppable.

Serena felt *true* love she had never known was

possible before. All the past lovers she had were all there to lead her to *him*.

She cried out, allowing her to climax to take her over the edge and looked into Zane's eyes as he followed right beside her. Pressing herself against him, she kissed him passionately as they both saw fireworks go off behind their eyes.

Together.

As it was meant to be.

"I love you," she whispered against his sweat-soaked chest.

"I love you too," he smiled, falling beside her and she grinned, snuggling against him more.

"Do you think we woke anyone up with our moans?" she giggled.

"Shit, I hope so," he smirked, leaning his head against hers. "I'd be kind of disappointed with myself if I didn't. I'm sort of hoping we also corrupted a youth."

"Oh, you naughty boy!" she smirked. "Is this the new Zane I am seeing here?"

"I don't know, is this the new Serena I'm seeing?" he smiled.

"Here to stay," she winked, beginning to collect her clothes and dress. He followed suit, throwing on the shirt she had ripped.

She looked over, realizing the shirt was more vest now. She had ripped it clean down the center of his chest and she grinned.

"What are you thinking?" he asked.

"Just that I made a fashionable improvement of that shirt," she laughed.

"Only *you* would think *this* an improvement!"

"Is it not?" she purred, moving closer and running her hands across his chest.

"Careful," Zane growled, leaning down and whispering in her ears. "I'm close to bending you over and taking you again!"

"Catch me and you've got yourself a deal!" she giggled, skipping past him and jumping off the ledge.

Chapter Twenty-Two
Nothing Ever Dies

IT WAS TOO GOOD TO BE TRUE...

Serena frowned, looking over at Zoey's troubled face and turned to Zane, who hadn't stopped clenching his fists since the news came out.

"Zane, we need to think about this for a minute," Serena frowned, turning to Zoey. "We can't just rush into this! I feel we should call The Council in on this!"

"Serena, it might be *too* late if we wait for their

arrival," Zoey shook her head. "We need to move fast."

"You can't be serious! I am usually all for jumping into a situation…but *this*?" Serena shook her head, "It's suicide!"

Zane shook his head. "We need to destroy him."

"Are you serious? By now he's probably got an army of dead minions!" Serena bit her lip, the sudden churning in her gut causing her to groan and clutch her stomach.

She knew this feeling.

She was afraid.

It was almost laughable if it weren't so frightening.

The great Serena Vailean—the beautiful, blonde, busty badass clan leader—terrified.

And all it had taken was a murder-happy death-wizard rapist gradually modifying a six-foot lizard into a devil-on-Earth.

Serena recited that back to herself.

Suddenly it didn't seem so foolish.

"It doesn't matter either way, Serena, because you are staying here," Zane said.

Serena blinked. "Wh-what? You expect me to stay while you go and—"

"Zoey? Can you give us a moment?" Zane took a deep breath.

Zoey, biting her lip, nodded and started for the door.

"You can't be serious!" Serena whimpered, "We're finally together again; we're about to have a family together… and you want to go off on a mission that you might not come back from?" Serena whimpered, "Please, Zane—*please*—don't go back out there! He's not your responsibility; he's *not* your fucking problem anymore!"

"But he is, Serena," Zane pressed his hands to either

side of her face and forced her to look up at him. "I can't allow my son—*our* child—to be born into a world with something like *that* in it. I *need* to do this for *us*. And *that's* why I'm going to succeed."

She shook her head, allowing the tears to finally fall, "And what if you *don't* succeed?"

"I can't allow myself to think like that, Serena." Zane sighed.

He began to pace for a moment, and she could tell he was working towards something and shook her head.

"Zane, what is it?"

Before he was even halfway down—before the knee of his pants had had a chance to marry the floorboards—Serena's eyes had flooded with tears as her body began to shake with both excitement and panic; her lips parting in shock, however no words were able to form as she watched in shock.

"Serena," Zane reached into his back pocket and produced the box, "I spent a lot of time wondering what I'd say if this day came"—he frowned and shook his head—"*when* this day came, and I'd always been so terrified that, when I finally pushed myself to be brave enough to get down on one knee, I wouldn't be smart enough to know what to say. Well, that day is here now and…" Zane stammered and chuckled at his own nerves, "And I can see that all of my fears—every concern I ever had about being too stupid to offer you the eloquence that you deserved—was every bit as accurate as a prediction could be…"

The two shared a nervous chuckle at that.

"But," Zane cleared his throat and looked up into Serena's eyes, "I'm also proud to say that, now that this day is finally here, I *am* smart enough to know that, now that I'm here, it isn't about how many poems I could—

or, let's be fair, *couldn't*—quote that make me want to write hundreds more about you, or about how many years I can—or *wish* I could—calculate in my head I'd want to share with you, or even about the names of great men I'd never be able to memorize who've come before me who had changed things for the better so that I could be here, saying what I'm about to say to you. Now that I'm finally able to speak these words, I know that no vocabulary that I'd made myself memorize would make a difference today could adequately say what the three most simple words could convey when each one carried with it the *truest* depth of its meaning: I love you." Zane opened the box then, and the ring caught the light as he held it up. "I truly love you, Serena Vailean, and I want to marry you."

Serena took a deep breath through her tears and looked up at him, "Zane Murdoch. You are *more* of an idiot than I thought if you think I'm going to let you go now."

"Then I guess it's good that I don't need your permission to let me go, Serena," Zane bit his lip. "I *need* to do this; I *need* to kill Maledictus. And I *will not* fail."

Serena whimpered as Zane slid the ring on her finger. She didn't want to admit it—didn't want to give in to the truth that she could see in her now-fiancé's eyes—but she couldn't bring herself to fight it.

"J-just swear that you'll come back, you asshole," Serena sobbed.

Zane nodded. "You know I will, baby, because I'm *your* asshole for life."

Frozen in shock, she watched as Zane pressed a kiss to her cheek, stood up and walked out the door.

"Zoey, keep an eye on my future wife, please; she *is* carrying my child."

SCARLET DUSK

And, just like that, he was gone.
Gone to kill a monster.

Chapter Twenty-Three
My Week as the Devil's Concubine/The Big BANG Theory

SO MANY YEARS OF HIDING AND PLAYING IT SAFE after that *one* stupid mistake had left Celine desperate for the protection of anybody stronger than her.

When she and Kristine had been caught feeding off of the then-human Zane—the act that had turned him in the first place thanks to Raith's interference—by Serena's younger brother, she'd thrown herself at his mercy. In exchange for safety from punishment for both feeding on a human and, ten times worse, actually *siring* a new vampire in the process, they'd gladly tossed the others in their group to Keith as a means of impressing The Council. For them, having a connection to somebody steadily climbing the ranks of the mythos government meant protection for them, and if all Keith demanded in exchange for absolute protection was their compliance, who were they to question it?

So when Keith ordered Celine to stick around the newly-turned Zane and his loyal lapdog buddy to make sure that no dangerous revelations were had, she didn't question the order. She'd actually gone above and beyond and gotten engaged to her unknowing "son"— though she hated to look at it like that—just so she could be certain that she was safe from recognition.

But the more she saw of what was becoming of Zane and Raith's friendship—the partnership they'd formed as mythos mercenaries; solving all sorts of mysteries and taking out all sorts of dangerous rogues—made Celine all the more nervous that she and Kristine might be found out. And if she and Kristine were found out, it wouldn't be long until Keith's deceitful efforts were brought to light, and so Keith ordered her to do the one thing she couldn't bring herself to do.

He told her to kill them.

All her life, Celine had just wanted to have fun. She lived to party and get crazy; never to fight or play the role of the dangerous life-taker. She might've been born a vampire, but all of her friends had teased that she was the most human of all of them. What had happened with Zane had been a stupid mistake; an accident brought about from too many stupid vamps in one place at one time and too many enchanted drugs in their systems. She couldn't bear to see her life ruined, or worse, because of one stupid mistake, but she also couldn't bring herself to remedy the risk by becoming a murderer.

So she did the next best thing: she arranged to have the taroe tribe Zane and Raith intended to steal from catch them. The taroe were a self-contained tribe of magic users up in the mountains; nobody bothered them and, in turn, they didn't bother anybody. But if they caught a pair of thieves in their village—if they discovered a plot from a couple of mythos to steal from them—then there was no reason to assume that they wouldn't just kill them as an example of what happened to any outsiders who came poking about.

It could've been so simple!

It should've been so simple!

It would've been so simple!

If only the taroe bastards hadn't taken the offense so seriously.

If only they'd just *killed* Zane and Raith.

If only they hadn't sacrificed the relic with the *Maledictus* curse in it to inflict their punishment.

That relic, as it turned out, had represented a sizable chunk of Keith's plans, and having it crammed inside the body of the vampire one of his rogue subordinates had accidently sired *had not* been a part of his plans.

That relic, as it turned out, contained the remains of a psychotic and sociopathic death-wizard, Meleilzsi Shaykh Naqshband, who, late in the tenth century, had gotten carried away in a power-struggle against an overly dramatic varcol—one of the first breeds of vampire to walk the earth—by the name of Utukku. According to Keith, Utukku had already amassed a sizable list of offenses with The Council of that time—enough that they'd taken two of his fingers as punishment for his crimes—and, when things with the death-wizard had gotten out of hand and he'd caused one of history's largest and most fatal earthquakes, Utukku had stepped in to prove to The Council that he knew enough to clean up the mess he'd made. The early reports, which Keith had gained access to because of his father's connections to The Council's records, stated that Meleilzsi Shaykh Naqshband had sacrificed himself to preserve his aura's essence—and essence that was said to be a festering and twisted breed of murderous and perverse evil—within his prized chalice, which, during the containment process, had been warped and caked in carbon, creating the dark, twisted relic that had eventually found its way to the taroe tribe.

And while the taroe had no clue what it was they'd acquired, the mysterious power it contained had enticed them and compelled them to keep it as a holy keepsake in the center of their village, which was *exactly* where Keith was content in letting it stay until the time was right.

The young vampire was, if nothing else, quite thorough in his scheming. Though the exact nature of the relic was a mystery, his research had shown him that anywhere the Meleilzsi Shaykh Naqshband-chalice went, chaos was never far behind.

It traveled far and wide during the Crusades.

It gained power and insight in Nazi Germany.

It tasted blood and terror during The Khmer Rouge.

Its impact over the centuries were clear to those who cared enough to research its history; those like Keith Vailean. After he'd pinpointed its location, he'd twisted and manipulated those around him so that he could, as nothing more than a son tagging along with his father, arrange to visit the site and, in doing so, found a pair of patsies who'd made a stupid mistake.

Content with letting the relic stay with the taroe and destroy the tribe from the inside, he needed only to wait. Then, with the taroe all dead, he could retrieve the relic and, with it, gain untold power within The Council as the young prodigy that solved a mystery of over a thousand years!

An incredible feat if one didn't speculate that the last Council member to actually *care* about the whereabouts of the Meleilzsi Shaykh Naqshband relic had given up the search in the early sixteenth century.

Which was *exactly* why Keith felt comfortable waiting for his prize; content that he wasn't in competition from any others seeking that glory. The relic was safe and sound within the ignorant grasp of the taroe tribe…

Until Celine, in an attempt at indirectly following his order to kill Zane and Raith, inadvertently brought the curse the only thing it needed: a host.

A 'cursed one.'

The *Maledictus*.

Terrified of the monster that returned when she was expecting a messenger bearing bad news, Celine fled, and Keith, not trusting the simple-minded sang with all his secrets, arranged to have her memories of all involvement with him secured. On his orders, a powerful auric had placed a protective bind on the memories that, if tampered with, would put the invading mind into a coma and, in cases of weaker aurics, kill them.

Satisfied that his secrets were safe and seeing a potential unraveling of all of his planning, Keith forced his plans into action ahead of schedule. Traveling to Europe with the excuse of furthering his work with The Council—a half-truth, since it *was* the mythos government's resources that he was after—he called upon Kristine to infiltrate a team of mythos hunters—posing as a fellow human expert in the field—and guiding them wherever Keith needed them to be. Once she had successfully gained the trust and control of the leader of the hunters, Devon—despite the threat of a budding romance that was blossoming between them—Keith knew he could, through her, point them at whoever he needed dead. Using this resource, he'd arranged to have his mother killed and his father implicated in the tragedy. Then, both his father's clan *and* his allies with The Council distracted by the tragedy, he was free to work around the unforeseen element of a walking, talking *Maledictus*; the exact nature of which he couldn't fathom, but, through what he'd established of its effects, was a destructive force that could easily represent one of biggest threats to both mythos *and* mankind.

A turn of events that, if properly manipulated, could be even *more* beneficial than simply tracking down an ancient relic.

But Keith needed leverage; an angle. Keith needed more power.

As luck would have it, his brash sister had taken the death of their mother far harder than he'd expected, and her father's hand in her death, though never proven, had been just enough to convince her to leave the clan, and, in doing so, forfeit her role as the next to lead the Clan of Vail.

Then, as luck would have it, his grief-stricken father, desperate for somebody to take under his wing with the loss of both his scorned daughter and scholar son, found and "adopted" the carrier of the curse, Zane Murdoch, as an apprentice warrior to the clan.

And, just like that, *everything* fell into place!

The power that Keith was a waiting heir to *exactly* the kind of power he needed to take down a threat as great as the one this Zane was carrying, and, now that he'd been brought into the Clan of Vail's walls, there was no longer any need to track him. The playing board was set for him to swoop in and kill the *Maledictus*; an act that would land him among the highest-ranking Council chairs practically overnight! But to claim the role quickly he'd had to arrange for his father to be killed in a way that none—especially The Council—would feel inclined to investigate.

He needed strength and effectiveness; he needed a killer.

Fortunately he still had Kristine and her team of mythos-hunters.

Unfortunately, Keith's sister had gone and seduced their leader, compromising Kristine's influence over the group. Proving herself to be the loose cannon he'd feared her to be—certain that it had been her influence that had tipped Celine to attack the human-Zane in the first place several years earlier—Kristine had crashed an engagement party between Devon and his sister.

Whether it was a jealous rage or a clever attempt at regaining control of the mythos-hunters through a mutual tragedy, she'd wound up murdering his sister's lover and, as a surprising bonus, driving her to become a shut-in.

Confident that his sister was out of the picture, he went about contacting the proper sources to murder his father, and while there *had* been a few complications—several loose ends that came close to tipping off Gregori Vailean of his son's treacheries—Keith had been able to see his father's clan left without a leader without a single hitch.

Except one...

Zane, his target, had been entrusted by Keith's father to bring his daughter, the rightful heir to the role of clan leader, back into their walls.

Suddenly all of Keith's plans—every carefully constructed piece of the puzzle—had meant *nothing*. Eager to see his plans finalized by his own hand, he'd returned home with the hopes of causing an internal collapse within the Clan of Vail with the assistance of local therions. If he moved fast enough, his sister would never secure the role of leader and, in all of the chaos, Keith could snag control, kill Zane, implicate his sister as he'd once implicated his father, and be hailed as a hero while his father's legacy collapsed, while his sister's interference was met with criminal charges, and while he secured his future as one of the most powerful mythos on the planet; capable of reshaping the world however he saw fit.

But, as both Serena Vailean and Zane Murdoch had proven several times over, they weren't happy unless they were, with every single step they made, interfering with *somebody's* plans, even if they weren't directly aware of them.

With Keith's deceit and treachery brought to The Council's attention, the young vampire had been put away, and Kristine and Celine—suddenly finding themselves potentially standing in a very dangerous spotlight—decided to use what little influence they'd acquired through their contact with Keith to *literally* construct their own solution, and, in the process, the means to take out a mutually despised interloper in their lives: Serena Vailean.

Kristine was eager to see Serena dead for her involvement with Devon and her interference with her hopes at obtaining power through Keith's plans.

Celine yearned to see Serena suffer for the humiliation she'd felt at how quickly Zane had moved on and her interference with her hopes at obtaining a lifetime of security.

With the confusion with the mythos government due to Keith's arrest and the wealth that had been redirected to them to keep them from being seized by the Clan of Vail, Celine and Kristine worked to create another clan within Vail's jurisdiction, presenting their stolen credentials and the excuse that the territory was left exposed to rogue influence with Serena still coming to terms with her new role.

And it *worked*!

The unlimited wealth and support and security of The Council was theirs!

Until an irate Serena, furious with Kristine for showing up and attacking Zane, exposed their new clan for the fraud that it was…

And killed Kristine.

Just like that, everything—*everything!*—that Celine had dreamt of came crashing down around her. She had no allies. She had no protection. She had nothing.

Until the monster—that *Maledictus*—that had been living inside Zane was *finally* removed. As rumor of the cursed Vail warrior's recent cure spread through the mythos underground along with claims that his lover, the new clan's leader, had been kidnapped, Celine dared to explore the potential that there might be hope for her after all.

But Zane, though clearly relieved that he hadn't killed her all those years ago, wouldn't let go of his incessant search for the blonde vampire who'd been a constant thorn in her and her allies' side for all that time.

Now, however, there was no safety for her, and, after fleeing from Zane after the auric hold on her memories had killed one of his fellow warriors, she'd fled to the only place that she felt any connection to: the building that she and Kristine had hoped to turn into their own clan. The place had been left in shambles after Serena and her crew had gotten done attacking the place—an attack that Celine had barely been able to escape from; one that had taken her only friend from her—but, with everything that had happened, she felt confident that she'd be able to stay there and let the chaos of Zane and Maledictus blow over before she planned out her next move.

Until the night Maledictus had showed up one week earlier...

Zane and the others had found him. They'd beaten him—nearly killed him—and taken Serena back. Then, in his weakened daze, he'd honed in on the only person he knew he had any control over.

Her.

Poor, weak, frail Celine.

In the face of her greatest fear, she'd panicked; promising anything and everything in exchange for mercy and protection from Zane and the others.

And, in her pleas, Maledictus had seen potential.

So Celine fell into her role as the new devil's concubine, and for a week she'd begrudgingly satiated any and all whims that the monstrous creature demanded. The tasks—humiliating and disgusting and, more often than not, uncomfortable or downright painful—however, represented a necessary payment for protection from what she knew was coming, and the self-loathing at the end of each night, when she'd replay the events over and over in her head in a vicious loop, was worth it if it meant that she'd be safe when Zane and Serena came for them.

Besides, it was better to be beneath the devil's loins than under his foot...

"Why are we here, exactly?" Nikki asked, looking around the hardware store.

Zane shrugged, grabbing boxes of nails and screws from the shelves and throwing them into a green plastic shopping basket. "Figured I'd spruce up the home; maybe hang a few pictures on the walls."

"Uh huh..." She looked into the basket, "And what about all the duct tape or the spray-paint?"

Another shrug. "I want to work on my tagging skills. Thought I'd start calling myself Z-Dogg—with two 'G's; that shit's important to kids nowadays for whatever reason—and start leaving graffiti all around the city in an effort to lure Maledictus out as a challenge."

Nikki shook her head. "You *do* realize how stupid all that sounds, right?"

"Yup," Zane nodded, turning away once he'd cleared the entire shelf of the nails and woodscrews. "Probably about as stupid as the questions you've been asking."

Raith and Isaac couldn't help but laugh.

Nikki smacked Raith before shooting Isaac a look. "Don't think I won't call in a favor to Zoey to beat the shit out of you on my behalf," She threatened as they followed after Zane to the checkout.

Isaac's laughter stopped abruptly.

As the clerk rang them out, growing more and more

unsettled by items, Zane stared off into the distance.

"You alright, mate?" Raith asked him.

Zane shrugged, "I guess." He smiled and looked over, "I'm glad to have Serena back, and… well, you know, all that," he paused and thought more of his upcoming role as a father, coming to like the idea more and more, "but I'm just… I don't know, anxious, I guess."

Nikki nodded, "Maledictus?"

Zane returned the gesture. "He's gotten stronger, and if even *half* of the intel that Zoey came up with is accurate, then we're pretty fucked."

One lane over, a woman shot Zane a glare, holding her hands over a young girl's ears. "Pardon me, sir! There is a child present!" she chastised him.

Zane didn't bother to look up at her. "Lady, don't get me started."

Raith chuckled and shook his head. "Typical."

Zane shook his head, "Typical pussy-ass whiners thinking the worst thing in the world is a few dirty words." He shook his head, "Maybe we *should* let Maledictus run a little rampant; show this lot of limp-dicks what *true* vulgarity is. I swear, if *one* more person complains about my love of the word 'fuck' I'm going to—"

The clerk's voice stammered as he finished totaling out the order, "Y-your total is—"

"Yea yea, here"—Zane handed the clerk the debit card attached to the Vail Clan's private funds. "Hey, do you guys sell propane?"

Isaac smirked, "And propane accesso—"

"If you finish that sentence, donkey-dick, I'm telling Zoey to turn off Cartoon Network for good!" Zane playfully jabbed the therion before looking back to the clerk, "Well? Propane? *Habla Ingles?*"

The clerk nodded, "Y-yea. Th-the tanks are outside. Let me just ring you up. One tank, right?"

Zane thought for a moment, "No. Better make it two." He smirked, "I wanna make a pretty big bang." Spotting a pack of Post-It Notes and lighter fluid above the conveyer belt, he pulled one down and handed it to him. "These too."

The clerks look of confusion and concern only grew as he scanned the sticky pads, fluid, and the scan code for the propane tanks. Handing Zane the receipt in a shaky hand, he told him that he could pick up the tanks outside.

"Great!" Zane scooped up the bags and started out, "Let's go kill this motherfucker!"

Behind them, the shrill voice of the clerk announced to his managers that he was taking his lunch break early.

Zane and the crew arrived on the rooftop of the office building neighboring what had been Kristine and Celine's clan headquarters. The rooftop they occupied was, though several stories shorter than their target-building, tall enough to allow for what Zane had planned.

Isaac held back a ways, mumbling something about heights, before calling out to the others, "Are you sure we're allowed to be up here?"

Zane laughed, "I think the more appropriate question would be, 'Do I care?'" He looked and shook his head, "Besides, I didn't see anybody stopping us on the way up."

Nikki scoffed, "And you think that might not have something to do with the fact that each one of us is covered in weapons and you're toting *two* propane tanks and a half-a-dozen bags of who-knows-what for who-knows-why?"

Stopping on the side of the building, Zane scoped the view of their target. Finally turning to Nikki—ignoring her sarcasm for what it was—he motioned for her to approach. "Think you can pinpoint what floor *he's* on?"

Nikki frowned, "Well, sure, but what makes you think he's even one *that* side of the building?"

Zane pointed over his shoulder, where the high-hanging morning sun shown down on them. "That asshole fancies himself a god—or a devil; whatever—so, naturally, he's going to want a good view of the action. Now, while I'm sure it's an absolutely lovely morning for those who *aren't* being cooked in their own skin, I *am* still very much a vampire and this *is* still very much a painful time to be out and about."

"Then why not wait for night?" Raith frowned, stepping up beside them.

Zane rolled his eyes, "'Cause this was the only time I could make an appointment. Really, Raith? We needed supplies *and* we need the element of surprise on our side; that walking fucking turd isn't going to be expecting us to attack with the sun out."

"Maybe for good reason," Nikki shook her head, "UVs turning you into an ass."

Zane sighed and nodded, setting down the tanks and bags and beginning to unpack the supplies. "Yea, that's not uncommon for my kind. Though we *are* talking about me, here, so…" he trailed off as he began to work.

"Raith, help me out here," he said, holding out one of the tanks and a roll of duct tape to his friend.

Raith frowned, "Help? With what? What is all this, exactly?"

"An entrance," Zane smirked, tearing a two-foot length of tape from his roll and securing three boxes of nails on one side of the tank before repeating the process on the other side. "Just do like I do, buddy; tape all this shit to your tank—nails, screws, spray-paint; all of it—and don't stop 'til there's nothing left."

Nikki's eyes widened, "Oh gods… you're not going to—"

"Whoop," Zane smirked, looking up at her, "there it is. I knew you'd love it."

Nikki smirked and shook her head, "I knew there was a reason I liked you, Zane."

"Yea yea, we'll kiss later"—he looked over as Raith shot him a look—"chill, buddy, it was a joke." He finished assembling his makeshift shrapnel bomb and stood up, "Now, I need to know where we're delivering these things, Nikki."

The taroe nodded and looked back to the building, her tattoos around her neck—the only tattoos that were left to see—started to glow.

Turning back towards Isaac, Zane held out his hand. "I'm going to need your shirt, big guy."

"My shirt?" Isaac frowned, "What for?"

"Because in this day and age women demand their werewolves to run around shirtless," Zane rolled his eyes. "Why do you think, stud? We gotta light these things with *something*!"

"So use your own shirt, dick! I like this shirt," Isaac glared.

Zane sighed, "Look, this is the only skin I got, big

guy. You and Raith, you're going to be going in there all Hulked-out and whatnot—nice, thick skins to protect you from *whatever*—and you're going to have to either lose the shirt before transforming *or* you're going to tear through and leave it in ribbons. Either way, you don't need it! So lose it and let me use it!"

"Fine," Isaac growled and shrugged out of the AC/DC tee, tossing it across the rooftop to Zane, "but you owe me a new shirt!"

Zane nodded and started to soak the shirt in lighter fluid, "Buddy, for this I'll buy you a whole new wardrobe. Deal?"

Raith, taking the hint, peeled off his own shirt—Nikki pausing in her task to admire the view—and took the lighter fluid from Zane, replicating the process on his end.

"So I get the tanks and tape, the screws and nails and the spray-paint, and I get the lighter fluid... but what's with the office notes?"

Zane smirked and started slapping a few of the sticky slips of paper along the side of one of the tanks—securing the loose corners with duct tape—before pulling out a Sharpie marker.

Nikki frowned, "Where'd that come from?"

Zane shrugged, starting to write his message. "Stole it from the hardware store."

Raith raised an eyebrow, "You *stole* a marker from the hardware store?"

Zane didn't bother looking up. "That's right."

Nikki looked back at Raith and Isaac, hoping for some sort of explanation. When none came from them, she looked back at Zane. "Why on Earth would you *steal* a marker when you'd already paid *hundreds* of dollars for all the other stuff?"

"'Cause I don't pay for writing utensils," Zane said flatly, finishing the first half of his message and beginning the process again on Raith's tank.

"Don't take this the wrong way," Nikki shook her head, "but that's, like, *really* weird."

Zane stood then, one tank in each hand, and shrugged again. "A man's gotta believe in something," he said as he stepped up to the edge of the building. "Now light these candles and tell me where I'm delivering them!"

Maledictus sighed, taking in the luxury of his post-orgasmic calm as he surveyed the city—bathed in the warm glow of the sun as it cut through the window like a spotlight—and smirked as Celine, chained at his feet, squirmed uncomfortably in the direct rays of the UV.

"I know you've been hearing this a lot lately," he smirked, reaching down and petting her head, "but you'll learn to like it, or you'll die enduring it."

"Yes, master," Celine whimpered.

"It won't be long now," Maledictus went on. "With all the bodies I've collected and with every day I've been left to focus my powers, I'm nearly ready to bring Hell to Earth."

Celine looked up at him, "M-Master...?"

Maledictus frowned, looking down at her, "Speak."

"If you... if you raise *all* the dead, are you sure that we won't be killed as well?" Celine shivered.

"Fucking fool," Maledictus backhanded her, sending her sprawling as far as the length of chain around her throat would allow. "I am a *controller* of death; it—like you—is my fucking bitch! You speak of it as others should speak of it—permanent and looming over all—but me? I *am* above death! And if you continue to obey me and be a good little whore, then you—as my servant—will be spared!"

"Y-yes, Master. F-forgive me," Celine begged, crawling back to his feet.

Maledictus scoffed, "A whore must *earn* forgiveness! Isn't that right?"

Celine shivered again, but still brought herself to rest her head against Maledictus' leg. "Yes, a whore must—" she stopped and squinted at something through the window, "Master, what's happening over there? On the roof; there…"

Maledictus frowned, catching sight of several silhouetted figures moving bout the ledge of the building across from them. "Oh my…" he smirked and stood, starting towards the window to watch, "Are they about to jump? How absolutely delightful! A fucking group suicide, and I'm at front-row-fucking-cent—" he squinted against the glare of the sun, "Wait…"

The figure closest to the edge threw something—a *pair* of somethings—with enough force to clear the distance between the two buildings.

"What in the blood-drenched fuck?" Maledictus jumped back as the two objects—a pair of tanks that had been strapped with a bunch of boxes and cans—crashed through the window and rolled across the floor, a pair of flaming cloths burning near the open valves. Across the side of one tank, Maledictus saw a row of yellow paper that read "KNOCK KNOCK" and, on the other—though its message was partially hidden by the angle it had fallen in—he could make out the word

"ASSHOLE".
 Maledictus sighed, "Fuck me…"

Chapter Twenty-Four
Suit Up

SERENA WAS LIKE A CAGED ANIMAL IN FRONT OF Zoey, who watched her friend as she continued to pace the room.

"I can't believe he'd just *leave* me like that!" she growled. "Asshole; total fucking *asshole*! Fuck, I love him so much! I'm… I'm going to *marry* that wonderful, spectacular, horrid, suicidal asshole! I should… I should just follow him! *That'd* piss him off—piss him off like he's pissed me off!—that'd show him! Yea… totally stick it to him! And you *know* he's going to need our help; it's the right thing to do! This is stupid; so stupid! Damn him! Suicidal asshole! Telling me to wait here like a good little woman! What's he thinking? He's probably in trouble, Zoe! Ugh! Okay! Let's go!"

Zoey sighed and nodded, "Would you believe that's pretty much how I expected this 'conversation' to go?"

Serena rolled her eyes, "Yes, you know me so well. Now are you coming?"

"Wouldn't be much of an accomplice if I didn't," Zoey smirked.

"There's my girl!" Serena grinned, "Alright, Zoe! Let's suit up! Momma's gotta go to war!"

"We're gonna need some big toys for this trip, Zoe!" Serena grinned, unlocking the doors to their munitions room and heading for the rear-storage that contained most of the clan's top-level weapons. "Ohh! I didn't even *know* we had this much selection!"

"Serena… let's try and at least pack a little lightly," Zoey paused, watching her friend grab a chainsaw. She sighed, "*That's* not even for fighting! That's for clearing fallen braches that fall in front of the garage! I doubt you're even going to *use* that thing!"

"Well, it's sharp, loud and can slice through shit! In my book, *that's* a weapon, toots. It's *exactly* what I need!" Serena smirked, opening another closet, "Oooh! Leather outfits? ZOEY, you dirty little deviant! Why didn't you tell me we had these awesome Charlie's Angels outfits?

Oh! This is *too* fun! Let's wear them!"

Serena started to undress, picking out the purple leather jumpsuit and admiring it as she slipped out of her pants and yanked her shirt off. She smirked, watching her naked leg disappear into the deep purple leather leggings of the battle suit and began to zip it up her stomach, admiring the way the leather pressed to her body. Smirking, she looked into the full-length mirror, seeing Zoey behind her in the reflection as she began to undress as well.

"It's probably worth mentioning that these aren't just *any* kind of outfits, Serena! I personally designed these to withstand high-*and*-low temperatures, underwater missions, *and* they are coated with a latex-infused, enchanted polymer that's flexible but can still guard against most attacks."

Serena stared at her, "Whoa!" She looked at her reflection with a greater admiration, "Can they stop bullets?"

Zoey bit her lip, "Uhh... sometimes."

Serena looked back, "Sometimes?"

Zoey shrugged, "Let's leave it at 'no' and consider anything else a miracle, okay?"

Serena ran her hands across the outfit. "Oooh. So sciency!"

Zoey rolled her eyes and continued to undress the rest of her body to fit into her own, blue jumpsuit. As she began pulling the zipper up along the front, her breasts blocked the teeth and she had to pause to tuck them in.

Serena looked over, a glimmer of light catching her eye. "Are those... no fucking way!"

Zoey turned bright red.

"Zoe, are your nipples pierced?"

Zoey bit her lip, knowing it was already too late to try to hide the jewelry adorning her nipples, and offered a nod, "Y-yea... Isaac says they're sexy."

Serena raised an eyebrow, watching the pair of jeweled tits disappeared into the blue jumpsuit before nodding. "Well, you can tell him he's right! Hubba hubba!" She turned back and began to lace up her boots. "So how come Zane or the others don't wear one of these?"

Zoey shrugged, "He said a while back that they looked too much like a prop from Charlie's Angels—small world, I know." She laughed, "After that, none of the guys wanted to be seen wearing them."

Serena frowned, "That's it? Vanity?"

"Well," Zoey cleared her throat, "*that* and the fact that I still haven't quite worked out *all* of the kinks."

Serena chuckled, "Zoe, between your pierced titties and my hot ass, these suits are rocking all the kink they'll ever need!" Serena grinned. "Plus... *color coded*! See, I get to rock my fave: purple, and you get one that matches your hair... and anything else that might be dyed blue."

Zoey blushed even more, "Alright then! Come on, Serena! Let's finish up!"

"Okay, okay! I'll stop!" Serena laughed, starting out of the munitions room and into the garage, "Now... for the ride that'll take us to Zane in style."

Zoey cocked her head, "You know, you seem *a lot* less jittery than before."

"I'm hormonal, Zoe. Either you take me out to kill monsters or you're going to have to watch me sob over Brigid Jones into a gallon of Ben&Jerry's while I complain that my labia don't glisten like they used to."

Zoey shivered, "So let's find a car, shall we? I don't suppose I could drive this time?" She looked back, biting her lip.

"Not a chance, girlfriend," Serena grinned, stepping over to Zane's cherry-red, 2014 Jaguar F-Type. *"That's my bitch!"*

"Oh god," Zoey coughed. "We're going to crash and die before we even get there!"

"Well, *that'll* give us a chance to test out the durability of these suits then, won't it?" Serena smirked, jumping into the driver's side. "Besides, let's be fair, when have I done you wrong? *Really, genuinely* done you wrong?"

Zoey smiled at her friend and shook her head. "Never. You have *never* let me down."

"Then, trust me to not let you down once again!" Serena laughed, twisting the key in the ignition and beaming as the car came to life. "Oh, Mama, yes! Their slogan is *so* true! It really *does* roar!"

Zoey sat next to her, still adjusting to the leather outfit and shook her head, "It is *way* too hot to be wearing leather!"

Serena looked to her friend as the garage door opened and she revved the engine. "All the more reason to drive *ridiculously* fast!"

Serena hit the gas then, and they shot out of the clan's garage, shooting down the private back road towards the onramp to the expressway. The wind slapped against Zoey's face and she took a moment to calm herself down before turning to Serena, who had cut her hair shortly after coming back to the clan to accommodate for the unevenness after all of Maledictus' torture had taken its toll on her locks. Now that she was sporting a lower-neck-length style, she looked more mature than she had before.

"So tell me, Zoe, why *do* you dye your hoo-hoo?" Serena asked.

Zoey blushed, "You *know* about that? I thought you were just bluffing!"

Serena smirked. "Well, I know now," she winked

"Damn…" Zoey sighed. "Well, I suppose it started more as an OCD thing for me—I didn't like the idea of having two different hair colors on my body—but when Isaac got a look at it…" she shrugged, "It just sorta turned into a thing."

"Makes sense," Serena nodded. "Speaking of which, what *is* your natural hair color?"

"Actually I'm a blonde, too." Zoey looked over and saw Serena grin.

"Well then I guess it's a good thing you dye it! 'Cause there can be only one blonde in this sisterhood, and I'd hate to have to kill you!"

The two shared in a laugh as they made their way into the city, and the two frowned, seeing a large crowd forming around the building that Kristine and Celine had acquired for their clan headquarters.

All around them were growing crowds, mumbling about explosions and shrapnel-related injuries and crazy people jumping off the rooftops.

"Well, Zoey, it looks like we're a little late to the show. I'm going to get out here. Would you mind parking this beast and keeping the perimeter clear of… well, anybody? I need to make sure no one gets through to the South Terrace block! If you spot anybody who's clearly seen too much, sweep their minds. The last thing we're going to need after all this is The Council creeping up our asses."

"Can and will!" Zoey nodded, "Good luck, Serena, and try to stay safe."

"Safety is my first priority, Zoe!" Serena smiled and slowed the Jaguar enough to give Zoey the time she'd need to take her place before she climbed out of the driver's seat. Moving to the back of the car as Zoey took control behind the wheel, Serena positioned herself on the trunk of the car.

"See you soon, girl!" she called back.

"I'll hold you to that!" Zoey shot back.

With that, Serena jumped off and, tumbling with the impact and effortlessly rolling to her feet and jumped into overdrive.

Here we go!

Chapter Twenty-Five
The Great Pandemonium

AFTER ALL THE THAT HE'D BEEN THROUGH, THE explosion from Zane's homemade shrapnel bombs was like a 4th of July celebration; every bit as beautiful and awe-inspiring as—

"GET DOWN!" Raith cried out, yanking Nikki to the rooftop as the screws, nails, and jagged bits of spray-paint cans peppered out from the busted window.

Zane let his mind slip into overdrive for a moment,

watching as the flying bits of shrapnel froze in the air and letting him appreciate the view. Maledictus, who'd practically been standing on top of the propane tanks when they'd went off, was caught in midair, his face twisted in shock and pain and most of his body already plastered in bits of scalding-hot metal and paint. Knowing better than to waste all of his energy in overdrive *just* to watch, Zane dropped to his belly and, in the process, back into normal time.

He couldn't stop laughing.

"Oh god! Raith! It was so *B-E-A-FUCKING-UTIFUL!* The motherfucker was all"—he twisted his face in a mock-imitation of Maledictus' agony.

Nikki couldn't help but giggle, "I take it you took a moment to admire it?"

"How could I not?" Zane smirked.

"God dammit, Zane!" Isaac growled, yanking several woodscrews from his shoulder, "You realize how many innocent people you just hit with all these?"

Zane looked back and chuckled, "Three things, Isaac: one—Zoey's gonna fuck the shit outta you when she sees how badass you look; two—Nobody's innocent; *nobody*; and three—while I'm sure all that clipped a few people—yourself included—I doubt it'll do much more than hurt like hell and give them an excuse to take the day off from work. Not like they were sitting at ground-zero—trust me, *that* is the sort of thing most people wouldn't survive—and, to be fair, a few nails to the noggin is a kiss from the angels compared to what Maledictus is going to bring down on the world if we *don't* take care of business. So let's take care of business!"

Nikki was still chuckling as they stood, shaking her head. "I gotta hand it to you; you sure do know how to make an entrance."

"So I've heard," Zane drew one of the two katanas at his back, spinning the sword in his palm to get a feel for the balance. *Three grams heavy on the handle*, he noted to himself, wishing he'd been smart enough to test the pair before he'd left. Taking a deep breath and trying to breathe out both his growing anxieties and the swelling irritation from the sun-poisoning he'd slowly been absorbing all morning, he took a few steps back and nodded to the others. "Don't wait up."

Raith nodded, the signs of his transformation already starting to show on his shoulders and arms. "Don't kill 'em all before we get there."

Zane shook his head, "I don't think that's going to be a problem, buddy."

Summoning the nerves to do what he had to, he took the first step, instantly throwing himself into overdrive, and sprinted towards the edge of the building, leaping in a suicidal hail-Mary for the gaping, jagged window frame. As his body soared through the air, the sounds of the city below him—humans trying to regain themselves after the chaos of the explosion that had just taken place above them—came into focus, and, from his bird's-eye view, he spotted a few of the onlookers pointing up at him.

The Council is not going to like this, he sighed to himself.

Prepping for impact, he gauged his trajectory and—

"Shit!" his eyes widened as he saw himself careening towards the window *neighboring* the one he'd been aiming for. *Dammit, Zane! Throw a pair of fucking bombs with pinpoint fucking accuracy, but the moment you're making the jump yourself you go and...* he didn't let himself finish his inward critiques as tucked his head and lead with his shoulder, willing the powers of the universe to grant him safe passage through the—

His world lit up with the deafening crash and waves of pain as his body broke through the glass, passed through half of the room, slammed him into the carpeted floor, and rolled him into the far wall.

Groaning and plucking a piece of the shattered glass out of his free hand, Zane shook the daze from his spinning head and forced himself to stand.

"Nice, Zane," he brushed some of the broken glass out of his hair. "Real nice. I bet the others are laughing their asses off back—"

The wall to his left—separating him from the room that the bombs had gone off in—burst outward and blinded him in dust and debris.

"You incessant fucking nut-mite," Maledictus' voice rattled through the haze. "Don't you know when to count your blessings and fucking quit?"

"You *really* didn't think I *wouldn't* be coming back for your scaly ass," Zane rebutted with a laugh. Keeping the katana brandished ahead of him, he yanked one of his Glocks free from the holster and flipped off the safety. Then, as a second thought, he switched the pistol from semi-automatic to fully-automatic. "I mean, just *look* at you: ugly as sin, annoying as fuck, and sort of a begging for an execution with all this 'change the world' death-wizard babble. I get that you're in the head of a stupid animal, but you *must* have seen this coming!"

"A stupid animal..." Maledictus grumbled, a hissing chuckle growing from the depths of the wavering dust-fog. "Well ain't *that* just the pot calling the kettle *BLACK!*"

Maledictus struck then, diving through the haze and lunging for Zane, who jumped back before the monster's outstretched claws could reach him and kicked out. Seeing the boot coming for his face, Maledictus moved his head to one side—letting the attack pass over his left shoulder—and moved to lunge at Zane. Recalculating the attack, Zane used his opponent's shoulder to push his airborne body back in a summersault that connected his left foot with Maledictus' lower jaw.

Maledictus stumbled back from the force—his jawbone, dislocated, hanging lamely at his throat—as Zane landed on his feet and charged forward, leading with his leveled pistol and squeezing the trigger.

The room went alive with the roar of automatic gunfire, and the already bloodied, shrapnel-adorned torso of Maledictus took the force of seventeen rounds in less than five seconds.

Though few of the bullets actually had a chance to pierce his scaly hide, the distraction had been enough to let Zane get close. The first pass of the katana—a straight-down swipe that would've cleaved Maledictus' skull down the middle—was sidestepped at the last minute, leaving an opening to the monster's windpipe for a pistol-whipping from Zane's now-empty Glock.

Zane gladly took the opening.

As the butt of the pistol slammed into Maledictus' throat, the monster heaved—its mouth gaping open—as it struggled to inhale. Remembering the horrors of what had emerged from that mouth in the past, Zane brought the Glock upwards; pinning Maledictus' jaw against his knuckles and resting the barrel along the length of Maledictus' jaw. Grinning, Zane ejected the spent magazine and—sheathing his katana for the moment—retrieved one of the elongated 32-round ammo magazine from the holster at his hip. Slamming in the magazine and pulling the slide, he drove his freed hand into Maledictus' face, dazing him further.

"Let me sing you the song of my people, asshole!"

Zane growled in his face as he squeezed and held the trigger, letting the stream of automatic gunfire roar directly in his enemy's ear as the heating barrel seared into his face.

Maledictus' eyes widened as he cried out, lashing forward in a desperate attempt to free himself from the torture and, after knocking Zane back a few paces, clutching his head and teetering on dazed legs.

"M-Mother... fucker!" Maledictus growled, his eyes spinning in his head as he tried to glare at Zane. "I'm going to make you—"

"Shut the fuck up already," Zane retrieved a second gun and, with a flip of a switch, leveled both automatic pistols at the staggering monster. "Just, for once in your miserable life, shut the fuck up!"

He let the bullets fly.

The task of getting the two therions across the gap and through the open window—well, the *first* open window; Zane had obviously felt that diving through an *open* window in the side of the building was too simple—wasn't too difficult for Nikki. After Raith and Isaac had transformed, a process that Nikki wasn't nervous to eavesdrop on at all the right moments—what was it about their kind that the gods saw fit to bestow such fantastic assets to? Not that she was complaining, of course—Raith had scooped her up in his bestial arms and awaited her orders. Though Isaac's fear of heights wasn't a secret by that point, he didn't let it slow them down when she gave the order and the two had leapt from the building's edge.

Halfway across the distance the three had begun to feel the tug of gravity, and *that's* when Nikki played her part. Calling upon her magic, she'd forced a swell of energy to push out from behind them. The force of the spell had lifted and pushed them through the first of the broken windows, landing them inside a room that looked like a submission from a struggling art student.

Littered in bits and pieces of this-and-that and caked in a rainbow array of the still-dripping spray-paint that, along with the *thousands* of screws and nails and metal shards, adorned every surface. Near the center of the room, just as much a pin-cushioned kaleidoscope as everything else, was a vacant length of chain and a makeshift throne that, as far as Nikki could tell, had been constructed out of human bones—the bottom-left corner of which were badly splintered; probably from a particularly concentrated burst of shrapnel—that had been fitted together to take the proper shape and then bound in, of all things, duct tape.

"What is it with men and duct tape?" Nikki had asked before remembering that neither of the "men" in her company could speak in their bestial forms.

To their left, the wall—or lack thereof—that had divided the room they occupied to the one that Zane had crashed through allowed them to see that both rooms were, in fact, empty, though the myriad of bullet holes and spent shell casings on the floor of the neighboring room offered enough hints that Zane had started his own fun.

So where was he?

Nikki drew her sais and nodded to Raith to set her down. "Alright, boys, time to divide and conquer, I guess."

Raith whimpered and looked at her with worried eyes.

"Don't worry, baby," she reassured him, petting his muzzle before planting a kiss on it, "I can handle myself. 'Sides, if I get into too much trouble I'll just whistle for you," she said with a wink.

Raith rolled his eyes, obviously not appreciating her brand of lap-dog humor, and started for the door.

"Huh," Nikki mused, looking around, "I wonder where that Celine-bitch wandered off to."

She knew it!

She'd known it all along!

But did *anybody* ever listen? Did anybody *ever* listen to poor, pathetic, dull-witted Celine?

No!

Of course not!

Nobody ever gave her the credit she deserved!

She cursed, dragging her fingers through the back of her hair and raking more of the paint from it before yanking the few nails and screws from the back of her shoulder that she *could* reach.

The moment that the homemade bombs had crashed through the window—the very *second* they'd entered the room—Celine had seen them for what they were. Then, it was only a matter of jumping into overdrive and kicking in the corner of Maledictus' repulsive bone-throne. With the broken bits, she'd been able to pick the lock to her chains—something she could've done at any time but had *purposefully* reserved for the right moment;

that moment—and sprinted for the door.

If it hadn't been for her stumbling with the damnable door, she'd have made it out without taking any of the blast at all!

"Fucking idiots! The whole lot of them; Zane and his pathetic bitch *and* that repugnant pervert of a lizard," she muttered to herself, working her way down the emergency stairwell, yanking a First-Aid kit off the wall as she passed. "Let the whole brain-dead lot just rip themselves to fucking pieces, then I can get away. Just wait for them all to *kill* each other before I—AH! Bloody fucking hell!" she winced as she poured some of the rubbing alcohol over the back of her shoulder. Breathing out the pain and shaking her head, she continued down the steps, "Can't believe he made me suck his—"

Something thudded and clawed at the bottom of the stairwell.

Celine froze, peeking over the railing and fighting the wave of vertigo from the view of the square-spiral of stairs beneath her.

"H-hel-hello..." she could barely get the air to fuel the word past her quivering lips. "I-is somebody there? P-please... I need some help..."

No response.

No spoken response, at least.

At the sound of her echoing voice, the thuds and scratches intensified—grew more frantic and eager—until, finally, a latch *click*ed and the basement door slammed open.

"S-Stay—" Celine stopped herself, clearing her throat and fighting her wavering nerves to sound confident and strong. *Pretend you're the blonde bimbo,* she thought to yourself, *Just act like Zane's stupid whore and you might get through this!*

Something rattled the railing at the base of the stairs and the sound of footsteps—more than one set?—started up towards her.

Just like Serena, Celine reminded herself once more. Then, "Whoever the fuck is playing with me better piss off before I decide to rip out my tampon and choke a motherfucker with it!" she gaped as the words flooded from her. *Bloody hell, did I say that? Holy shit! I'm a total badass!*

But the sound of lumbering footsteps on the stairs didn't falter.

Thinking better of trying to back up her newfound vulgarity with any real action, Celine turned and started back up the stairs.

Maledictus wheezed as his aching throat screamed for oxygen. Zane's cheap shot on his throat had been bad enough without following it up with a headache from hell—ironic as that was—and finally proving that he *wasn't* bulletproof.

As it turned out, when over fifty bullets were shot at him fast enough, at least a dozen did what they were supposed to do.

Good to know.

He made a note to thank Zane—over and over and over again—for helping him discover this about himself.

In return, perhaps he'd formally introduce him to each and every one of his internal organs; one by—

"Do I not have your attention, shit-eater?" Zane

growled, slamming the pommel.

Maledictus stumbled. The pommel? He recalled a visit from a Japanese traveler teaching him that his people called it the *kashira* of a katana. He blinked. When had he had a Japanese traveler?

Furthermore, why in the hell did it matter?

"You hear me, Maledictus?" Zane lunged, drawing back the katana for another strike, "Time to—"

"Oh, I hear you loud and fucking clear, Zaney-boy!" he hissed, blocking Zane's attack by bringing his forearm under his wrist and pushing him back. "I'm just having a bit of an identity crisis." He kicked Zane, connecting with his stomach and forcing him back down the narrow corridor. Shaking his head, he scoffed at their surroundings, "Can you fucking *believe* that those dumb cunts actually picked this shit-hole as the headquarters for their limp-dick clan? Place is a bigger fucking nightmare than anything even I could come up with!"

"Kinda doubt that," Zane glared, jumping into overdrive to end him.

Maledictus followed after him, spotting the pair of katanas coming straight for his eyes. Ducking back, he wedged both of his arms between the blades and pushed them apart; slamming Zane's wrists against the walls of the hallway. Gripping the vampire warrior's shoulders, he charged forward, forcing Zane off his feet.

It's been fun, old friend, but it's time to—

Zane, using Maledictus' hold on his upper-body, brought both knees up and into the Leiche's belly—shifting the contents of his organs and forcing several of the bullets to roll uncomfortably within his guts—and head-butted him in the nose. Reeling back, Maledictus stumbled and faltered out of overdrive, carrying Zane, who started to slip free of his grip, with him.

"—time to *end* you!" Zane growled, baring his fangs and, dropping the katana from his right hand and letting it fall behind Maledictus' shoulder, drove a sharp right-hook into his ribs. Yanking his hand back, he darted his open hand under Maledictus' arm, catching the still-falling katana and stabbing it into the back of the Leiche's right calf.

Maledictus hissed and stumbled as his right leg went limp under his weight, and Zane facilitated his condition by jamming his extended elbow into his freshly cracked ribs and slamming him against the wall.

And now Maledictus had a pierced lung.

Zane was such a giver.

He really had to think of a way to repay him.

"What the fuck are you laughing at, asshole?" Zane growled, punching him in the face.

Had he been laughing?

Oh well, roll with it.

Maledictus smiled. "I've got some company coming to join us."

Raith growled.

Though the act had barely registered with him, the echoes of the deep, ferocious sound reverberated along the length of the elevator shaft he was occupying.

Hearing it come rolling back up, however, he realized that he agreed with himself and, aware of this new one, issued another, longer growl.

He didn't like the idea of splitting up; didn't like the idea of Nikki wandering this waiting house of horrors to spring to un-life and turn into Maledictus' war scene. He knew it was coming, and he knew Zane knew it was coming. Though, for the life of him, he couldn't begin to fathom *how* it was going to come.

A Leiche...

Damn!

It was bad enough when the *Maledictus* was just a curse—some enchanted program that the rage-infected taroe tribe had cooked up as a punishment for him and Zane poking around their village—and was parading around in his own ykali body. Bad, but nothing compared to *this*. The Leiche essence—whatever his name had once been—had acquired Zane's vampire traits and Raith's own shapeshifting abilities, turning him into something that the world had not only never seen, but reawakening something that the world had already suffered from over a thousand years earlier.

And Nikki was on her own in a building that all of *that* had been squatting in for going on a week!

Who knew what sort of dangers occupied all those floors...

Climbing, upside-down, down the lift cables of the elevator shaft, Raith kept his sensitive ears open for any sign of something on the lower floors.

As well as the chance of Nikki's whistle.

He only hoped that her pride wouldn't keep her from calling for help if the need arose.

As he started to pass the third floor, he heard something and paused; his hands gripping the cable as he craned his neck towards the door. Sure enough, something—or, rather, many things—were crashing about on that level. Thinking that Zane and Maledictus' battle might have taken them down further than he'd expected or that any of others may have encountered some sort of trouble, he righted himself on the cable and then jumped to the ledge. Pressing his ear against the door, he verified the suspicions that *someone* was causing a great deal of damage, but, unable to hear any voices, couldn't identify whom.

Growling again, Raith wedged his clawed fingertips between the sliding elevator doors and yanked them apart, coming face-to-face with…

A zombie?

Raith blinked at the alien sight of a lumbering, *living* corpse—half of its face torn away to expose the rotting meat and vacant, maggot-infested right eye socket and a decent chunk of the back-left area of its skull caved in—before noticing shortly after that, just beyond the equally bewildered risen corpse, was even more like it.

Well… shit! Raith thought to himself.

The corpse, which seemed just as astonished by the sudden appearance of a therion just on the other side of the magically-opened elevator doors, finally shuffled to face him and let out a high-pitched, guttural sound from its throat.

Then *every* corpse was facing him, and then approaching.

Raith kicked out. The attack hit the corpse in the hip, making a wet popping, and—as a wet, clotted stream of reeking black blood began to trickle from the corpse's rot-coated shorts—it slowly began to fold over under the caved-in portion that Raith had just torn out.

Oh, gross! No fucking thank you! Raith stabbed his claws into the doors and slammed them shut before turning and jumping back to the lift cables, eager to get to the higher floors and warn the other of the massive—and disgusting—army that Maledictus had no-doubt brought into being.

Nikki was eager to figure out what had happened with Zane and Maledictus.

Though she knew that neither she nor Zane nor Raith had been responsible—let alone deserving—of the monstrosity that her people had released unto the world in an act of dark rage, she still felt, in some way, like she had to oversee its destruction.

That, and she was more than just a little curious as to how a vulgar and destructive vampire like Zane and an equally vulgar and destructive monster like Maledictus could've gotten lost in the short time it had taken her and the others to arrive.

After Raith and Isaac had split up, she'd stepped over the gaping divide between the two rooms and looked around for any clues. The area around the door, which hung open on one tortured hinge, was littered in bullet holes that, from a distance, created an almost comical outline that was far too tall to be Zane. Exploring the floor around that area, she'd found a number of warped bullets that hadn't punctured Maledictus, as well as enough fresh ykali blood to prove that at least some of them *had*.

Nikki smirked at this, whispering "You go, Zane!" to herself as she searched for any sign that Maledictus might have gotten a hit in, as well.

Her smirk became a smile when none turned up.

Keeping her sais poised at her side, she'd followed the "trail" through the door and into the hall—remembering that Raith and Isaac had parted at this point—and, scoping both directions, caught sight of a small smearing of ykali blood on the push-handle to the staircase two doors to her left. She followed, pushing open the door with her hip and holding up her weapons as she peered inside.

Though nothing immediately presented itself, the sounds of something—*a lot* of whatever the things were, from the sounds of it—echoed from the bottom of the stairs. Sneering at the sound for a moment, Nikki decided that she didn't want to know what was making all that racket; not on her own, at least.

Luckily for her, a few drops of ykali blood leading upstairs gave her a simple enough out from exploring whatever *it* was.

She continued after the trail up the double-flight— pausing to appreciate a sizable dent in the steel railing— and through the doorway to the next floor, once again preparing for any risk on the other side.

But there was nothing there. Just an uncomfortably narrow hallway lined with office doors. To her right, where the hall ended abruptly, she noticed a trail of twin scratches leading down either side of the walls that led to a dead-end with a set of bathrooms—men's on the left; women's on the right—and the mangled remains of a drinking fountain that gushed belching torrents of water all over the carpet and a lonely, blood-coated katana.

"Gods above and below, Zane," Nikki marveled. "It'll be a miracle if the building's left standing!"

Starting towards the water-soaked dead-end, Nikki puzzled herself with a riddle:

Would a pair of horny bastards decide to take this into the women's washroom, or would they sooner compare dick-sizes at the urinals in the men's?

Zane silently thanked the powers of the universe that he wasn't responsible for cleaning up the mess that he and Maledictus had made in the men's bathroom.

After being thrown into the side of the first stall and, under the force of the impact, taking out more than half of the four stalls in a painful Domino mockery, he'd made a note of putting Maledictus' increasingly bloodied face through each and every sink. As the tile floors had grown slippery with the payoff from so many destroyed plumbing lines, he'd had no problem throwing the top-heavy Leiche through the only intact stall—smirking as he faltered and broke through the toilet and, using the overhanging framework of the stall barriers, delivering a swinging kick to the dazed monster and sending him through the wall and into the conference room on the other side.

Stumbling in the process of following Maledictus through yet another hole in the wall, Zane lost his footing and, by the time he'd righted himself, had given his opponent enough time to break an office chair across the side of his head.

Dazed, Zane had barely registered the pain from slamming into the office wall, only a few feet from a window on either side of him.

He barely had enough time to count his blessings that he hadn't been thrown from the building before he caught sight of Maledictus coming at him and ducked in time to have another chair shattered against the wall. With the Leiche fumbling with his balance over him, Zane was free to deliver an enraged uppercut to his enemy's groin.

Maledictus just looked down at him and laughed.

"Oh fuck…" Zane sneered in disgust, "*That's* never happened befo—"

"PERKS OF BEING A FUCKING MONSTER, ZANEY-BOY!" Maledictus roared as he grabbed him by the shoulders and spun him around, picking up speed and momentum, and prepared to throw him through the window.

Seeing what was coming, Zane drew his remaining katana and stabbed it through Maledictus' hip.

The ear-splitting shriek of shattering glass rang in Zane's ears for the second time that morning.

A cool breeze from outside swept up his bangs, and he watched the silver-and-black strands of hair pass in front of his eyes as he squinted against the rays of the sun.

Below him, the noise of the city offered a new tune from the night-song he'd come to know so well.

And, with his sword hooked in his enemy's side and a driving need to share the fall he'd been condemned to, he dragged Maledictus into the start of that day's afternoon in the human world.

Chapter Twenty-Six
End of the World
(as we know it)

CELINE WAS SO EAGER TO BE RID OF THIS PLACE; this place and everyone—every-*bloody*-one!—associated with it. With the way her life had been going ever since she'd made the mistake of attacking and turning Zane, she was beginning to wish that she *had* just been arrested.

Hell, execution is looking goddam great *at this point!*

But there was, however, the recent discovery of how

good it felt to *not* go through life as a victim pathetically begging for protection. And while she wasn't particularly thrilled with crediting Serena Vailean as the inspiration of this discovery, she was comfortable in the awareness that, in whatever new, bolder life she established for herself after all this was over, she'd never have to credit anyone but herself ever again.

Least of all *her*.

Celine scoffed, playing out different scenarios of various things she'd do if she came face-to-face with the blonde bimbo. Though she'd gotten herself a bit lost in the building—she'd yet to explore *all* of it since she and Kristine acquired it several weeks earlier—she was certain that, so long as she avoided direct conflict with either one of the two warring sides, she'd figure out a way to get away from the building.

She smirked, perhaps she'd make her way to the rooftop and make one of those exciting-looking jumps to a neighboring rooftop that everyone seemed to be doing. After all, if the likes of Zane or Serena could do it, there was no reason that she—

She heard something approaching behind her and smirked, a swell of confidence growing within her, and she clenched her fists. She'd been reciting the line from before over and over, and she was certain that she'd perfected it.

"Whoever the *fuck* is dicking with me had better piss-the-fuck-off before I'm forced to rip out my tampon and cram it down a motherfucker's throat!"

She spun around, eager to shoot her practiced death-glare at whoever dared to—

Celine's breath caught in her throat.

"Nice try, you stupid bitch!"

Serena smirked as she walked—seeing no need to break a sweat with running—towards the bug-eyed Celine; feeling a swell of pride at how her hips swayed in Zoey's sexy "battle suit."

When all was said and done, she promised herself to take this outfit into the bedroom and torture Zane with it.

Celine's wavering aura had begun to deflate at the sight of her, but, as she'd recently acquired a few forged pages from the big book of the badass Serena, she pumped herself up that she could take her…

If she only *believed* in herself.

Believe all you want, cunt-nugget, Serena reminded the arrogant she-vamp that she could pop inside her head whenever she wanted, *it ain't gonna make it true!*

"I'll show you!" Celine hissed, baring her fangs, "I'll show all of you!"

Celine lunged.

Serena didn't falter in her pace as she threw her right elbow out, clocking the incoming Celine across the left side of her jaw. As the realization that she'd made a terrible mistake dawned on Celine's aura, Serena broke out in a wide grin and let the back of her now-perched right hand lash out in a blur against Celine's neglected right cheek.

The she-vamp toppled to the side, throwing out her hands to stay her fall against the wall and taking in an audible breath against the waves of pain.

"I thought…" she whimpered.

"You thought wrong, bitch!" Serena scoffed.

Celine growled, "You stupid bimbo! You think that just because you were brave enough to put up with Zane when that *thing* was in him makes you right for him?" She pushed off against the wall for another attempt at Serena.

Serena ducked under the wide punch and twisted Celine around from the shoulder, forcing her to face away from her.

"No, honey, I think that us being right for each other makes me right for him!"

Taking the sides of Celine's head in each hand, Serena twisted sharply and giggled at the sound of her neck breaking.

"And *that's* how it's done, bitch!" Serena spat on the corpse of the she-vamp who had done *everything* to ruin her man's life. "There, now that *that's* done..." she smirked and turned away starting back down the hall towards where she'd left the chainsaw. "Sorry about the holdup, Bruce, but I didn't want to dirty your chain with the likes of *her*," she slung the retrieved tool over her shoulder and started back towards Zane's aura, "Now let's go find Daddy—ooh! I like the sound of that."

Zane was rather enjoying the sensation of freefalling. There was a certain freedom—albeit a loaded one given what awaited the end of it—that just felt right.

Or maybe it was how his fists felt as he drove them repeatedly into Maledictus' face.

Either way, it was euphoria!

Shortly after Maledictus had thrown them out the window, Zane had been able to rotate the two of them, using the larger Leiche's bodyweight as a means of seeing to it that he met the street before Zane. Finding his katana firmly jammed in his opponent's side, Zane had sacrificed his grip on the handle and started letting loose a chain of overdrive-fueled punches to preoccupy the already lengthy fall.

As soon as they crashed into the street—no matter how many humans were around to witness the spectacle—he was going to retrieve his Glocks and empty every last bullet he hand into—

He looked past Maledictus' battle-damaged face at the street below, frowning at the total lack of humans. There were no cars, no pedestrians—no bicyclists or dog walkers or joggers or jittery business folk on their "too short" lunch break—no *anything*!

Then he spotted it...

Zane's eyes widened. *Is that my Jag?*

Maledictus did, indeed, impact before Zane...

Directly on the hood of his prized, cherry-red 2014 Jaguar F-Type!

The two of them—between the force of gravity and Maledictus' bony, barbed, and otherwise weaponized body—caved through the glistening, sleek metal and threw everything that made the beautiful car purr into a useless hunk of dented metal.

"WHY THE FUCK IS MY CAR PARKED OUT HERE?" Zane roared, forgetting all about his plans and taking out his rage on the only living thing around him: Maledictus. "IT CLEARLY SAYS 'NO PARKING' RIGHT THERE!" he pulled the Leiche's head up from one of his horns and thrust a finger at a nearby, curb-mounted sign. "WHY DOES THE UNIVERSE—"

"FUCKING ENOUGH!" Maledictus roared, grabbing Zane by the jacket and hurling him onto the sidewalk. Standing, Maledictus focused on healing—his body and all the damage that had been inflicted on it beginning to mend—as he yanked the katana out of his side and twisted it into a knot.

Zane sighed, "Now you're just adding insult to injury."

"No, Zane," Maledictus started towards him, "now I'm fucking *ending* this nut-fuckery for good!"

Serena growled as she approached the room that she'd sensed Zane in, suddenly feeling his auric signature on the floor below.

Then the floor below that.

Then the floor…

"Oh no…" Serena spotted the broken window. "Oh shit, no!"

She took off in a sprint for the stairwell, moving in overdrive through the door and down the steps, feeling her body howl from the exertion. Five floors down, she sensed Nikki, Raith, Isaac, and over a hundred dull, gray auric signatures with the stink of Maledictus all over them. Slamming through the door and starting towards the energy signatures, she let herself fall out of overdrive and into a human Olympian's pace as reached ahead of her with her aura.

Nikki had been fortunate enough to catch up with Raith and Isaac *before* Maledictus' horde of walking corpses reached them. The first few had gone down easily—they *were* only corpses—but, as the horde grew more and denser, it became a struggle just to hold their ground.

A struggle they were steadily losing.

Trying to replicate the attack that she and the auric Michael had used at the asylum, Nikki had found the enchantment far weaker against the magic that had been used to bring the shambling, undead army back from the dead. Every wave of magic she hit them with, though succeeding in knocking the mass over, seemed to get absorbed into them and make them that much more resilient to the next spell.

Fighting them, even more than casting against them, was proving a useless effort. The therions learned quickly that biting into the corpses was more unpleasant for them than the horde, and any other attacks only served to remove a few of the horde from an equation that seemed to spring two in the place of every fallen. Even worse, any attack that *didn't* render a corpse immobile only served to remove pieces, which, though they hardly seemed to notice, was creating another cloud of toxic rot that was steadily choking the three.

Nikki was beginning to run out of ideas when…

Guys, Serena's voice chimed in their heads, *Zane's in trouble; big trouble. Maledictus took the fight outside, and I can feel him preparing for something. Whatever you're facing now is happening outside on a much larger scale, and if we don't take him out* **now** *then all this is going to spill out across the city.*

Nikki frowned, looking back and focusing her thoughts to Serena, *It's an army! A damn horde of corpses! My magic is only making them stronger, and if Maledictus' is powerful enough to do* more *of this than I don't think we have much chance of stopping him, let alone an even bigger army of these evil, dead bastards!*

Then we gotta keep Maledictus from getting any stronger! Serena called out, coming around the corner behind them and starting towards them at a full sprint.

Nikki wasn't sure if she wanted to kiss Serena or kill her. Showing up when they needed her most was a *definite* perk, but…

"How in the hell are we supposed to keep Maledictus from getting stronger?" She shouted across the hall as Raith and Isaac fought to hold back the horde of corpses.

"He's a death-wizard, right?" Serena asked, catching up to them. "So we don't die; we don't die, we don't let Zane die, and we don't let Maledictus claim a single other life to add to his tank of death-energy. Now move!"

The three obliged. Serena could see each of their auras spiking as they noticed the chainsaw strapped to her back and, with her entrance and everything at stake, decided that it was best to do as she said.

Using her aura to push the horde back—condensing them in the narrow hallway—she took a sharp inhale and drew back her arm, replicating the act of firing an arrow from a bow.

For so many years she had used the motions she'd learned as a little girl in archery to *also* direct her auric attacks, often losing a great deal of respect from those who saw it followed *immediately* after by a greater swell of admiration at how effective it was for her. Envisioning her aura as arrows and "firing" them from an imaginary bow had become so engrained in her muscle memory that her subconscious, at a young age, had begun to create a bow-shaped anomaly within her hand, until the day came when the act became so much a reflex that anybody capable of seeing auras was certain that Serena *was,* in fact, wielding a shimmering, semi-translucent purple bow with matching arrows. Training herself further, she'd learned to manipulate this even further; taking control of the "arrows" after they'd been fired through a target to move them, or fabricating other weapon-shaped anomalies with her aura.

Now, however, she was calling upon something far greater…

Focusing all of her auric control, Serena Vailean closed her eyes and allowed the dull-gray orbs occupying the darkness to be mapped out; giving her a sense of each and every corpse that was shambling within the hallway.

Three auric threads snaked back to each of her friends as she began to draw some of their energy in an effort to further fuel the attack, and the energy in her hands grew as her aura swelled and vibrated in her hands…

"Nikki," Serena spoke in a low tone, forcing herself to remain focused.

"Y-yea?" Nikki answered, uncertainty saturating her voice and her aura.

Serena let out a deep breath and prepared to release the attack. "Just promise me that you'll catch me…"
Just hold on, baby. Just hold on a little bit longer…

Nikki had barely registered what Serena had said before her left hand opened and released the auric "bow string."

Serena had tried to describe the process to her a while back, and, though Nikki couldn't see auras and, for her, it simply appeared that Serena was firing make-believe arrows at her enemies. Granted, they were make-believe arrows that Nikki had *watched* pierce and pulverize many enemies, but, unable to see the process with her own eyes, she had simply come to trust the process as Serena's own.

This time, however, was far more jarring.

As Serena's hand opened, the room went alive with a roar like static that made Nikki want to cover her ears. However, as Serena had warned her—albeit rather suddenly—her hands were needed.

The skull of every corpse occupying the hallway whipped back then, the eyes of those that still had them peeling back in a mockery of shock a split-second before every one of their heads erupted under the force of the attack.

And Serena, eyes fluttering, fell back into Nikki's arms.

Zane rolled free as Maledictus' foot came down for a kill shot, leaving a crater in the pavement where his head had been.

"Hold still, you cancerous nut-wart!" Maledictus growled, "Just let me kill you so I can move forward with my fucking life as the devil this world deserves!"

Zane glared at him, rolling to his feet and standing. "You were a devil to me and my friends, Maledictus," he narrowed his eyes at the Leiche, unbuckling the stifling and constricting leathers and letting them fall to the pavement. "And you're even dumber than I thought if you think for one fucking second I'm going to let you be a devil to anyone else ever again!"

"We'll see," Maledictus leered.

Zane let his fangs extend as the memories of the past few years rolled in his mind; each and every horror he'd woken up to and been forced to take responsibility for due to the being inside of him that now stood before him. All because of that damned relic and the binding taroe tattoos that he'd been tortured with enduring when the curse had been set. Every time he'd lost control after that, those tattoos—channeling the energies through the taroe's enchanted ink—would begin to glow, and he'd grown to despise the tattoos as a symbol of what was lurking beneath his flesh. Now, however, facing down the monster and everything he represented, Zane realized that the tattoos didn't need to represent his curse or his rage…

They could represent his perseverance.

They could represent his survival.

They could represent *him*.

And, seeing the potential for a new world *without* Maledictus, he smiled.

"Thank you," he said, sincerity catching both Maledictus *and* himself off guard.

The Leiche staggered and glared, "The fuck is that supposed to mean?"

Zane nodded, pulling off the black tee-shirt and tossing it along with the other gear, finally taking pride in letting his tattoos be totally visible for the world to see. "Just that: 'thank you.' Thank you for giving me the chance to *personally* square off against everything I ever hated about myself."

In the back of Maledictus' mind—deep down where the auras of all those he'd killed were kept, teeming like fine wine in a rocking chalice—he felt something churn, and he could swear he heard applause.

A necessary tragedy.

A necessary tragedy.

He growled as the marine's words echoed incessantly in his mind, and he felt his blood go hot with rage at a realization that he refused to let come to light.

A necessary tragedy.

"Come on, Serena!" Nikki chanted, patting her

friend's cheek and feeding more and more of her magic into her, "Come on, girl, we need you up. We gotta go help Zane!"

Serena's eyes fluttered open, "H-huh? Zane?" She sat up like a bolt, feeling a fresh wave of vitality from whatever Nikki had been feeding into her. "Jesus H—Nikki, my sister from another mister, there is some serious juice in what you're packing there!"

Nikki's aura settled then as she smiled and shook her head, "Yea... well, after the show you just put on I had to do *something*; might not have been as badass as all that, but..."

Serena smiled, jumping to her feet. "Trust me, it was *truly* badass," she nodded to them, getting a firm grip on the chainsaw, "I gotta go save my baby-daddy. Think you guys can scout for any stragglers that I might have missed?"

Nikki chuckled and nodded, "You mean more corpses? I kinda doubt you left any for us, but—yea—we'll make sure they're all dead... er, deader... uh, dead *again*."

Serena nodded and looked over at Isaac, "Zoey's outside redirecting traffic, and she's looking *really* hot in her jumpsuit." She started off and paused again, "Oh yea, and *great* choice in piercings!" She winked.

From behind her, she felt a swell of curiosity from Nikki's aura. "Piercings?"

Then a swell of embarrassment from Isaac.

Serena saved her laughter, certain there would be more than enough time for it *after* she kept Zane from getting murdered by a death-hungry lizard rapist.

Zoey-girl, do you read?

Serena felt Zoey's auric signature swell. *Loud and clear, Serena. How's it going up there?*

Oh you know, it goes. Blew up a bunch of zombie heads after breaking a jealous hussy's neck; now I'm hauling ass like a pregnant Valkyrie into broad daylight—thanks to you, by the way; great job—so that I can use a chainsaw to carve a self-made devil from his pocketed crotch to his ugly, leering face. Same ol', same ol'. Thinking I'm gonna get myself laid after all this and then take you out to a strip club so you can see what a normal dick looks like.

There was a rolling sensation in Serena's head as Zoey laughed. *I knew you were my best friend for a reason, you crazy bitch!*

You know, sister. Look, I know you're busy and all, but do you think you can give me a distraction in about fifteen seconds? Nothing major, just a little something-something to take Maledictus' mind off of Zane for, like, half a second?

There was a momentary pause. Then, *Fifteen seconds? Like fifteen seconds from—*

Yup, from this moment right now!

Sure thing, Zoey confirmed. *One distraction in thirteen seconds.*

Serena smirked and began counting to herself as she threw her aura ahead of her, bursting through one of the office doors—sensing Zane's aura just outside of the window and a few floors down—and shattered the window before diving through it.

Eleven... ten...

Maledictus snarled, growing more and more enraged by Zane's newfound strength.

A massive, bony-knuckled fist cut through the air.

Zane ducked it in one fluid roll and countered with a series of jabs to Maledictus' ribs; breaking them all over again.

Maledictus roared in pain and tried to kick him away.

Zane sidestepped it and drove his boot down on the monster's grounded foot, shattering two of the three talons and causing another pained roar.

Maledictus glared, "You can't beat me, *boy*! You're fucking *nothing* without me!"

"That's where you're wrong, komodo-cock," he smirked, driving a fist into Maledictus' face and following it with an uppercut from his other hand that threw the Leiche back into his totaled car. "See, you were *something* when you were ripping the world apart with *my* body. Now, you're nothing more than an ugly rerun; a festering side-effect of some truly heinous assholes doing what assholes do." Zane fought to resist looking over his shoulder at the sound of a window breaking and silently prayed that it didn't represent a loss for them. "Sorry to break it to you, Mega-dick-fist, but you were an accident."

"Zane!"

"What the?" Zane turned, his eyes widening at the sight of Serena running towards him, her body framed in the reflection of the sunlight in the one of the windows behind her, and suddenly Zane remembered his dream.

As furious as he was that she'd left the clan—as enraged as he was that she'd once again ignored his requests and just stayed safe—he couldn't help but love her all the greater at that moment.

Nine... eight...

Serena kept feeding the auric countdown in his head.

"Hate me later, lover, but I couldn't stay away!"

Seven... six...

"Besides," she swung a chainsaw around and held it up, "I brought you a gift! What do you think?" She hurled the chainsaw towards him, it shifting in the air as she snagged it in his aura to ensure safe passage to his hands.

Five... four...

Zane threw out his hand and caught it just as Serena used her aura to start it in his grip.

Three... two...

Zane smirked as the tool roared to life in his hand. "Groovy!"

"Gah! I can't believe you said it! I'm gonna fuck you so hard tonight! Oh yea, and *ONE!*"

Zane frowned, "What's the countdown fo—"

Sorry, Zane, Zoey's voice chimed in, *Serena asked me to do this.*

Zane turned, spotting a mailbox on the other side of the street beginning to rattle.

Maledictus growled, turning towards the sound. "What the fuck?"

Serena smirked, seeing Zoey's blue aura twist and rend the mailbox—making all sorts of racket—before finally tearing it from the concrete and hurling it like a giant bullet towards Maledictus, who dove to avoid being liquefied by the metal projectile.

Hitting the pavement right in front of Zane, whose aura swelled excitedly.

"DO IT, BABY!" Serena cried out, throwing her aura out and wrapping it around the roaring chainsaw, reinforcing the weapons bladed belt.

The weapon sank into Maledictus' back, sending him into instant pained convulsions as he tried to worm free of the attack, only to have Zoey's aura suddenly wrap around him and pin him to the street. Driven by the monster's cries, Zane, aura swirling with the excitement, continued to saw through the monster's body. Halfway through, the reinforced blade squealed against something cold and hard—the cursed relic that had once been the ancient Leiche's prized chalice—and momentarily erupted in a stream of sparks from the ever-widening wound. Maledictus' eyes bulged in agony, his cries growing in intensity as his aura whipped and writhed with the realization that he'd been beaten.

Finally, the blade broke through it, and Zane, no longer held back by the obstacle finished sawing through the already dead ykali.

Serena stared, awestruck, as the shimmering remains of the chalice rolled free and clattered on the sidewalk. As the magic in the relic began to die down, she became aware that they were being watched and, letting her eyes drift towards the city skyline, she spotted the ghostly silhouettes of the thousands upon thousands of auras that had belonged to the victims of the death-wizard, Meleilzsi Shaykh Naqshband. A short distance from the body, a shimmering green aura took shape; fading in-and-out as a man who, in his lingering moments, saluted her before turning to Zane and repeating the gesture.

Then, all at once, the auras dissipated and swirled like smoke in the wind and vanished.

Tears welled in her eyes as Serena suddenly felt overwhelmed by the combined feelings of gratitude from each and every passing energy signature.

The top-half of the relic—still rolling to-and-fro on

its uneven corners—came to rest, and the magic glow faded to obsidian-black. As the last of the magic left it, two more auras appeared over Maledictus' body—an older looking man and a young girl who could've been Serena's twin—and stared at one another for a long moment before moving towards one another and colliding in a misty embrace; their combined auras swirling and melding until they, too, vanished.

"Serena? Are you alright?" he dropped the chainsaw and hurried to her, wrapping his hands around her waist and beginning to inspect her for any injuries, "What is it? What are you looking at?"

"Just some restless souls that you've freed, baby." Serena smiled and looked at him, taking in the sight of his exposed torso and his tattoos, which, while he probably wouldn't like her admitting it, had grown on her. "Now why don't you take me home and free me of this jumpsuit?"

Zane smirked, "And into a pair of pregnancy pants?"

Serena punched him in the arm and immediately after let herself fall into his arms, "Asshole!"

Zane wrapped his arms around her. "Yea, but I'm *your* asshole."

Serena smirked and nodded, "Damn right you are."

Epilogue
~2 Years Later~

"ZANE, PUT HIM DOWN THIS INSTANT!" SERENA called out, her voice carrying across the living room of their private quarters inside the Vail Clan's new building.

Zane turned in time to see his wife careening towards him and grinned at his son, "Uh oh! Looks like the Murdoch boys are in trouble, little buddy!"

Gregory smiled widely at his father's tone, exposing one of his fangs as he let out a stream of cackles. "Uh oh, Daddy! Twouble!"

Zane laughed, setting Gregory down and turning to Serena, who had finally made her way to the two. "Zane! Your son's birthday is *tomorrow* if you haven't forgotten! And, despite it being *two hours* past his bedtime, he's *still* awake and hasn't even had his bath yet!"

"Bedtime? Bath? On the eve of his *second* birthday?" he laughed, looking down at his son as he waddled to his parents' sides. "What do you think of all that, Greg? Any of that sound like fun for the soon-to-be birthday boy? Boo! Boo to strict-Mommy and boo to pre-birthday baths and bedtime! Boo, I say; boo!"

Gregory laughed again and jumped excitedly, "Boo! Boo boo boo! Boo, Mommy! No bath! No bed!"

"And you, ya little parrot?" Serena couldn't hold her stern face as she scooped up her son and planted a set of raspberries on his cheeks, earning another round of laughter. "Is a bath *really* so bad? Hmm? You know that's when you get to play with Bertil, your squeaky bat-toy!"

Gregory's eyes lit up and he clapped, most of the passes of his hands missing and making him giggle more. "YAY! Bertil bath bat! Bertil bath bat!"

Serena smirked and shot Zane a dirty look, "Now who's got the cheers?"

"Spoil sport," Zane pouted.

Gregory laughed and mimicked his father's pouting face as Serena turned and started towards the bathroom. "'Poil port! 'Poil port!"

"Your mother's right, Greg; you *are* a little parrot!" Zane laughed as he followed after his wife and son.

Serena laughed, "Be nice to your father, Gregory. He's probably just as excited about the big day we have planned for you tomorrow, too, and it's *definitely* past his bedtime!"

Zane frowned, "Bedtime my a—"

Serena spun around and leveled her pointer finger at him before he'd fully had a chance to stop himself in mid-sentence.

"No! No, I stopped myself! Don't take this one away from—"

"Dollar. Swear jar. Now!" Serena spoke through clenched teeth.

"Uh oh, Daddy in twouble!"

Serena nodded and turned back, "That's right, baby, and he'd better pay up or it'll be his ass in a ha—aw, crap!"

Zane erputed into laugher. "Ha! Who's paying the swear jar now, bi—eh, heh heh heh. Nope, not getting me that easy."

Serena groaned, "He's going to have enough to buy his own island by the time he's *five*."

"Ooh! You hear that, little buddy? Our very own island!"

"Don't encourage your son, Zane."

Zane frowned, "Why the hell not? Damn! Damn… dammit… ah shit!" he sighed, "Fuck." He finally dropped his face into his palms, "Just get the kid into the tub before I wind up owing him an entire continent?"

Serena smiled and nodded, turning away and planting another raspberry on Gregory's cheeks as she walked away.

Zane smirked, admiring the view from his angle. The past two years had done nothing but amplify everything that had made her irresistible to him on the night they'd first met. She had grown into an even more beautiful woman and an absolutely perfect mother. She was everything both Gregory and Zane could ask for *and* more. And at that moment, watching his son and wife together gave Zane the peaceful feeling he'd always been looking for.

Things had finally come together for them.

He smiled, waving to Gregory as he and his mother disappeared around the corner and headed for the bathroom.

It all seemed like a distant nightmare now.

Maledictus. Keith. All of the psychotic plotters and schemers.

Every one of them had become nothing but an unpleasant shadow in the past. The Clan of Vail had grown in numbers over the years, Serena's role as leader was solid and productive, and things were, at long last, peaceful.

At least, they were *more* peaceful. Zane was thankful that there was still enough rogue activity and swells of crime to keep him and Serena in shape and far from being bored.

But for how long?

He knew that trouble, as it had a way of doing, would come back around to them sooner or later. Between the tales of the Maledictus-monster's defeat by the taroe-cursed Zane and his crazy clan-leader lover and the ever-growing and trouble-brewing Xander Stryker, the craziest of the crazies were bound to come gunning at some point.

Xander Stryker…

The son of the legendary Joseph Stryker, and every bit the insanity magnet, it seemed.

What next?

"Zane?" Serena's voice called out to him, "Incoming!"

"Huh?" he looked up; seeing Gregory—naked and dripping—running towards him, leaving a trail of cackles and water behind him and waving his squeaky, bat-shaped bath toy in the air.

"Fwy Bertil! Fwy! Mommy's gonna get us!"

Zane broke out into laughter, falling off the couch as he watched his son's antics. Gregory, seeing this, dropped the toy and started laughing as well.

"Mommy! Daddy and Bertil go boom!" he laughed.

"Zane! Really?" Serena sighed, "I swear! You're just as bad as he is!"

"Ha! I guarantee you I'm *at least* twice as bad as him," he smirked up at her.

She rolled her eyes, "Give it time."

"You give it time, Mommy!" Gregory laughed.

"Do you even know what you're saying anymore?" Serena tried to grab at him, only to have him squirm away from her grip and starting running around the living room again. "Geez, where do you get your craziness, kid?"

Zane scoffed, "Really? Like you don't know?"

"Okay! Fine! Maybe I do!" she laughed, eying her son's movements like a predator before scooping him up. "Ha! Got'cha! Now let's go! We still gotta get you dry, then I'll send your father in to tell you a bedtime story." She paused and looked back at Zane, "But *no* scary stories this time!"

"Aww!" Zane groaned, "But the scary stories are the most fun! Come on!"

"Yea, Mommy," Gregory pouted, "De scawy stories are fun!"

"Oh my—fine! Geez you two are a damned handful!"

"Ha!" Zane pointed at her, "Another dollar for the

swear jar."

Zane smiled, following the two to Greg's bedroom and he watched as Serena helped Gregory with his pajamas, before stepping over and lifting their son up to tell him a story of two brave-yet-stubborn warriors who met on a scarlet night and came to be king and queen of a great kingdom after freeing them from the terror of the lizard-wizard. Finishing his story halfway through when he noticed his son's eyes had already shut and the gentle snores had begun, he smiled, placing him in his bed before leaning down and kissing his forehead.

"Goodnight, my little badass prince," he smiled. "And happy birthday."

Finally joining Serena in the living room, he plopped down beside her on the couch, letting out a heavy, relaxed sigh.

"Did you have a chance to talk to Zoey and Isaac?" Serena frowned, looking over. "Do they *really* have to leave tonight? I mean, Greg's birthday is *tomorrow*?"

"I tried to talk them into another day, and believe me when I say I could tell they wanted to," Zane sighed, shaking his head. "But The Council is pressing pretty hard. It's pretty serious, I guess. They're already steaming that they weren't on the plane *yesterday*."

"What could be so bad that it would have to be so urgent?" Serena sighed, "And why them?."

Zane shrugged, "Who knows? 'Cause she's an ass-kicking genius auric and he's what James Bond would be if he could transform into a towering wolf-beast and had a dick the size of baseball bat," he paused to let Serena's laughter subside. "Either way, they've got a job to do and—you know what?—so do we. Whatever it is, they've got it handled, and we have Greg's birthday party to orchestrate."

"Yea, I guess you're right." She groaned and leaned back, "I heard that Nikki's got some weird plan in mind; something that her tribe used to do it on her birthdays," Serena smirked. "It better not be some voodoo, skull-and-crossbones kind of thing."

"Oh stop!" Zane laughed, "Besides, you *know* Greg would LOVE that!"

"I guess so," she chuckled.

They made their way to the garage, in time to see Zoey and Isaac packing up the car. Serena grinned, giving Zoey's shoulder-length purple hair a tug hair before taking her into a tight embrace.

"Does the carpet *still* match the drapes?" she giggled.

"Oh no…" Zane frowned.

Isaac coughed out a laugh before Zoey sent him a glare and he straightened up, quickly taking a deep breath.

"You'll just have to wonder, I suppose," Zoey smirked. "I'm glad you came by."

Serena nodded and smiled, "I'm glad we caught you. We had to chase a naked, soaking-wet parrot-child around the living room."

"Sounds like something I had to do with you when you got into your dad's stash of elixers," Zoey laughed.

"Oh! Thanks!" Serena nudged her.

"So, you're off then?" Zane stepped forward, "You know that Greg is going to miss you tomorrow."

"Are you sure you have to leave so soon?" Serena bit her lip.

"Unfortunately, The Council is pretty insistent. Seems like this World War Two experiment is causing quite the commotion."

"Well, considering his past, it doesn't surprise me," Zane sighed, "they *vivisected* him and experiment with his organs! I mean, I've seen some shit, but—YEESH!"

"Vivisection…" Serena shivered. "Please, Zoe, be careful. If you hit any trouble don't hesitate to call us, okay?"

"Sure thing, hun," Zoey smiled and hugged Serena tightly. "I'll miss you!"

"Come back soon!" she smiled, hugging her back.

"Take care," Zane nodded to the two and stepped back with Serena.

The two stepped out of the garage and towards a waiting car. A short moment later, they were off, heading into the night under the full blood moon. Watching their friends' ride disappear into the distance, Serena leaned her head against Zane's chest.

While the road ahead was uncertain, she felt more confident than ever before with Zane by her side.

Taking a deep breath and smiling up at her lover, Serena Murdoch, under the glow of the scarlet night, kissed the vampire she'd fought so hard to call her own.

PREVIEW TO NATHAN SQUIERS
CRIMSON SHADOW: NOIR

Chapter One
Rituals

Another night.

Another chance to finally die.

Pulling the cigarette from his mouth, Xander set it into the old glass ashtray on the nightstand to his right and let out a deep, smoky breath. To his left, lying in wait on the floor, was the wooden box bearing the Yin-Yang symbol on the lid. As he let the taste of smoke and regret linger a moment longer, he allowed his fingertips to brush the polished surface and dared another exhale, hoping it would be one of his last.

For the moment, however, he let himself remember.

SCARLET DUSK

After all, it was the only time of day he allowed the memories to come.

Reaching away from his cigarette—not daring to move his other hand from the box—he reached up to his bare chest and lightly ran his fingers across the pendant.

His mother's pendant...

It had looked so much better—so much more appropriate—around her neck.

But she wasn't around to wear it anymore.

Not since Kyle...

She wouldn't want you to keep doing this to yourself, you know. Trepis' voice was soft, almost unnoticeable inside his head. His involvement with Xander's ritual varied from night to night, but one thing was clear: he was never in favor. Xander didn't blame him. Under any other sort of circumstances he probably wouldn't be either. The painful truth of the matter, though, was that things were bad enough five years earlier to warrant the attempt, and they certainly hadn't gotten any better. *I certainly don't want to see you doing this to yourself.*

Xander shook his head, "Then close your eyes."

They're your eyes too, smartass! Trepis' scorned voice was a tickle in Xander's mind.

"Don't worry, then," Xander said, sliding the lid off the wooden box. "I'll close them for both of us."

Oh, aren't we cryptic.

Xander ignored his lifelong friend's sarcasm and, giving only a brief, sidelong glance, drew the solid black, eight-chambered revolver from the satin-lined interior, leaving its ivory twin untouched.

Yin and Yang, his late-grandfather's custom-made pieces, were, other than the pendant, his only treasures. Ever since he'd first come across the guns and the remaining round in Yin's chamber he'd performed the ritual:

One bullet.

Eight chambers.

Once a night.

For almost five years his solitary, suicidal game had gone on and not once in all that time had Yin's hammer ever found purchase on anything but an empty chamber.

That dull click haunted him each night in his dreams.

Please! Trepis said, pulling Xander from his thoughts. *Can you stop doing this to yourself?*

Xander shook his head, "Tonight might be the night, Trep."

You say that every night! And every night proves to not be 'the' night. Doesn't that mean something to you?

"Yea," Xander smirked, "that I'm not trying hard enough."

That's not funny.

Xander weighed Yin in his hand and let it hang loosely in his grip, "Sure it is." He thought for a moment and frowned, "What do you think it means?"

There was a soft tickle over Xander's ear as Trepis scoffed. *It means that fate or destiny or whatever-you-think it is DOES NOT want you dead!*

"You know that's not what I believe," Xander said, scowling.

Then what do you believe, Xander? Huh? You sure don't believe strongly enough in dying, or you would've just done it by now! The fact that this has become your only potential way out and that it's not working has got to mean something.

Xander bit his lip, focusing on Yin's barrel. "It means it wasn't my time."

That's right!

Xander nodded, "But tonight could be it."

Dammit, Xander, no! That's not—

Before Trepis could get another word in Xander popped the cylinder open and checked—though he was certain that it was there—to make sure the round occupied one of the chambers. Spotting his would-be prize, he spun the wheel and slapped it back into place. With Trepis' words still rattling in his head he jammed the barrel into his mouth and thumbed back the hammer, feeling the resonation rattle against his teeth like it did every night. With his right hand still tightly wrapped around his mother's pendant he clenched his eyes shut and pulled the trigger.

A flash of red and black tore across the vast darkness behind his eyelids like a bloody bolt of lightning.

A rustling around him like a whirlwind; across the room, some papers on his desk shifted and fell to the floor.

A dull, empty click.

As the energies settled around him Xander relaxed his muscles, his left arm sagging and drawing the revolver out of his mouth. Before the gun hit the floor he stayed his hand, glaring at the piece.

Trepis stayed quiet then as Xander let out a heavy sigh—one of many till the next night would arrive—and set Yin back inside the box with Yang and slid it under the bed. Certain that the twins were hidden from his grandmother for another day he picked up the ashtray and clenched the cigarette between his lips as he set about getting ready for bed.

He'd been condemned to another day.

ABOUT THE

Literary Dark Duo

Megan J. Parker lives in upstate New York and is normally found lounging in the writing office with her fiancée and fellow author, Nathan Squiers.
Since the debut of her first novel, Scarlet Night, Megan J. Parker has gained international recognition and has been a bestseller in paranormal romance and dark fantasy. Her first novel, Scarlet Night, also was a runner up for 2013's Best New Series Award on the blog, Paranormal Craving.

Nathan Squiers (AKA The Literary Dark Emperor) resides in Upstate NY with his fiancé and fellow author, Megan J. Parker. Nathan is usually found in his writing lair where he is either typing away at his latest work or staring out the window as he plots a new idea in the subspace of his mind. His first series, Crimson Shadow, is a bestseller on Amazon in both Dark Fantasy and Horror categories. Along with that, his Death Metal novel two awards in 2013 for best paranormal thriller and best occult. Nathan Squiers was awarded 2012's best indie author of the year and has since then been rampaging the literary world with his take on vampires and the paranormal world.

ALSO AVAILABLE BY MEGAN J. PARKER:

SCARLET NIGHT
SCARLET DAWN
**ORIGINAL SIN
GONE WITH THE SIN
*THE LOVER

*A prequel to the Scarlet Night series
**A prequel to Crimson Shadow (by Nathan Squiers)

ALSO AVAILABLE BY NATHAN SQUIERS:

CRIMSON SHADOW: NOIR
CRIMSON SHADOW: SINS OF THE FATHER
CRIMSON SHADOW: FORBIDDEN DANCE
CRIMSON SHADOW: THE DIRTY DOZEN (SHORT STORY COLLECTION)
**SCARLET RISING
A HOWL AT THE MOON
*S(a)TAN
*FORBIDDEN PAINTS ON A WICKED CANVAS
**THE FIGHTER

*A prequel to the Crimson Shadow series
**A prequel to Scarlet Night (by Megan J. Parker)

Made in the USA
Charleston, SC
07 February 2017